ROGUE LII

By John R. Monteith

Braveship Books

PROLOGUE

Lieutenant Commander Reza Jazani gulped tea and burned his tongue. He pressed the porcelain cup into its holder and inhaled to cool his mouth. "Damn it."

His executive officer, a small-framed lieutenant in his late twenties, glanced up from a computer console. "Sir?"

Jazani waved him off. "I was talking to myself."

"Right, sir."

Reflecting upon the waning and uneventful three-week patrol within the cramped confines of *Ghadir-957*, Jazani glanced at a sonar display for evidence of an elusive enemy. The United States Navy kept its surface ships out of Iranian waters, and its stealthy *Virginia*-class submarines evaded detection. Sighing, he doubted he'd detect any hidden nautical trespassers.

Seated forward of the *Ghadir's* commander, a thin man kept his nose in a display while speaking. "The dolphins have acquired a submerged contact."

Unaware the cetaceans were within acoustic range of his submarine, Jazani was surprised. "You're sure?"

The young sonar technician looked at his commander while pointing at his headphones. "The dolphins just sent out a detection alert. I can't tell you if it's accurate or not, but there's no mistaking that they've reported finding something."

Jazani's kept his hopes low, like those of outmaneuvering an American *Virginia*-class submarine. Russian coaching had let his nation's fleet deploy its first dolphin team, but the return on investment to date was confused mammals, frustrated submarine crews, and false alarms. "Very well. Does the mothership know?"

"I'm waiting for the next command, sir. It should come any moment now. Not yet. Okay, still waiting."

Remembering the thin sonar technician's talkativeness, Jazani raised his palm. "Just tell me when it comes."

Seconds later, the sailor glanced at his commander. "The mothership just sent the order for the dolphins to investigate.

They also order all capable ships to relay the order. We're the closest to the dolphins, sir. We need to relay it."

"Very well, then. Relay the order."

The thin technician nodded. "I'm relaying the order to the dolphins to investigate their reported submerged contact, sir." He pressed a button that sent a sequence of recorded cetacean calls through *Ghadir-957's* bow-mounted hydrophones.

Curious, Jazani slid his headset's muffs over his ears. The echoing undersea sounds mimicked nature to his ignorant human hearing but carried an unnatural interspecies message to a militarized dolphin duo. Then he heard rapid clicks as a response.

The talkative technician bounced his voice off his console. "They've acknowledged the order, sir."

"That was hard to tell. You're sure that was the acknowledgement?"

"That was them, sir. It's easy to miss if you're not trained, but all the waterfront sonar staff got training on it last month."

"Understood." Jazani eyed the other sonar technician who sat forward of his executive officer. The quieter of the young sonar duo nodded his agreement of the dolphins' confirmation.

The talkative sailor seemed to enjoy proving his knowledge. "Per protocol, the dolphins will swim to the unidentified contact and photograph it from thirty meters away. After that, they'll surface and broadcast the images along with their location. Their transmissions are limited in range since they need to keep high resolution, which is why we need ships nearby to receive them, but they actually use satellite data for–"

Jazani raised his voice. "Thank you. That's good to know, but I assume we need to raise an antenna to listen?"

"That's right, sir."

"Very well, then." The *Ghadir's* commander turned his head towards his second-in-command. "Bring us to periscope depth."

"I'm bringing us to periscope depth, sir."

As Jazani sipped his cooling tea, he teased himself with the dolphins' newfound contact being a *Virginia*-class within range of his torpedoes. He jammed his teacup into its holder, and while the deck angled upward, steadied, and rocked, he stared at his console. He kept his gaze upon a monitor showing the input of the photonics mast, and he watched water shift from opaque to translucent. Nudging the optics clockwise with his finger on a joystick, he saw tiny whitecaps. "Raise the radio mast."

The executive officer's tone was businesslike. "I'm raising the radio mast, sir."

Jazani heard humming hydraulics lifting the antenna.

After the hum subsided, the *Ghadir's* second-in-command sounded enthusiastic. "Sir, we're getting the imagery broadcast from the dolphins. They're already on the surface."

Disciplined, Jazani kept his eyes–his submarine's best asset for avoiding heavy oil tankers in the busy strait–on the sunlit water. "Can you make out the images yet?" Lacking a response, he risked two seconds to glance towards the curiosity on the room's opposite side. "What is that?"

Remaining seated, the short executive officer extended a tablet to his commander's lap showing the mammals' gift. "You have to see for yourself, sir. I'll watch the periscope for you."

Accepting the tablet, Jazani glared at an impossibility. It was a submarine, but its framed dimensions suggested that his tiny *Ghadir* ship dwarfed it. The torpedo tubes, external and below the intruder's belly, placed the vessel under fifteen meters in length. Then a redundant image from the second dolphin confirmed the discovery. "It can't be."

"But it is, sir. Unmistakable."

"I'll watch the periscope feed, XO. You turn us around. Maintain depth, but get us away from that abomination." Jazani reached for his console's handles to brace himself as the deck rolled. "Get this image to the mothership... Belay that. Get this image to the mothership and to staff headquarters with our best targeting solution."

"What message should I include with it, sir, if any?"

"Tell them, the rumors of the Americans using undersea robots in our home waters is confirmed. Tell them, any nightmares we've had of such robots being armed have just come true."

CHAPTER 1

Standing over seated shoulders, Commander Andrew Causey glared at the lines forming on a sound display. "Five blades?"

Beside him, his sonar supervisor pressed a single muff against his ear, listened to sounds from the sea, and nodded. "RPMs correlate to a speed of three knots."

"You got anything I can use for range? Wave front curvature? Hole-in-ocean from background noise? Triangulation with the bow or conformal arrays?"

The short man with dark eyes and a tight, brown, regulation mustache shook his head. "We've only got it on the towed array, sir. If you want to try for a range, a broadside turn would help."

Causey contemplated the request but denied it in favor of letting his submarine's velocity alter the position relative to the target over time. If he remained patient, his vessel would handle the geometric dance in silence. "I'll drive true bearing to resolve the range."

"Got it, sir." The short supervisor brushed his commander's stomach while tapping one of his technicians on the shoulder. "Sorry, captain."

Consistent with his intense and quiet demeanor, Causey remained silent about being bumped. Tight confines required the sacrifice of personal space, and he considered pleasantries and other trivial words wasteful.

After chatting with his sailor, the supervisor reestablished himself next to his commander. "The target's drifting down the array, sir. Do you want to turn to resolve ambiguity?"

Drawing a plot in his mind, Causey envisioned two imaginary lines from the cable of hydrophones trailing his vessel, the *Indiana*. Since his towed array sonar system lacked a backstop like the other hydrophones attached to his boat, he had to guess if the sound came from the left or right.

"Sir? Do you want–"

"I heard you. I'm deciding." The *Indiana's* commander considered investing the time of turning to resolve the question, but he had other evidence. Heading sensors spaced along the wire defined the towed array's deviation from a perfect line, and measurements of phase differences of the frequencies hitting the hydrophones gave clues about the left-right conundrum. The answer on the screens below him agreed with his expectations of the target's location. "No. I believe the target's to the northwest."

"To the northwest, aye, sir." The supervisor huddled over four sailors to tighten their attention in their commander's decreed direction.

The *Indiana's* commander stepped away from the sonar technicians, creating space for his executive officer to approach the men responsible for listening to the water. As the man stepped in front of him, Causey examined him and considered his qualifications.

With an average build and a softness of physique, the executive officer stank of mediocrity. He'd graduated in the middle of his class in every institution ranging from the United States Naval Academy, Naval Nuclear Power School, and his Prospective Executive Officer Course. Competent, but risk-averse, he lacked a spark, and his speech came with a taciturn reluctance. "By procedure, we should turn to verify the ambiguity, sir."

Causey choked back chastising thoughts about the man's rampant conformity. "Captain's override. Time will prove me right as we approach, or we'll adjust if I'm wrong. Make sure the sonar team keeps three men listening for threats. Counting submarines, Iran has at least a dozen warships in our operations area."

"Aye, aye, sir." The executive officer awaited a sign from his boss before moving.

The *Indiana's* commander offered his back as the sign and then joined his navigator officer by a local chart. He pointed at a blue circular icon. "Is that the distressed robot?"

Keeping the unmanned undersea vehicle's proper title, the navigator nodded. "That's our distressed UUV, sir. More specifically, that's the location of the latest distress call, four hours ago."

"Sonar just heard it making turns for three knots. Draw an area of uncertainty around it allowing for three knots from the last distress call. Also allow for the currents."

As the navigator worked a stylus, a blue circle arose, skewed and bulbous to account for the one-knot current pushing the distressed American undersea robot. The northern portions of the area tracked over the Iranian coast. "I'll overlay the sonar bearing, sir."

Causey watched the line of sound from the *Indiana's* towed hydrophones slice the bulbous circle. "Looks like it's drifting with the current."

"Four miles east of its last distress call. Yes, sir."

"Maybe I will do our sonar team a favor and turn."

"To get ahead of it, captain?"

"Yes. Plot a course to deploy our drone to intercept the UUV while we stay two miles away from Iranian waters."

The navigator worked a stylus over the plot, and the requested course appeared, showing three hours until the *Indiana* would slow and launch its drone.

Causey turned and raised his voice. "XO!"

With fear of disapproval livening his steps, the second-in-command darted to his boss. "Sir?"

The *Indiana's* commander lowered his nose to the display. "I've plotted the bearing to the UUV on the navigation chart. I believe our distressed robot's drifting with the current."

"That makes sense, sir."

Causey tested the man. "What's peculiar about this situation?"

The executive officer frowned. "You mean other than a UUV calling for help deep in Iranian waters?"

"Yes."

Desperate eyes looked upwards towards the overhead hydraulic piping for inspiration. "Um... this is the first ever repair mission for a UUV in a hostile nation's waters."

"It's a repair mission only if repairs are possible. If not, it's a salvage mission. And if that's not possible, it's a destruction mission, but I'll allow the optimism. Your optimism actually highlights what's peculiar."

Despite the cool air from a vent blowing his hair, the second-in-command blushed.

"Would you like a hint?"

"Yes, sir."

"We just picked up the robot's screw, and that gave us two pieces of data. Compare and contrast those pieces."

The examinee offered a blank stare, but then his eyes sparkled. "I think I know."

Causey hushed him. "Take your time and make sure you know before you tell me. It's important that you develop an instinct for this game I'm playing with you. I'm leaving you in charge for at least twenty minutes. Take us on the course I've plotted with the navigator and contact me if the UUV shows signs of changing its behavior."

"Aye, aye, captain. Where will you be?"

"With the divers." Causey departed. After a short walk and climb, he reached the control station of the nine-man lock out chamber.

A burly lieutenant with a sculpted build argued with a thinner, taller man, his team's senior chief petty officer. Their banter ceased as the *Indiana's* commander entered their space.

Recognizing divers as a special breed, Causey credited their silence to curiosity instead of deference to his rank, and he sensed their need for a distraction. "No need to stop fighting just because of me."

The senior chief relaxed his tense frame. "Hell, sir. It's nothing new. You know me and the lieutenant squabble like an old married couple."

Lieutenant Hansen rolled his eyes. "Speak for yourself, you salty dog. My joints don't crack when I move."

"Of all the insolent, surly, snot-nosed officers in the fleet, I have to get a wanna-be comedian."

"And I get the crustiest old bastard Neptune ever shat out his nasty ass."

Causey raised his voice. "Gentlemen!"

Senior Chief Spencer frowned, crinkling the brown skin around his nose. "I'm no gentleman, sir. I work for a living, and I know who my parents are."

Hansen opened his mouth to address the double-insult against the officer class, but he shut it when Causey raised his finger.

"Men, please. If you need marital counseling, I charge three-hundred dollars an hour, and I round up to the quarter hour."

Blank stares.

"Okay, I see you're suffering from sticker shock. I'll do you a favor. The first ten minutes are free." Causey leaned his buttocks against a workbench. "Tell me what you're arguing about." He lifted his nose to the lieutenant. "You first."

Lieutenant Hansen pointed at the pressurized chamber over his head to accentuate his argument. "I want to send our newest divers to inspect the robot for the experience. There's no other way for them to learn other than training on the job. But the senior chief wants to send out our best two guys. How the hell's anyone supposed to learn their job if they can't do it?"

Causey recalled the dive team's complement of six men. Hansen was in charge, Spencer was his senior enlisted man, and the role of true leader remained unsettled between the troubled spouses. He faced the taller man, inviting his rebuttal.

Senior Chief Spencer countered. "Yeah, I sure as shit want to send out our best. The new kids are good divers, but this is way too important to risk the newbies."

The *Indiana's* commander agreed with the senior chief. Attempting the first repair, retrieval, or destruction of a malfunctioning UUV involved defining the mission's goal onsite and reacting to any surprises in Iranian water. The task required experience, and he hoped to lead the lieutenant to that conclusion. "You've considered mixing your teams? One newbie, one veteran?" He knew the answer but let his feigned ignorance propel the discussion.

The senior chief shook his head. "We could do that, but that's just not right, sir. The guys have trained as buddies and know how to finish each other's sentences."

Lieutenant Hansen nodded. "Yeah, it's generally okay to switch pairings for training, but when it comes down to it, the guys work best with their longtime buddies, sir. That's one thing we agree on."

Causey folded his arms. "Alright, I got it. It's either newbies or veterans. And I suppose they all want to get out there?"

Senior Chief Spencer frowned. "We all want to get out there, sir. Unfortunately, four of us have to stay behind and watch."

The *Indiana's* commander recognized a disconnect. "You mean four of you have to supervise and support."

"Yes, sir. That's what I meant."

"But you made it sound like a spectator sport. You'll have two backup divers pressurized while you and the lieutenant monitor breathing gases, vital signs, and communications. That's important and complex work. There aren't any spectators on your team."

"Well, sir. That's why I want the best two out there."

Lieutenant Hansen shook his head. "I want the senior guys in here with the full view of the picture. We've trained on the robots before. They're not that complex, not compared to diving manned submarines or wrecks. The new guys can handle it out there."

Causey ended the debate. "In isolation, the robot's a simple vessel, and I agree. But it's not in isolation. It's in shallow water deep in hostile territory. The Iranians may know it's distressed and could be waiting. They may even have sabotaged it. Whatever's out there, you need your veterans on point to sniff it out."

Lieutenant Hansen shrugged his broad shoulders. "I can't argue that point. It's the lost training opportunity I don't like."

"Focus first on doing it right. Then teach the newbies from what your veterans learn."

The muscular young officer blushed as he realized the weakness of his argument. "You're right, sir. I can live with that."

"Good. Be in the control room in three hours to monitor the drone with my tactical team."

"Three hours, aye, sir."

Causey retraced his steps to the control room, and the eager eyes of his mediocre executive officer pleaded for approval. "I figured out what's peculiar about this, sir."

"Go ahead."

"Our robot's blade rate suggests that it's moving at three knots, but based upon its last distress call and its present bearing, it looks like it's drifting with the current, which suggests it's moving at zero knots through the water."

The *Indiana's* commander nodded. "Good. What's that mean to you?"

The man's supple build seemed to deflate.

Causey encouraged him. "There's no right answer. You used logic to identify the disconnect. Now use intuition to resolve it."

"It's got a stuck rudder, sir."

Recalling the theories flowing between civilian engineers and naval technical experts since the distressed UUV had radioed its first cry for help, the *Indiana's* commander agreed. "That's probable. We have a diagnostic trouble code for a control surface failure, and everyone believes that's the problem. But why's it stuck?"

Embarrassed, the executive officer gave a sheepish grin. "A fishing net got caught in it. Or a piece of driftwood. Maybe some broken wreckage."

Satisfied with the thought exercise, Causey declared it complete. "Good. We obviously won't know until we see it, but those are good guesses."

"If you don't mind me asking, sir, why'd you say our blade rate data was peculiar? We expect a jammed rudder, and we've measured the Doppler shift to verify that it's going in circles. So, whether it's making three knots or max speed, it's going to look like it's just drifting with the current over an extended time period."

"I know, XO. My point is, what we're expecting, is peculiar. It takes a lot of bad luck for something to jam a hydraulic rudder, even on a vessel that small. Whatever's happening is abnormal, and I want you to remember that we're trying to make it look routine. But keep the bigger picture in mind–something's wrong other than a UUV going in circles."

"I understand, sir."

Three hours later, Causey slowed his ship to bare steerageway and announced his intentions. "Attention in the control room. I've slowed us to deploy the drone, which I'll use to investigate the distressed UUV. We're two miles outside of Iranian waters, but our drone will take station on the robot five miles inside Iranian waters, which means that we're violating international laws. Stay alert for Iranian submarines, surface ships, sonobuoys, aircraft, and divers. That's all. Carry on."

Standing behind a seated technician, his executive officer looked up with the pained eyes of someone who feared a misstep. "The drone's ready, sir."

"Very well. Launch the drone." Causey glanced at a monitor and watched numbers tick upward showing the increasing speed of the human-controlled probe swimming from his submarine's torpedo tube.

After half an hour of a patient technician driving the drone towards the distressed UUV, the executive officer moved to his commander's side. "The drone's two miles from the robot, sir. Do you want to try an active search?"

Causey shook his head. "Keep it passive."

"We can't hear anything, sir. The robot secured its screw."

"It'll come back on. Be patient."

Fifteen minutes later, the sonar supervisor stooped over a technician's shoulder to stare at a screen. He straightened his back, revealing his short frame. "Captain, we've got the robot again, on the drone and towed array. Blade rate correlates to three knots. That gives us a good enough fix to drive the drone in. I recommend a five-degree steer to the right."

A glance at his monitor gave Causey his confirmation. "Steer the drone to the right five degrees." He considered the dangers of micromanagement. "And from now on, we're trusting our drone operator to do this without backseat drivers."

A young technician looked up from his screen.

Turning his head to the young drone operator, Causey continued. "Keep it below the surface, keep it off the bottom, keep it passive, and above all, keep it from banging against the robot. Assume the Iranians are watching and listening."

"Yes, sir. I'll get it done."

"I know." The *Indiana's* commander turned towards a monitor showing the view through the drone's camera, which showed the water's darkness. "And I'll be watching."

Ten minutes later, the sonar supervisor pressed a muff against his ear while stooping over the drone operator's shoulder. "The robot's coming around in a circle. We should see it on this pass."

His eyes glued to his monitor, Causey saw nothing from the drone's camera. "Maybe not."

The supervisor glanced at his commanding officer. "Dang it, sir. It passed below and just off the drone's starboard side."

From his seat, the young drone operator called out. "I can get it. I'll chase it."

Although avoiding micromanagement, Causey recognized the need for validation. "Remember not to bump it. Be cautious instead of aggressive. I don't like having my drone in Iranian waters, but don't hurry. We've got time."

Within minutes, the drone technician stirred. "I'm following it, five meters behind. It's driving in a pretty wide circle. I'm moving in closer to see it."

Breathing shallowly, Causey watched his monitor as bright lights from the drone illuminated five rotating blades within a protective shroud.

Several men called out the visual confirmation of the robot's propeller, and then the drone operator pushed for more visual information. "I'm moving in closer for a better view."

Thirty seconds later, the straight stern planes and canted rudder appeared on the unmanned submarine's tapered tail. Then the robot's blades coasted to motionlessness.

The young technician called out. "I'm slowing the drone, diving under the robot to help slow down."

As the remote camera moved below the UUV and then looked upward, Causey saw the problem. A torn T-shaped piece of a metal hung from the rudder's underside. He spoke under his breath. "What are the chances of that?" Glancing at his second-in-command, he raised his voice to pressure him into risking the first verbalized opinion. "What do you think of that, XO?"

The careful response lacked authority or fear, toeing the line of neutrality. "It's possible that the robot collided with the mast of a submerged wreck, sir."

"I agree that's what it looks like, but I can't say if that's what happened, or if that's what a saboteur wanted it to look like." As the camera swam through varied perspectives of the jammed rudder, Causey sought concurrence of his conclusion. "Lieutenant Hansen, do you agree that this condition appears salvageable?"

The burly diver looked up from his seat among the tactical team. "Yes, sir. I do. We'll go out armed and ready for any saboteurs. We'll also need to make some noise cutting that off, but it should be quick work. I also want to inspect the whole robot closer to see if there's any damage."

"Agreed. Join me and the XO at the navigation plot." Causey moved to the table where his navigator hunched over a chart, and he waited for his second-in-command and the dive team's officer to join him. "How close do I need to get you?"

Lieutenant Hansen cleared his throat. "Since we're shallow enough to use rebreathers, my guys can make good speed. If you can get us ahead of the robot's expected movement, two hundred meters would be enough."

Causey stated the obvious. "It's settled, then. We're going into Iranian waters. XO, plot an intercept course to get us on the robot's track, two hundred meters ahead of it. Also, get a message drafted to fleet headquarters with our intent and send it out on a communications buoy with a thirty-minute delay."

Two hours later, Causey approached the control station of the nine-man lock out chamber and heard the divers arguing. "What's wrong now?"

Slouching to keep his tall frame under a run of hydraulic piping, Senior Chief Spencer scowled. "The lieutenant wants the guys to attach themselves to the robot with lanyards."

"Okay. What do you want?"

"When it's drifting, nothing. When it's moving at three knots, they can hold on with their hands or swim. I don't want them in lanyards so that they don't get caught up in moving parts."

The muscular lieutenant shook his head. "I get that. But you'll be doubling their time out there if they can't work while it's moving. We're in Iranian waters now and need to minimize our time."

Before Causey could intervene as a counselor, a voice over a loudspeaker chilled him. "Torpedo evasion!" As the deck angled through a turn and the ship trembled into its acceleration, he darted down a ladder and turned into the control room.

His executive officer met his gaze. "Sir, we've got high-speed screws identified as two torpedoes, both coming from the northwest. Minimal bearing rates."

The *Indiana's* commander snapped his jaw towards a monitor showing raw sounds from the seas. With his sonar team tracking the weapons, cursors marked the direction to the incoming torpedoes. They struck him as good shots, fencing him in from either side. "State the ordered course, XO."

"One-one-zero, sir."

"Very well. I have the deck and the conn. Steady on course one-zero-five." As fear rose within him, Causey protected his second-in-command's dignity. "You made the right call ordering a torpedo evasion and turning, but I'm easing up on the course to escape the weapon to the left. It's easier to evade one torpedo than two. Also, order the drone due south into deep water to sink itself when its battery dies. Cut its wire."

Looking up from the sonar screen over which he crouched, the executive officer revealed fear–the right amount per

Causey's judgment. "Aye, aye, sir."

"Get a tube ready to take out our robot."

"I'll use tube two, sir."

"Where's my reactive weapon?"

"Tube one's ready for a reactive firing down the bearing of the incoming weapons. I recommend firing, sir."

Unsure who shot at him, how they'd found him, or if he'd survive, the *Indiana's* commander was terrified. But recalling his duty as a naval leader, he forced a loud and confident voice as he released his desperate retaliatory weapon. "Shoot tube one."

CHAPTER 2

Seated in the cramped control space of *Ghadir*-957, Lieutenant Commander Reza Jazani felt his pulse racing, and his eyes darted between monitors. One display rendered a flash photo taken from a dolphin's head showing the conning tower of a submerged *Virginia*-class submarine trespassing in his waters. The other showed the location of the two 324-millimeter torpedoes a frigate had launched. "That's another victory for the dolphins."

Beside him, the small-framed executive officer pressed a muff against his ear and shook his head. "Amazing. First, an American robot. Now, a *Virginia*."

"Put cameras on dolphins' heads, teach them a few basic commands, and otherwise unthinkable opportunities arise. A sabotaged robot as bait. An arrogant navy sending its finest ship into a trap."

"Right, sir. And now we have a fleeing adversary. I can't believe how loud an American submarine can be."

Jazani scoffed. "Every ship's loud at flank speed."

"Still, sir. This is amazing. We're recording it for future reference. We're capturing a lot of good information."

As the *Ghadir's* commander studied the lines showing the sound power levels of the American submarine's narrowband noises, one of the fainter lines disappeared. "It's still quieter than I expected. We just lost... what was that, a reactor coolant pump?"

"Yes, sir."

"We lost a reactor coolant pump at this range while the target's running for its life."

As a swell rocked the shallow submarine, the executive officer showed his commander a scowling profile. "Isn't that an exaggeration, sir, at least per the intent of the geniuses among our political leaders?"

Tempted to feed the cynicism, Jazani reminded himself of a commanding officer's need for stoicism. "Be careful expressing opinions against a mission you've been ordered to support."

The small man challenged the warning. "Come on, sir. You know that someone with too much rank and too little common sense defined this trap. Shooting small torpedoes to avoid snapping the American ship in half is a noble gesture, but even the smallest torpedoes are designed to sink submarines."

Agreeing with his second-in-command, Jazani found his admiralty's plan dubious, but he defended the orders. "We're giving the Americans a chance to survive."

"We could've done that with a heavyweight torpedo, by detonating it early. Try that with a frigate-launched weapon!"

While seated in the tight confines, Jazani often bumped shoulders with his executive officer. The closeness demanded leeway in formalities. "You're arguing a hypothetical."

Missing the hint to relent, the short officer continued his rant. "If we'd been allowed to detonate a heavyweight, we'd be guiding it in with a wire. Then we'd send them a shockwave that would cripple them and get the message across. If not, we'd send another, and then another until the dense Americans figured it out."

"I don't think they're dense. Don't underestimate our adversary."

"But here they are looking like fools."

Jazani wanted to end the talk about the unchangeable decision. "That would've been difficult, XO. A heavyweight shockwave can kill from farther away than you might think. Lightweight torpedoes minimize such a risk and give us a chance to study and possibly capture a wounded ship. The less metal we vaporize and twist into useless shards, the more we can salvage."

"That's a simplification and wishful thinking. You're talking like a politician, sir, with all due respect."

The *Ghadir's* commander scoffed. "With all due respect, stop baiting me, and I'll stop talking like a politician. I've given you enough leeway in this debate."

"I'll stop now, sir, but my point about the small weapons

being unguided still concerns me. I don't like our options if they miss."

Jazani expected the two-torpedo salvo, which a frigate had launched toward the point where the dolphins had surfaced, to accomplish the goal of stranding an American submarine in shallow Iranian waters. "I don't think they'll miss. Look at the data."

His executive officer returned his attention to his display and shrugged. "I guess you're right, sir. The southerly torpedo is vectoring away, but the northern one's closing with a fifteen-knot speed advantage. Our tracking system predicts impact in eight minutes."

"Keep watching. The Americans are arrogant because they're good. Don't be surprised if they try something cunning and perhaps... unorthodox."

"You mean the same Americans who let two riverine command boats get captured near Farsi Island a few years ago?"

"I said they were good, not perfect."

The executive officer leaned forward, exchanged words with the soft-spoken sonar technician, and looked to his commander. "The Americans' reactive weapon is heading into oblivion, and they've probably lost their guidance wire to steer it."

"Or they've lost their ability to listen and order a proper steer. Either way, the shooting frigate will escape unharmed. Tell me what you know about the weapon headed for the robot."

"It's going to hit, sir. That can't be helped."

"So be it. The robot's already served its purpose."

Seated forward of Jazani, the thin, talkative technician turned and brushed one muff behind his ear. "May I speak frankly, sir?"

Jazani rolled his eyes and sighed. "When have you not?"

The sailor scowled. "Good point, sir. I believe I speak for the bulk of the crew, if not everyone, when I say that we don't like being out here supporting a bunch of surface ships and aircraft in half measures."

"That's too complex a discussion for the moment. We're tracking a hostile exchange. A real one, I remind you." Jazani tried to keep his gaze on his screen, but he turned and narrowed his eyes at his submarine's best sonar expert. He anticipated the answer but wanted to hear the thin man say it. "You're incapable of listening attentively until you've spoken your mind, aren't you?"

Blushing, the sailor shrugged. "Sorry, sir. You know how I am."

"Very well." Jazani darted his eyes between his display and the sailor. "What do you mean, specifically?"

"Lightweight torpedoes. Letting the Americans live. Why such weakness when we should be displaying power?"

The *Ghadir's* commander scoffed. Again, a man on his crew wanted to debate the unchangeable, but he respected the sailor's independent thinking. Submarines won battles and returned home with dry innards thanks to sailors who knew when to follow orders and when to question them. "Would you prefer detainees for political leverage, or would you prefer martyrs to incite the Americans?"

The technician looked away in thought before responding. "Hmmm. I'd say they're already incited. They're always incited. Americans have always been cluttering our waters with submarines, looking for a fight. We're the first generation of sailors who can give them one. I say, let them suffer some pain."

"Don't be so fast to pass judgment."

Unconvinced, the thin sailor faced his commander. "And what happened with the American sailors we captured three years ago? I'll tell you what? We videotaped them and gave them back to their lazy, pampered mothers and wives the next day."

Jazani snapped. "We were under international scrutiny for nuclear negotiations back then. I assure you it's entirely different now."

The thin man opened his mouth.

The *Ghadir's* commander shut it as he raised his voice. "And those sailors were led by a young officer. A *Virginia*-class submarine's captain is a respected commander, and there could very well be more than one hundred survivors. This mission offers powerful leverage."

Unfazed, the talkative man assumed a cynical tone. "It would be cleaner with zero survivors and video footage of two halves of their submarine sinking."

The executive officer intervened. "That's enough, sailor. He's your commanding officer."

Jazani raised his palm. "No, XO, it's okay. I give leeway because we're a small crew, and I can't afford men suppressing their dissent." He turned to the loquacious sailor. "But I don't take killing lightly. Not even Americans. Fortunately, our admiralty thinks the same way. If you can't keep quiet about your discontent in my actions and the intent of the Islamic Republic of Iran Navy, then find a relief for your watch station and reflect upon your career until you can."

Inhaling through his nostrils, the thin man gained his composure. "I'll keep my opinions to myself, sir."

"Do so." Jazani returned his attention to the weapons and liked what he saw. The northern torpedo had shifted to active searching and had gained contact on the American submarine's hull. "This looks promising. So far, everything's going to plan."

As the ship rolled, the executive officer cocked his head. "I don't believe that battle plans are supposed to survive engagement with the enemy."

Appreciating the camaraderie of the growing and competent Iranian submarine fleet, the *Ghadir's* commanding officer admired and respected his men. Unlike the submarine commanders of the world's lesser navies, he trusted the infrastructure that trained his technicians and officers, and he appreciated that his second-in-command's skill allowed him to sleep during long patrols. "Sometimes, with good training and a competent team, things work out as intended."

A shadow overcame the small officer's face.

"What's wrong?"

"Today we had a chance to prove our submarine's combat abilities, but instead we've accepted roles as observers."

"I thought I put all debates on hold, XO."

"Sorry, sir. You did."

"But now that you've said it, tactical observers are vital to combat, and we're providing value by tracking the scenario, whether we pulled the trigger or not. Keep your focus and that of our crew on your duties."

"I will, sir."

Moments later, the northern torpedo's destiny remained promising, but the thin sonar technician stirred. "I heard launch transients."

The announcement jarred Jazani from an encroaching sense of complacency. "A weapon?"

As the talkative sailor raised a finger to request silence, the two other men seated at tactical consoles pressed muffs against their heads.

In silence, the *Ghadir's* commander awaited his team's consensus.

His short executive officer began the inquiry. "I didn't hear anything. Did you?" He looked towards the quieter sonar technician.

"No, sir. I'm tracking the torpedoes. He's tracking the Americans. It was outside my sector."

Jazani saw through the apparent contradictions. "I know what it was. It was a communications buoy." He tapped an icon on his screen, unmuting the boom microphone on his single-ear headset, and called out with his submarine's mission name. "Task force commander, this is Shark One. Over."

Seconds later, a deep voice entered his ear. "Shark One, this is task force commander. Go ahead. Over."

"Task force commander, Shark One. I believe the target launched a communications buoy. The coordinates are marked in our data feed, and I request you have an asset investigate. Time is of the essence to prevent a message from being broadcasted. Over."

"Shark One, task force commander. I see the coordinates. I'll send an asset to investigate. Out."

When he muted his microphone and turned his attention back to his team, Jazani saw concern in the profile of his second-in-command. "What's wrong?"

"We're losing the target." The executive officer stood and then stooped over the thin technician's shoulder to glare at his display.

The talkative sailor confirmed the loss. "I've lost half the target's noises, and they're fading fast. Distance is becoming a factor, and the target's last deployment of countermeasures deafened me in a five-degree sector."

"But the torpedo went through the countermeasures?"

"Yes, sir, and then I picked up the target again, but with fewer noise sources. Our northern torpedo's converging on the target's bearing, too, which is making it harder to hear."

"Losing the Americans was inevitable. We can't match the speed of *Virginia*, nor do we desire to while listening." Jazani toggled the mute icon. "Task force commander, this is Shark One. Over."

"Shark One, this is task force commander. Go ahead. Over."

"I'm losing the target. I request you assign tracking to Shark Two or Shark Three. Over."

"Negative, Shark One. Shark Two had to reposition to avoid the retaliatory torpedo, and Shark Three is too far to the west. Over."

"Do you have any other asset you can assign to tracking? Over."

"Negative, Shark One. The task force's nearest helicopter is committed to retrieving the target's communications buoy. You're the only one with contact on the target. Over."

Jazani scanned his screen and saw the lines to the American submarine's noises fade. "I just lost contact. Over." After muting his microphone, he called out to the talkative technician. "Get me the ping cycle of the northern torpedo."

Obeying, the sailor tapped a calculation upon his screen. "It's range-gating, sir. The distance correlates to three hundred yards between the weapon and the target."

The task force leader's deep voice shot from the earpiece. "Report the status of our weapon. Over."

Jazani unmuted his microphone. "It's range-gating, sir. The target's three hundred yards from the weapon. It's a solid lock, and per my calculations, the weapon has plenty of fuel. Over."

"I've ordered Sharks Two and Three to make best speed towards the expected impact point for assessment, but you're in the best position to listen. Gather all the information you can. Out."

As a swell rocked the tiny submarine, Jazani called out to his team. "Our task force commander says we're still in the best position to hear this. The information flow's about to become challenging when the warhead detonates. Stay calm, listen, and share whatever you even remotely suspect's worth sharing."

With concern, the executive officer looked to his commander. "The American captain's running out of time to abandon ship. He must know he's been defeated."

During seconds of curiosity and reverence, Jazani took off his communications gear and picked up a sonar headset. He pressed muffs against his ears. The racing torpedo accelerated its shrill ping cycle as it shortened the distance to the submarine. The *Ghadir's* commander lowered the headset and announced his conclusion to the team and, in disbelief, to himself. "If he doesn't surface immediately, he's a fool. Or worse."

CHAPTER 3

Causey tried to silence the nagging internal monologue. He'd failed. He'd made a mistake. He'd led his crew, his submarine, and himself to their deaths. Despite his efforts to stop them, internal accusations cycled through his subconscious mind.

With mortal fear pasted on his face, his second-in-command stared at him. Under pressure, the man seemed useless.

Causey tried to bring him back to life. "Recommendations, XO?"

A blank stare.

"XO, do you have anything on your mind?"

"No, sir."

"We're dead in minutes unless we do something. You're sure you have no ideas?"

"It's crazy, but..."

"Spit it out."

"We could surface and abandon ship."

"That's not crazy. It's what I'd order if I didn't have another idea, and I want your opinion. I say we aim our bow at the weapon, bottom the ship, and hide in the engine room until we're rescued."

Appearing relieved that the decision belonged to someone else, the executive officer lauded it. "Yes! That could work. We're in shallow water and will have the minisub hatch for rescue."

"I appreciate the sanity check. We'll do it."

"I'll get a message of our intent out to fleet headquarters on another communications buoy, and I'll assemble the crew back aft."

"Put as many men in the tunnel as will fit and assemble everyone else forward in the engine room. In case the weapon hits farther aft than I hope, we'll run back into the forward compartment."

"Yes, sir."

"I'll make the announcement. You've got less than two

minutes. Move out!"

"Yes, sir." The executive officer marched away.

Causey grabbed a microphone. "This is the captain. A light-weight torpedo will hit us in less than two minutes. I'm going to maneuver the ship so that it hits us forward. I want every man who's not in the control center to evacuate the forward compartment within ninety seconds. We'll stay in the engine room with the ship bottomed while we await rescue. Corpsman, bring any vital medications. Divers, bring diving equipment. Engineering, prepare to take local control of the rudder and stern planes. Galley crew, bring plastic wear and high-calorie foods like peanut butter, beans, and rice. Stay calm but move with urgency. Carry on."

Lieutenant Hansen stood and faced the *Indiana's* commander. "Sir, I'll grab four rebreathers and–"

Causey interrupted him. "Do you need a decision from me?"

"No, sir."

"Follow your instincts. Go!"

The burley diver darted away.

Causey cast his voice across the control room. "I need the navigator, the sonar supervisor, and the ship's control stations to stay with me. Radio operator, you're free after our communications buoy is launched. Everyone else, grab whatever food you can carry on the way back and leave now. No heroes. That's an order."

Sailors in blue jumpsuits stood and cleared the space.

A pot-bellied man wearing a khaki belt around the expanse of his blue cotton jumpsuit swiveled his chair at the chief-of-the-watch station towards his captain. "Sir, do you want me to pump the forward trim and drain tanks?"

The *Indiana's* commander thought about it. With the forward spaces about to flood, he agreed with keeping the compartment as light as possible. "Yes. Pump the forward trim and drain tanks to sea. Also, blow the forward sanitary tanks." He twisted his torso towards the charting table. "Navigator, what's the water depth?"

"One hundred and eighty-two feet, sir, with a slight downward slope to the west. Verified on the fathometer."

Causey called out to the seated man who controlled the ship's depth. "Make your depth one-seven-zero feet."

Reaching the shallow depths proved quick and simple for the *Virginia*-class hull.

As the deck steadied from its gentle angle, the radio operator declared the satellite communications buoy launched and floating to the water's surface with its message about the bottoming plan.

Causey released two more men. "Radio operator, go. Navigator, go. Take the local paper charts with you."

The liberated men departed.

Stooping his short frame over a console but ready to flee, the sonar operator trembled with adrenaline. Holding one muff of a headset against his ear, he faced his commander. "I heard the communications buoy hit the surface."

"Very well. How about the torpedo?"

"Unchanged. I'm tracking it at ninety-eight seconds away, but it's a guess at this point since there's no bearing rate. It's just a tail chase."

"Very well. You're free. Get out of here."

The supervisor darted aft.

With three men seated at the controls of the ship, the *Indiana's* commander stepped to the pair seated in the forwardmost station. "I only need one of you."

The younger petty officer looked up over his shoulder. "I'll stay, sir. I'm single. He's got a wife and three kids."

Causey tapped the father on the shoulder. "Go. That's an order."

After thanking his colleague, the man marched away.

Starting a mental countdown, the *Indiana's* commander tallied eighty-five seconds before impact. "Are you ready for some abnormal driving?"

The single sailor sounded scared but compliant. "Yes, sir."

Considering an untested scenario beyond the dreams of the

Indiana's builders, Causey visualized his final moves. Once he envisioned the steps in sequence, he instigated them. "Right full rudder."

The deck angled during the turn.

Ninety degrees later, the *Indiana's* commander pushed his ship to its limits. "Rudder amidships."

"My rudder's amidships, sir."

Causey tapped a button. "I'm ringing up back emergency."

Laboring in violence against its flank-speed momentum, the ship shuddered, and a digital display showed its speed plummeting.

Causey's mental clock gave him fifty seconds. "Left full rudder."

"My rudder's left full, sir."

"Set me up to talk to the engine room directly."

The sailor tapped a button. "You're on an open circuit with maneuvering, sir."

Causey spoke into a microphone. "Maneuvering, control room. Do you hear me?"

He recognized his engineer officer's voice issuing from a loudspeaker. "Control room, maneuvering. We hear you, sir."

"Take local control of the rudder. Once we've reversed course from our evasion course, set the rudder amidships. Got it?"

"Set the rudder amidships after we've settled on the reverse course of our evasion course. Understood, sir."

"Also, take local control of the stern planes and use them to keep us level. Start with ten-degrees rise."

"Rise, sir?"

"We'll be going backwards and we'll be light forward. I'm having the forward compartment trim and drain tanks pumped dry and sanitary tanks blown."

"Understood, sir. I'll take local control of the stern planes and start with ten-degrees rise to keep us at a level deck."

"Then once the torpedo hits, bring us to all stop and go silent."

While hesitating in his response, the engineer revealed his

uneasiness with running backwards from an incoming weapon and stopping after it would detonate next to the hull. "Uh... once the torpedo hits, come to all stop and go silent, aye, sir."

"That's it. We're heading aft now."

"Sir, do you want us to isolate the engine room electric buses from the forward compartment?"

The *Indiana's* commander appreciated the question. With the rapid pace of ideas, he'd forgotten to separate the sections of his submarine's power grid that would remain dry from those awaiting immersion. "Yes."

"I'll include the main battery, sir. Except for systems with local battery backups, you'll be completely in the dark.

"I know. Make it happen."

"I'll have the engine room buses isolated, sir."

Causey stood and glanced at the single sailor and then the portly chief of the watch, who pumped weight out of the forward compartment. "Go. Both of you. Grab a flashlight. I'll follow."

The crewmen stepped across the control room and ducked through a door.

As the *Indiana's* commander followed them through the galley, he heard the incoming torpedo's seeker pinging off the hull. Compounding the assault on his senses, the compartment went dark.

The single sailor ahead of him illuminated his light, and a cone of white cut the blackness.

Causey withdrew a small flashlight from his belt and aimed it at the deck plates. When he reached the open door to the reactor compartment's tunnel, he scurried through it and helped the nearest sailor shut it. With the watertight boundary sealed between his crew and the spaces he expected to flood, he studied the men jammed into the thin corridor.

Their faces showed fear, and the air stank of body odor.

Causey shouted. "Brace for impact! Grab something! Bend your knees!" He obeyed his own order while clutching the watertight door.

Like death, the torpedo's seeker pounded the hull with a haunting shrillness. Like death, the warhead exploded with a deafening thud. Like death, the deck shook and rattled.

Like salvation, the reactor compartment held.

Causey regained his footing. "To the engine room. Everyone. Go!" He took several steps behind his filing men, but curiosity compelled him to reverse course. When he backtracked to the watertight door, he stooped and looked through the porthole.

Suggesting heightened humidity, droplets clung to the window, but the compartment appeared dark and dry.

Hoping the pressure hull had somehow retained its integrity, Causey realized his desire's folly as the deck dipped. With water filling half the submarine and rotating its football-field-length, the bow plummeted twelve feet and into the mud. The deck lurched, and the *Indiana's* commander stumbled. After recovering, he watched rising water shimmer and reflect the scant light from his portal, and then he retreated into the engine room.

Confused sailors blocked his path.

"Make a hole!" Causey pushed through his people to reach a ladder ascending to the submarine's upper deck. He climbed and then reached the engineering room's sealed control center, maneuvering. Among the watch team and the engineering officer, he found his second-in-command. "We're bottomed, XO."

"I assumed so, sir. Our speed fell off abruptly to zero."

"Head out into the spaces and get a status of any injuries. Also, spread the word that we're in ultra-quiet mode, and get a command center set up for the officers."

"Aye, aye, sir." The executive officer departed.

"How's the plant?"

In delayed shock, the thin and tall engineer officer offered a blank stare but uttered his report. "We're still running for high-speed operations. Given our present situation, I recommend shifting the plant to our quietest mode, per your order of ultra-quiet."

"Agreed. Do it. And remember not to use any announcing circuits. Pass orders to your team by word of mouth. God knows who's listening. Also, take manual control of the aft trim tanks to bring the stern to the bottom. Get the deck level."

"Bring the plant to ultra-quiet operations without using announcing circuits and take manual control of the aft trim tanks to bottom the stern and achieve a level deck, aye, sir."

Causey stepped from the maneuvering center, descended the ladder to the middle deck, and landed among a horde of dazed sailors. "Everyone pass the word through the ranks to get the diving officer up here."

Sailors repeated his order throughout the throng of lingering men.

In a moment of unexpected calmness, Causey realized he was recovering from mortal fear and no longer trying to cheat death. His heart raced but his breathing began to slow, and he felt the air shifting behind him as a body approached.

"You wanted me, Captain?" Lieutenant Hansen stank of nervous sweat and clammy skin.

"Did your team salvage enough equipment to head into the forward compartment? I want your guys to assess the damage."

The diver strained to speak in full sentences. "We did, sir. The problem's going to be... it's going to be compression and decompression. Decompression is the biggest challenge... I mean a challenge.... without a lockout chamber."

"You can use high-pressure air to pressurize the tunnel."

His brush with death hampering him, the young diver wrestled to express each thought. "It'll take some attentive control to avoid giving my guys the bends... real attentive control. We'll need to monitor and hold the pressure... hold pressure in a real tight band. But if your ship allows control over the pressure in there... in there... then maybe..." The muscular officer gazed into an undefined distance.

His need to lead inspired Causey with strength. He placed his hand on a thick shoulder. "Hey? You're alive."

A tear streaming down his cheek, the lieutenant said nothing.

The *Indiana's* commander shook the catatonic officer. "Hey! I said you're alive."

The diver blinked and then released a cathartic chuckle. "Holy shit, captain. Only by an ass hair."

"Do you know what to do next?"

Lieutenant Hansen wiped his tear. "Get my guys into the forward compartment."

"That's right. Check with the engineer for the air system diagrams and draw up a plan."

"I'll need about thirty minutes to check everything before I send my guys in."

Causey suspected the young officer's overconfidence. "Remember to get Senior Chief Spencer's input. In fact, get your whole team's input. The more experienced minds you can bring to bear on this, the better."

"Of course, sir."

"And do it right instead of doing it fast. There's no hurry. We're not going anywhere."

"Can I have the tunnel and the area by the watertight door as a staging and control area?"

"Yes, and you can have the area around the control valves to the air pressure reducers, too. This is your show."

"I'll get it done, sir." The diving officer disappeared into the confused crowd.

Causey started into throng of sailors with a slow pace, inspecting faces to measure his men's mettle. With each pair of eyes he checked, he saw courage and hope rising behind the waning terror. But an appropriate fear remained within his sailors as an anxious awareness of a hostile adversary and the inability to run or fight.

Escorting a master chief petty officer with a big head, his second-in-command appeared oddly confident and eager to update his boss. "I commandeered the engineering lab for officer meetings. It's private and has just enough space."

The mediocre man's first post-torpedoing move impressed Causey. "Decisive and appropriate. Good."

"Also, I've asked the chief of the boat here to set up muster areas for each division. This mindless milling about isn't doing us any good."

The *Indiana's* commander nodded. "That's two good easy but important decisions. So, you've got your head on straight, which means you're not in shock. I wonder how many of the crew are."

As quickly as it had come, the executive officer's confidence vanished. He sounded timid. "I wasn't really looking for shock, sir. I was inspecting for injuries as you asked, and there was nothing in need of treatment. Everyone's fine physically."

With an inspiring spring in his step, the big-headed master chief stepped forward. "I was looking. I'd say about fifty-fifty on guys who look dazed. You'd have to be dead not to be affected."

"They'll recover."

"They sure will, sir, and you did your part making sure of it. I heard a few guys exaggerating about the abnormally large size of your testicles by turning the ship around and bottoming it."

Causey snorted. "I'll take that as a compliment."

"No question about it. I'll get working on the muster stations and put together a map of which division is where. I'll also get an inventory going on the supplies we managed to bring back here."

"Good idea. Get on it."

"Done, sir." The master chief marched away.

Realizing he needed help passing an order, Causey called out. "Cob!"

The chief of the boat stopped and listened.

"Pass the word for all officers to meet in the lab. Let the division chiefs handle musters."

"I'll pass the word, captain."

A new idea entered the *Indiana's* commander head. "One more thing. Have everyone think of a way out of this mess. You may all believe I've got oversized testicles, but they only took us this far. I have no idea if the fleet received our message and is helping, or if we're stranded in hostile territory to fend for ourselves."

"I'll ask, sir."

"Encourage everyone to volunteer whatever comes to mind.

No idea's a bad one. No idea can be worse than our reality."

CHAPTER 4

Jake Slate slapped the small primate's paw from his pocket. "Back off, you little imp!"

The rhesus macaque eyed his human opponent, shrieked, and scurried around a corner.

Walking beside him, Jake's wife giggled. "I told you they trained monkeys to grab wallets."

Jake glared at his guide, a man in his early twenties who claimed to hail from Bangalore.

The native Indian offered a meek smile and spoke with a British accent. "Your beautiful wife is right. So many bad people taking advantage of tourists."

Letting his cynicism flow, Jake revealed his suspicions. "Yeah. A busy place with rich tourists. I wonder how the little monkeys select their targets."

The guide gulped, redirected the conversation, and pointed at the calligraphy on the Great Gate. "This is a wonderful line of poetry. 'O Soul, thou art at rest. Return to the Lord at peace with Him, and He at peace with you.' Very beautiful, isn't it?"

Jake scoffed. "How poetic."

His wife smacked his chest. "Be nice."

"Linda!"

"Stop complaining."

"I'm not complaining."

"I don't like your attitude."

"You never like my attitude. I thought that was a qualification of being my wife."

Linda thumped his chest again and followed up with a swat against his shoulder. And then another backhand to his chest. In Chaldean Aramaic, she called him a fool. *"Daywanna!"*

Jake raised his eyebrows and dared her to repeat it. "What'd you call me?"

"Daywanna!" She turned her nose upward and followed the failed monkey-thief's suspected accomplice-guide through the gate.

Defeated, Jake walked after his wife and mumbled. "*Day-wanna*, it is, then. Let's check out the gardens." His phone chimed, and as he lifted it from his pocket, he recognized his boss' name. He placed the microphone against his cheek and tried to sound perky, but his tightening throat betrayed his anxiety. "Hello, Pierre."

"Good afternoon. How goes the trip to the Taj Mahal?"

Jake judged the question sincere, but he sniffed Pierre Renard's ulterior motive. After pleasantries, he expected his French boss to issue an order. "Not bad, other than a monkey trying to take my wallet. This place is impressive. Definitely worth the trip."

"I'm glad you're enjoying it, and I'm happy to hear that one of my submarine commanders was able to match wits with a primate."

"Enough monkeying around. I know you. You usually call for business only."

"Right. Business. You won't believe the opportunity that was just placed before me."

Enjoying his vacation, Jake wanted to continue decompressing. His last mission had been an unwelcomed stressor since its unwanted inception, and he appreciated his time away from mercenary naval combat. "Do tell."

"Not over the phone. Not even on an encrypted line."

Jake grunted. "Cyber-security's not my area of expertise. I'll have to trust you."

"I don't trust the security of the cellular infrastructure in India, especially while my fleet's parked in the dry docks of its nemesis."

"Fair enough. When do you want me back?"

"I've chartered a flight for you and Linda from Agra to Karachi."

Jake considered letting his wife continue her tour of India but remembered the growing risk of his position as the commanding officer of the submarine, *Specter*. As Renard's man, he was becoming a renowned target for enemies the Frenchman had created during a lifetime of arms dealing, military advising, and naval strikes. He tried to hide his chagrin. "At what time?"

"You get one more hour to finish your tour of the Taj Mahal, but I want you eating dinner in Karachi. I'll text the details to your guards."

Glancing at the two veterans of the French Foreign Legion who served as his armed escorts, Jake considered his life a bizarre blend of parole and witness protection. The game was tiring him, and his heart sank as another ripple in the world's unpredictable instability invaded his private life. "I'll tell Linda."

"Why do you sound so glum? I thought you lived for our adventures."

"I do. But if that's all I'm living for, isn't that sad?"

"Come listen to the opportunity. Then you can answer that for yourself."

Four hours later, Jake swallowed a mouthful of shredded beef while scanning the table's other faces. His mercenary fleet's leadership ignored him during the silent probing of their savory family-style meal. Anticipation consumed him, and he saw eagerness in his colleagues' faces.

On his right, his French mechanical systems expert, Henri Lanier, sported a designer blazer and a head of impeccable silver hair. On the mechanic's right, Terrance Cahill, commander of the fleet's flagship *Goliath*, reached for cubed chicken with a lively jab of his fork. Jake attributed the Australian's sparkle to his growing romance with an Israeli intelligence officer.

Liam Walker, Cahill's second-in-command, sat by his countryman and appeared distant, seeming unsure how a frigate sailor should process the company of lifelong submarine officers. Beside Walker, Dmitry Volkov, commander of the *Wraith*, wiped an olive-oil based dressing from his short, graying beard. To Volkov's right, his translator uttered a Russian phrase and then accepted a bowl of bulgur wheat from his comrade.

Between the translator and Jake sat the circular table's primary occupant, Pierre Renard. The Frenchman sipped from his mineral water, lowered the glass, and then gazed at it with pensive eyes. As some unknown spark catalyzed his energy, color rose to his cheeks, and he nodded at the security team's leader by the club's main door.

Jake glanced around the empty officer's club of the Karachi naval submarine base, which he assumed Renard had rented for this evening. The six bodyguards closed each door to the dining area, assuring the privacy of the mercenary fleet's leadership.

Renard cleared his throat. "Gentlemen, I'm ready to share the news. Olivia McDonald has brought an opportunity to me, to us, that we must pursue."

While the Russians exchanged words of translation, the fearless Australian commander challenged his boss. "Yeah, we got that part, mate. You said the CIA Sheila was working on something."

Renard smirked and waggled a finger at Cahill. "No, my friend. Miss McDonald had been helping me arrange a different opportunity, one that now seems so... I wouldn't say unimportant... perhaps, mundane, compared to the mission she's just requested."

Jake raised an eyebrow. "Requested?"

The smile growing across Renard's face was reminiscent of child in a candy store. "Yes. She requested. You see, it seems an American submarine may be stranded on the bottom of the Strait of Hormuz."

Before he knew it, Jake was standing and looking down on Renard. A decade had passed since he'd last helped his countrymen, and he sensed his first chance to assist a United States submarine. "Seriously?"

"Jake, please sit."

"Sorry." He lowered himself into his chair. "It's just..."

"I know. You smell opportunity beyond all our dreams. And for you specifically, redemption."

Remaining silent, Jake shrugged.

"You have a good nose, but events are unfolding too quickly for me to negotiate any extra clemency at this time. We'll do what we're asked and trust the goodwill of our partners after the outcome."

The dreamlike hope of a presidential pardon evaporated, but Jake knew his boss would arrange appropriate rewards for their fleet, and he embraced the chance to help his old team, the United States Navy. "What happened? What can we do?"

"Less than ten hours ago, the USS *Indiana* was struck by a lightweight torpedo in Iranian waters. Prior to being struck, the *Indiana* sent a message via a communications buoy that it would present its bow to the weapon and attempt to bottom the ship with the crew assembled in the engine room. American assets heard the explosion, but nobody's found the *Indiana* yet."

While Jake's mind raced with questions, problems, and solutions, Cahill's mouth let loose with carefree curiosity. "How in the hell did an American submarine let itself get hit?"

Renard shook his head. "That was my first question to Miss McDonald. Either she doesn't know, or she won't tell me."

"Well it's important, mate. Were the Iranians trying to sink it or weren't they? Was it intentional or not? It makes a world of difference."

"Indeed, it does. She told me to assume hostility on the part of the Iranians, but she had nothing more to say about it."

With independent wealth granting him free time, Jake had developed a habit of reading international news, and he recalled a relevant situation. "Aren't the Iranians involved in a peace settlement in Syria?"

Renard sipped his water and then lowered the glass. "Correct. And like all multinational negotiations, it is a complex matter. The Syrians must demonstrate a government-led ousting of ISIS, which will earn them a lifting of bans on their oil exports to the United States and Europe, which will create competition with other oil producers, such as Iran, which in turn demands its export markets are protected from Syrian expansion in the negotiations."

"Markets, such as America?"

"Always in the mix are your countrymen, my friend. It's the hazard of being a superpower."

After replaying the chain of diplomatic events in his mind, Jake summarized it. "That means that America and Iran are at least faking some sort of friendship at a bargaining table."

"Correct."

"But American submarines still have to spy on Iran, since they're growing their navy like gangbusters."

"Correct."

"And they're concentrating their navy in the Strait of Hormuz, which controls a ton of oil flow."

"Correct. Twenty percent of the world's petroleum passes through the strait."

"And the Iranians are good at building and operating submarines."

"Correct."

As his translator relayed the conversation to the Russian commander, Volkov offered his assessment in broken English. "In Russian Navy, we teach Iran good. Maybe too good."

Renard used the break in Jake's questioning to reassert himself. "As you might expect, I have a plan. However, this situation is so sudden and unusual that I'm open to brainstorming if desired. The mission itself is even open to challenge, but I've tentatively defined it with Miss McDonald's concurrence as returning the *Indiana* intact with its crew to a friendly port."

Jake furrowed his brow. "Friendly includes Pakistan?"

"For the sake of our mission, yes. But Oman is preferred as a destination, since its shorelines are closer to the *Indiana's* expected location."

As Jake continued the questioning, he suspected he was the commander most interested in the welfare of his fellow Americans, if he dared to consider himself a citizen. "Expected? We don't know?"

"The Fifth Fleet has a good idea based upon the communications buoy's location, the reported course the *Indiana* was on during its torpedo evasion, and a best estimate of the location of the detonation. But it's uncertain until proven."

Jake's anxiety rose. "So, who's looking, other than two dozen

Iranian submarines?"

"The Americans are looking, too, I assure you. The shallow water is noisy, and the *Indiana* will be silent, but the Americans have coordinates and know the ship's track."

Sensing he'd become more emotional about the mission than his colleagues, Jake tried to appear relaxed by crossing his ankle over his leg and leaning back. "Then what about our constraints? The Americans won't want us stepping on their toes, and we all want to make sure we don't shoot each other."

"Assuming the situation becomes violent, the United States doesn't want to destroy the entire Iranian fleet, especially during the peace talks in Syria. Neither side wants a war. So, you can imagine that we've been commissioned to use our slow-kill weapons to compel interfering Iranian assets back to their piers."

Jake snorted. "The situation's already violent. I mean, the Iranians torpedoed an American submarine."

"Aside from that."

"What do you mean 'aside from that'?"

Renard's face softened with a pensive expression. "There's no saber rattling. There's no bragging. There's no warning to the Americans to stay out of Iranian waters. There's just diplomatic silence. It suggests uncertainty in the Iranian perspective of the event. It might even suggest a mistake."

As the scenario angered him, Jake grimaced. "Come on, Pierre. There's more to it than that. If it was a mistake, there'd be an apology. Olivia's leaving something out."

Renard raised his voice. "An American submarine got caught deep inside Iranian waters. What more must you know?"

An uncomfortable silence overfell the table.

"I'm sorry, Jake, but from what I understand, the Iranians had every right to strike, and they were humane in their selection of a lightweight weapon. It's only their diplomatic spin about it that's defying explanation, and that's not presently our concern."

The words hurt Jake. "You know damned well that America's

been putting its submarines in hostile waters for decades to help preserve world security. We–I mean they–have been policing the world for everyone's benefit with their asses on the line since before we were born."

Cahill sliced the growing tension. "You mean before most of us were born. Pierre's getting long in the tooth, and me mate Henri's not far behind him."

After suppressing a weak smile, Renard regained control of his group. "Regardless of the philosophies and the ages of our team, we have a mission, one that might be legendary in scope. But we must agree upon it."

Seeming to sense his moment to contribute, the Australian prophesized his ship's role. "I assume you'll want me to do the heavy lifting?"

The French boss nodded. "Indeed."

"Well then, I see three obvious questions. Maybe your Taiwanese engineers can help model the answers."

Renard shook his head. "I doubt it. We're in a race against time. We know that the Iranians are looking for the *Indiana* as well."

"Alright then. The first concern's getting the *Indiana* into me cargo bed. I assume half the ship's flooded. Getting underneath it's going to be tough."

Eyes sparkling, the Frenchman shared his solution. "I believe we can get the *Indiana* to rotate its stern up enough for you to get under the bulk of it."

"How will the crew know when to rotate? I don't imagine they'll be waiting for me like that."

"Communications is one-way at the moment. However, once you're in close range, you'll be able to communicate on an encrypted digital sonar. The Americans will share their software with us, which will handle the encryption and provide a regulated volume control to avoid broadcasting unnecessary sound."

The Australian cocked his head. "I suppose that could work, but you're limited in how far I can rotate me ship before the rail-

45

guns would break the surface."

"I didn't say it would be easy." Renard raised his glass of bubbling water towards Cahill. "I would trust only a world-class commanding officer to handle the job with the appropriate skill, instinct, and judgment."

"I appreciate the confidence, mate, but I still have concerns about the weight. A *Virginia*-class half-filled with water may be too heavy for me. And if I can carry it, a third concern's the torque on the *Indiana's* hull. It could cause its bow to break off."

"Which takes me to my next point. You'll carry the *Indiana* to safety underwater."

"The whole way?"

"Yes."

"That limits me to something less than thirteen knots, depending how bad the drag is on a *Virginia* hull. I won't be able to run from torpedoes."

"You'll have to slip away without attracting one."

Through his translator, Volkov voiced a concern. "You want Jake and me to shoot the Iranians. That will protect Terry. That will also protect the Americans. And since we're the ones shooting, we'll be the ones being shot at."

"Correct. The *Specter* and the *Wraith* are still the only ships in the world armed with slow-kill weapons. Until that changes, you and Jake are the only ones who can deter the Iranians without escalating this into a full-scale war."

Jake wanted to offer the less-than-lethal weapons to the American submarines, but he wondered if the *Virginia*-class tactical system could handle the modified Black Sharks. "Can we give some slow-kills to the Americans?"

Renard swallowed and lowered his glass. "I'm having six slow-kills flown to the Fifth Fleet from our inventory, as well as six limpets. They'll attempt to mate them to at least one submarine for the rescue mission, but I'm not hopeful. The problem is timing. There's already one American submarine searching for the *Indiana*, and it won't have the time to load our weapons. Therefore, the bulk of the combat, if not all of it, will fall to you and Dmitry."

Jake tried to avoid cynicism, but an inner voice hampered his enthusiasm for the forming mission. It nagged him with the ugly truth that part of him had wanted the *Goliath* to be destroyed when stolen three months ago, so that he could escape the wearisome cycle of flirting with and cheating death. "I don't mean to be an ass, but what are the Americans doing to fix their own problem?"

The Frenchman frowned. "They're deploying a legion of decoys to overwhelm the Iranians with false targets. That's no trivial matter in hostile waters. Given the tension, there won't be any overt violation of Iran's national boundary, which means no surface ships or aircraft. So, as you can imagine, an American submarine must handle the task. I'm not sure, but they may be doing it manually by releasing divers."

Eyeing the shredded beef on his plate, Jake jabbed a fork into the meat and then took a bite. While chewing, he noticed others at the table eating in silence. He swallowed. "So, that's it, then?"

Renard washed down a bite of spiced chicken. "Unless anyone wishes to add ideas or challenge what we've discussed. I was truthful when I said I invited brainstorming."

Jake watched heads shaking. "I guess not. It's crazy, but it's perfectly crazy, just like the type of mission we're designed to handle." The mission's concept was already burdening him with anxiety, but his hope for redemption compelled him. "When do we leave?"

"As soon as your American riders get here."

Jake rolled his eyes. "Was it too much to ask them to trust us without babysitters?"

"Far too much. But don't worry about them slowing us down. They'll be at your ships before we finish dinner. The Americans understand the urgency. Your ships' provisions will be loaded soon, and you'll all be underway before midnight."

CHAPTER 5

Jazani considered the mood in *Ghadir-957* sullen. Secrets between eighteen men on a hundred-foot vessel were rare, and whispers and facial expressions revealed the truth. Although his small crew performed their duties, they knew something had gone wrong, and they were worried.

In a moment of full candor, he realized his men were scared.

After waking from a fitful nap in his miniscule stateroom's bunk, he brushed his teeth, grabbed a cup of tea from the galley, and walked to the control room.

Seated forward of his undersized executive officer, two sonar technicians listened for the sounds around their submarine.

As Jazani took his seat beside the smallish man, he addressed his second-in-command, whose drooping eyes revealed a struggle for alertness. "Are you finding real combat boring?"

The executive officer slid a muff behind his ear. "I find this quite boring, sir, but I wasn't aware this qualified as combat."

"Under the sea, ninety percent or more of combat is finding your enemy." Jazani scowled as he realized he'd accepted the Americans as his enemies. Until the ambush on the *Virginia*-class, he'd considered the undersea gamesmanship a miniaturized version of a Cold War between rivals. He wondered how the gambit with the hostile weapon had redefined the game.

Seated forward of the conversation, the talkative technician slid a muff behind his ear. "It seems to me that we found our enemy twelve hours ago but let him escape."

The *Ghadir's* commander sighed. "Don't start with that again."

"I thought a complaining sailor was a healthy sailor."

"There's a limit to the effectiveness of rehashing the past."

The thin man offered a coy smile. "But you said you can't afford men suppressing their dissent."

"Did you really just quote me verbatim?"

"Yes, sir. I have a pretty good memory."

The executive officer interrupted. "He can quote the entire

Koran. I've seen him recite some uncommon verses, and the entire crew thinks he's a genius."

Modest, the sailor qualified his ability. "I once had it all memorized, but I forgot half of it. It takes constant practice to maintain proficiency."

"Impressive." Jazani waved his hand. "But that's no reason to push my generosity."

"I agree, sir, but it's frustrating being overlooked in this scenario. Everyone on board knows we should've shot a heavyweight torpedo. We all wanted to, and we should've been allowed. I know you wanted to, also, sir. But you can't complain because you're the captain."

Jazani enjoyed the matching of wits and technology with the Americans, but killing was a separate matter. Afraid to look inward for the answer, he baited his second-in-command to end the dissent. "XO, what's your opinion?"

"You know my opinion, sir, and you can trust me to keep it to myself. I'm a naval professional, and I follow the orders of my commanding officer, as long as he follows the lawful orders of my admiralty."

"There you have it." Jazani turned to the thin sailor. "We are but a military asset under orders. As its commanding officer, I helped target the American submarine. By helping coordinate the dolphins' movements, you helped me with the targeting. Parts in a proficient machine, all of us."

The talkative sailor's tone became pensive. "True, but why is our machine not working now? The dolphins were doing great, but now they're struggling. The mothership reports that they've rested and fed, but they can't find our target."

"How long until their next break?"

"Any time from ten minutes ago to almost two hours from now."

"Do we have local control, or is the mothership in charge?"

"The dolphins veered too far from the mothership about two hours ago. So, they gave me local control. But you're making a good point, sir. I should send them back before they go too far."

"Agreed. Send them to their mothership. They'll be more useful in the daylight anyway."

Jazani sipped tea from his cup, lowered it, and aimed his voice at his executive officer. "Any update from the divers?"

The short man shook his head. "Nothing. They're walking through the mud, confused like everyone else. Do you want to head shallow and stream their video?"

"Yes. Take us shallow and raise the radio mast. Get the periscope up, too, and see what's around us. Snorkel and top off the battery while you're at it."

As the submarine ascended, the wind-blown swells rocked the deck. The panorama from the photonics mast showed a starlit night, the rumbling diesel engine confirmed the charging of the *Ghadir's* main battery, and the video from the pair of Persian divers on the strait's floor showed conical swaths of light. The bright cones illuminated stirred mud and the anchor chain holding a frigate above the location where an American submarine should have been.

"Have you seen enough, sir?"

"Yeah. This is disconcerting." On his monitor, Jazani shut off the view of the divers. "But keep the radio mast up. I want to hear what's going on with the task force. Maybe somebody's found something to clear up this mess."

"You sound like you blame yourself."

Jazani canted his head and waved dismissive fingers.

"We weren't the only ones who heard the explosion, sir. There were a total of five assets, including two other submarines. The data's accurate. The Americans should be here."

"But they're not, are they?"

The short man shook his head.

"The dolphins didn't find them, our swarm of submarines haven't heard them, and divers can't see them. We know we hit something right here, but there's no sign of it. What does it mean?"

The executive officer shrugged. "The obvious answer is that we hit a decoy."

Jazani grunted. "Too easy. That's the lazy answer, and I'm sure many of our brethren are tempted to think that way, but fortunately our admiralty isn't."

"I understand that, sir, but I think that sending fifteen submarines, ten surface ships, and half a dozen helicopters to search four-hundred miles of water is too much."

"How can any amount be too much, given the quarry?"

"If we present too many targets to the Americans, they may be tempted to shoot back."

The *Ghadir's* commander snorted. "That risk is business as usual in these waters. I prefer to verify the result of our torpedo rather than lazily assume its failure."

The thin technician curled forward and pressed his muffs against his ears. After several seconds, he announced his findings. "I've got something. American *Virginia*-class propulsion noise. I'm sending the bearing to the system."

As the technician tapped a key, Jazani watched a line form on his monitor. "XO, get this information to the task force on a data feed. Secure snorkeling. I have the deck and the conn. Coming right to course two-two-zero."

"I've sent the data to the task force, sir."

Fearing a trap and an incoming American weapon, Jazani moved cautiously. "XO, lower all masts and antennas. I'm slowing us to three knots and bringing us down to twenty-five meters."

As the deck dipped and then leveled, the spikes representing narrowband sounds from the target rose above their noise floors.

After analyzing the data for ten minutes, Jazani risked believing he'd found an American submarine, but doubts lingered. "XO, how much faith do you have in our wave front curvature algorithms?"

"For the usual fast Americans, not much. But I see your point. This one's hardly moving. That gives the integrators time to process the phase differences between our towed hydrophones."

Jazani rubbed his palms. "If I believe it, it's three miles away making three knots towards us."

"Agreed."

"I'm coming shallow to share the data with the task force."

"You don't want to shoot, sir?"

Unsure of the truth within his heart, Jazani gave the dutiful response. "Our orders are to find, not to sink. A helicopter's better positioned to handle it."

The executive officer grunted. "That's an opinion, sir, but I commend your loyalty to our superiors for stating it as a fact."

"You'd prefer to launch a weapon yourself?"

"I'd like it to be an option."

"Don't be so quick to dole out death. And don't be so quick to believe that we've really found what we're looking for."

"I want to find our wounded animal, and it seems to be limping towards us. Why should I be so quick to ignore a gift?"

"Because I doubt it's a gift. I suspect a curse. Wounded or not, American submarines at three knots can't be heard from three miles away. Keep your head on straight and be thankful that we're not tasked to engage it."

Twenty minutes later, the talkative technician called out. "I hear our helicopter over the target. It's lowering its dipping sonar. And now, it's emitting active pings."

Jazani eyed his monitor, which showed a history of the American noises following a straight line at three knots. "These aviators waste no time announcing themselves." To his surprise, the American target continued along its path, despite the airborne hunters broadcasting their sonar search.

The thin technician became animated. "Two loud splashes."

Jazani half-stood from his seat. "Air-dropped weapons?"

"I don't hear any screws, sir."

"What the devil..." Not wearing his headset, Jazani tapped an icon on his screen, unmuted an overhead microphone, and called out. "Task force commander, this is Shark One. Over."

Seconds later, a deep voice issued from the speaker above him. "Shark One, this is task force commander. Go ahead. Over."

"I just heard two drops from Angel Three hitting the water. What's going on? Over."

"Angel Three is dropping divers. Over."

"Understand divers. Out." Jazani considered his non-submarining comrades foolish until he thought through the scenario. He realized divers in fins could catch a three-knot contact, and the best sensors to identify the target were flashlights and eyeballs.

Shaking his head, the executive officer faced his boss. "I guess we're just observers again, sir?"

"For the moment. But keep observing. I consider this deep drama in shallow waters."

"You should be a poet, sir. A poet-warrior."

"I'll settle for a warrior, if, as you wish, I'm ever allowed to shoot a weapon."

"That may require a lot of patience."

"Patience is the hallmark of a good submariner."

Fifteen minutes later, the executive officer announced his assessment of an updated data feed. "I'm afraid I may have misjudged the situation."

Jazani glanced at the incoming news, which identified the submerged target as an American unmanned undersea vehicle. "We have a major fleet exercise looking for a wounded American submarine, but all we can find is a robot."

"There's more, sir. If you keep reading, the frigate's going to launch a Hoot at the robot. We're tasked to track the Hoot."

Survival instincts compelled Jazani to check the geometry between the relevant vessels to verify his *Ghadir* was clear of the supercavitating torpedo's future track. Convinced of his safety, he looked at his second-in-command. "Tell the task force we acknowledge the tasking and will support it."

"I'm sending the acknowledgement, sir."

Ten minutes later, Jazani received the launch announcement and pressed muffs over his ears. A splash preceded the hiss of the submerged weapon's self-generated steam shroud as it accelerated to its sustained speed of two hundred knots. "Impressive."

On his monitor, lines of bearing to the Hoot fanned away from his ship, following the torpedo towards the robot. To his dismay, the weapon raced by its target. "That's a miss. Let the task force know."

His executive officer stirred. "I'm typing the note and sending it, sir. Shall I recommend that we handle this ourselves with a Type 53 torpedo?"

"Don't embarrass us like that. You know the fleet wants to do this with our newest homegrown weapon. Instead, recommend that they dial down the speed against such a small target."

"I will, sir."

Five minutes later, Jazani heard the half-speed Hoot, running at only twice the speed of a conventional torpedo, detonate under the American robot. "That's a hit. Can anyone hear evidence of the robot's sinking?"

Two young heads shook.

The short officer summarized the lack of evidence. "The robot's parts are too small to hear. There'd be nothing left but shards. No compartments collapsing. No air escaping. Just like rocks falling."

"Very well. Inform the task force of the obvious. There's one less American robot infesting our waters."

After the executive officer sent the message, he became animated. "Sir, check the data feed. Shark Four just picked up a submerged contact making the same sounds we heard. Another *Virginia*-class propulsion plant. Except this one isn't moving."

Jazani read the data and frowned. Then he replaced the downward corners of his mouth with a smirk. "You know that this means, don't you?"

"Another decoy, but probably not a robot."

"Meaning probably what?"

"A sonobuoy?"

"It was a trick question, XO. It could be a robot set to zero knots. It could be a submarine-launched self-decoy set to zero knots. Or it could be a sonobuoy set to broadcast *Virginia*-class noises while it drifts with the current."

The short man shrugged. "So, we don't know until we look."

"And we will look. And we'll look at the next, and then we'll look at the next, and so on and so forth until there's nothing left to examine."

"When do you think that might be?"

"I have no idea, but I know these decoys will become troublesome."

"Then why are you smiling?"

"Decoys are intended to fool hunters, which means the Americans are protecting something. And that means we hit something. That wounded *Virginia*-class ship is out there, and I intend to find it."

CHAPTER 6

Within the quiet engineering lab, Causey studied the *Indiana's* movement history. The penciled trace showed the ship moving three knots in reverse during the first half hour of its backwards crawl. Thereafter, the speed showed a quieter two knots. "We're not really making three knots."

His face unreadable, the executive officer offered cautious agreement without independent thought. "No, sir."

Causey qualified his assessment. "Since our bow's on the bottom, we don't move with the currents, but our speed sensors can't account for that since they measure the water's speed over our hull. So, we're making three knots as measured, but only two knots over ground, if I believe the charted currents."

"Agreed. Let's say it's really two knots, sir. That should get us into Pakistani waters in just under two hundred hours. That's more than eight days, but we can't go any faster without shaking. We can sustain the turns for all-back nine knots and hold the two knots over ground, but that's it, captain."

The *Indiana's* commander accepted that the muddy bottom negated his nuclear-powered escape speed, but two knots beat zero. "We'll hold two knots, at least while the divers work outside."

In need of leadership, his second-in-command looked up.

Causey spurred him. "Not sure what to do next?"

"No, sir."

"I'm going to check on the divers. I want you to have the Cob calculate rations for nine days and determine if we need to send the divers in to get more canned goods. Once you've got him started on that, I want you to review possible Iranian search plans with the department heads and any free officers. Think of ways they could find us."

"Understood, sir. I'll take care of it. Uh... captain?"

"Yes?"

"Do you want me to account for any visible trail we might be leaving on the seafloor?"

Causey had considered the exposure, but he'd crossed it off his list of risks due to the impossibility of its exploitation. Submarines and assets that hunted them ignored shallow tracks in mud. "Why would that concern you?"

"Well, sir, I've been racking my brains trying to figure out how we got targeted in the first place."

Encouraged by his second-in-command's unsolicited input, Causey wanted to learn more. "Go on."

"The only way it was acoustically was if we crawled right by a submarine that was drifting dead in the water."

"That's plausible. Right now, it's my top theory."

"But what if it's some unknown thing we haven't considered, sir. Iran could be using robots, dolphins, or divers, just like us."

Causey grunted. "I can't say either way, but I'll have our divers investigate our trail in the mud. It's worth knowing how bad it is, now that you mention it. Good thinking." He stepped from the enclosed engineering lab and found his way to the tunnel's watertight door.

The burly diving officer turned at the sound of sneakers tapping the deck plates. "Good timing, sir. The guys are at the hull breach."

"How's the tunnel holding?"

"At this depth, it's fine. We've got a wire jammed through the door to keep communications with the team, but that's giving negligible leakage. Some water got in, of course, but I bet your reactor's still dry enough."

"That's just about the least of my concerns."

"Why not go in and take a look, just to be sure, sir?"

"We can see through windows, and it looks fine. I'd like to enter and check for a slow leak, but I'm not hungry enough to eat my own sailors. So, I won't send them in to be cooked by a critical reactor."

"Oh, yeah. Silly me."

Wanting to give orders, Causey checked himself. The divers had become invaluable, and he made sure to demonstrate respect. "Don't beat yourself up. I'd give all your men the bends if I supervised them."

Despite the somber and anxious mood pervading the crippled submarine, the young officer chuckled. "Yeah. You'd probably put them in front of a seawater valve."

Causey had made his engineer shut down intakes on the starboard side of the engine room to avoid proving the diver correct. "No, I'm not that clueless. Can you show me what's going on? You said my timing was perfect."

"Sure. Let me knock and give the signal. Then you can look." Lieutenant Hansen wrapped his knuckle against the portal, and a diver's face appeared. The officer pointed to his eye, and the pressurized man nodded.

A second later, a waterproofed display appeared showing a video feed of two flashlight beams dancing off the jagged shards outlining the hole in the torpedo room. Causey nudged aside the lieutenant and the silent senior chief to see better. He tried to hide his gasping. "That hole's got to be ten feet across."

Seemingly unimpressed, the lieutenant shrugged. "At least. A lightweight warhead is enough to put a submarine on the bottom. Lucky for us it was shallow water."

"I'm not sure how much of it was luck. Something tells me they could've vaporized us if they wanted to, but there are too many unknowns to speculate."

"All that matters is that it was only one weapon and it wasn't any bigger."

"What's next, lieutenant?"

"I figured I'd see if we could take manual control of the torpedo tubes."

Causey raised his eyebrow. "That's good thinking, but we don't have a way to generate targeting solutions. I think you're looking at step four when we need to solve steps one and two."

"If you've got a better priority, I'm all ears, sir."

In a welcomed show of solidarity, Senior Chief Spencer supported his young officer. "Yeah, sir. I agreed with the lieutenant about checking out the torpedo tubes. You got something better in mind?"

The *Indiana's* commander prioritized his thoughts. "My first concern's for your guys. Make sure you get with the engineer and monitor your men's radiation. The tunnel's a high-exposure area. The engineer can tell you where they should stand and sit to minimize their exposure, and you'll need to rotate your teams and have their dosimeters read often."

Both divers nodded their agreement.

"My next concern's a question. Have either of you guys thought about welding enough sheets of metal over the hole to pump the compartment dry?" He expected modest ridicule but needed to know their opinion, and he was impressed with the seriousness of the senior chief's response.

"We kicked that idea around, but that's a lot of work. Getting material in place, covering that full area of the blast damage, and staging the equipment. It would take days, and it would be loud."

"We've got days, but let's discuss the other concerns before committing to any loud repairs. Actually, my next two concerns can be achieved in one operation. Do you think your guys can drag the towed array from the stabilizer to the front of the ship?"

Both divers shrugged as the lieutenant answered. "Yeah. I'm sure we can. But 'how far' is the question. I don't want the guys getting too far away from the boat."

"Any length you can give me is good. It's our only chance of hearing."

Lieutenant Hansen frowned. "How could you access the data?"

"There's a diagnostic port back at the towed array system's control station we can tap into with a laptop and headphones."

"Huh. So, we could hear, and we could have torpedoes, too."

Causey recalled his third concern. "That's my intent, but the ideal situation is to remain undetected. So, while your guys are deploying the array, I could use their assessment of the trail we're leaving in the mud."

Both divers narrowed their eyes, and the senior chief challenged the comment. "Does that mean you expect enemy divers in the water? I mean, who else would be looking for our tracks?"

"I don't know. I'm asking for the assessment as a precaution."

"The lieutenant and I had talked about arming our guys, but we decided against it for this first reconnaissance trip. But given what you just said, I say we arm them before they leave the hull."

"That's another thing we agree on. Bring them back, senior chief. Let's put some weapons in their hands and have our guys pull the towed array sonar in the wrong direction like the captain said."

The *Indiana's* commander remembered his final immediate need. "As long as they're coming back, can you have them retrieve a half a dozen communications buoys?"

Lieutenant Hansen reached to the deck for a whiteboard. "I'll write it out for the guys to send the word. Can you still write messages into the buoys after they've been immersed?"

"We should, but we'll find a way if not. I'll want your guys to take one out with them on their next trip and release it to the surface."

"Consider it done, sir. But why not just send one of my guys to the surface with a global satellite phone? They'd need to ascend in stages with delays, but they could do it."

Appreciating the good ideas coming his way, Causey left the latest one undecided. "I like it except for the risk of detection. If the Iranians sniff it, they'll know it's us. I still prefer the option to have the communications buoys transmit with a delay, but I'll keep your idea as backup plan. But getting a GPS fix passively would be useful."

"I can do that."

"Great."

"I can also have my guys swim off our track and back again to put some lateral distance between us and the buoys."

"Yes. As far as they can go without losing them."

"Don't worry about them, sir. The biggest risk is that they'll like their chances better without us and swim to shore. They're swimming machines. I wouldn't worry about their safety. I'd worry about them running away."

Though the officer's tone was joking, the concept of swimmers abandoning the submarine took hold in Causey's mind as he walked away. He questioned if his crew could quit their ship to save themselves. As he marched around the corner of an equipment cabinet, a second-class petty officer he recognized as an electronics technician inspected a huge breaker box, the size of a man's torso.

The sailor's businesslike visage showed courage over his underlying fear. "Captain."

Causey doubted the man would abandon the ship unless ordered. "What are you up to?"

"Checking for arcing and sparking. The chief wants to make sure the impact didn't set us up for nasty shorts."

"Good thinking." As the *Indiana's* commander followed a meandering path to the lab serving as his command center, he heard the gentle hiss of steam and rumble of turbines. While it worked at low output, the power plant throbbed through his feet. The slight down angle lifting the stern from the mud made the walk aft an uphill trek.

The first group of sailors he found was sitting in a circle playing Texas Hold'em. A middle-aged chief petty officer looked up defensively. "It's just for bragging rights, sir. No money's exchanging hands."

"That's good. Who's winning?"

"Gomez, sir. He's got X-ray vision or some wicked voodoo working against us."

"Keep playing for bragging rights. I don't want to hear any whining if he takes all your paychecks." Causey stepped away to hoots and appreciated the men finding distractions from their dilemma. The mood fit the reality–a cautious optimism that they'd limp to safety, but the question nagged him about which men would leave the *Indiana* if offered a rescue vehicle. His intuition told him none of them wanted to abandon their ship, but he reminded himself to keep tabs on their mental endurance.

When he reached the lab, he found his second-in-command

huddled over the chart with several officers.

"XO, I just spoke with the divers, and they've agreed to deploy the towed array sonar forward. They'll also inspect our trail in the mud like you suggested."

"I'll work with the sonar chief and divers to deploy the array, sir."

"Very well, but there's time for that later. First tell me what's on your mind here."

The executive officer tapped a pencil on the chart. "Here's where we were when we were hit." He moved the pencil. "Here's where we are now. We've covered twenty-five miles, best estimate from our speed over ground. That puts a lot of uncertainty between us and ground zero."

"The Iranians have already figured out that we're not at ground zero. What's their next move?"

"I'm assuming our trail is wiped clean at ground zero, sir. The current's strong enough that it should be erasing our track everywhere we've been within hours of our passing."

"To be verified, but that's probably true. Go on."

"The first thing they'll do is a circular search outward. They have enough submarines to do it."

"That would be role reversal. They normally wait for us to come to them. It'll be a slow search with slow submarines. They can't make more than twelve knots on a good day."

The executive officer's eyes lit up. "Agreed, sir. This is where it gets challenging. If they think this through, they'll conclude one of two things. Either they hit something other than us and we got away, or we're alive on the bottom. In the first case, they'd give up and go home."

Causey nodded. "Of course. And we'll ignore that case as good luck we couldn't hope for."

"Right, sir. In the second case, they have to consider that they hit our engine room."

"Like ninety-nine point nine percent of all torpedo tail chases."

"So, they'll think we're stranded without propulsion but

with a functional tactical center and fully loaded torpedo room. They'd be scared to get near us because we'd be silent and lethal until our battery runs out, which is days running just hotel loads."

Causey narrowed his eyes. "That possibility may be driving them crazy. They should expect us to be stranded but able to fight. That could slow their search a lot."

"Right, sir. Thanks to that, the odds are in our favor of us slipping out of here and into Pakistani waters."

The *Indiana's* commander raised his palm. "Not so fast, XO. Let's say the Iranians somehow figure out what's really going on. We need to account for that. Then what?"

Squirming in discomfort, the executive officer glanced around the table for support from his juniors. The nods he received compelled him to speak. "We discussed this. If they catch on, then it's a tough road ahead. They'll realize we're attached to the bottom, and they won't need to know where we are, because they'll know that we're going to Pakistan."

"Not sure I follow you. Is it really that obvious?"

"They'll know that we can't cross the Gulf of Oman."

"Why not? From where we are, we could theoretically drag ourselves to the bottom of the gulf and back up again. What are we looking at? Six hundred feet at the deepest point? The question would be if our power output could get us up the other side."

"That's right, sir. And we'd also be at risk of sliding and rolling on the way down this side of the gulf. I don't think we can change depth anymore, so to speak. The Iranians may think we're crazy enough to try it, but we're not. We need to follow the bottom at a constant depth, and they'll probably figure that out. So, they'll look for us along their two-hundred-foot line."

Causey appreciated the thorough thoughts from his second-in-command and probed further. "In that case, they still have to consider that we could backtrack to the Strait of Hormuz and then cross to Omani water, right? That would be a lot shorter than heading to Pakistan."

"We could, sir, but that's right back into a legion of submarines. Their numbers are just too dangerous to head back into the center of their power."

"Good conclusion. Keep going."

"We also can't head north, because that only beaches us on the Iranian coast."

Again, Causey probed further. "That's the shortest path to surfacing and simplifying any attempt at repairs. Have you considered how fast we could weld the damage enough to make us seaworthy again?"

Revealing his fear of failure, the executive officer stared blankly. "No, sir."

"Don't worry. Neither have I. But it's an option we need to consider. When you're in the spaces next, check with our mechanical division chief about the possibility. Also check with the dive team about underwater repairs and have them draw up a plan. I discussed it with them briefly."

"Yes, sir."

Causey lowered his nose to the chart. "If the Iranians figure out the truth, they'd be smart ambush us somewhere to the east. It's our least risky way to safe waters."

"There's not much we can do about that without help, sir."

The conversation headed in the direction the *Indiana's* commander had predicted. "Then we should request help. If we can get some confidence about where we're going and that we're not leaving a trail, we can tell the fleet what we need."

Again, the blank stare. "But any help we'd get would require illegal entry into Iranian waters, captain. We'd be asking the fleet to risk starting a war for us."

Before Causey answered, a loud scraping noise, like metal abrading concrete, grated his ears. He cringed. "Damn."

"We're running over something, sir."

"No shit. I hope it's not as loud outside as inside."

"I wouldn't dare to guess, sir. But it's bad. We have to hope for the 'large ocean concept' to protect us from being heard."

Half a minute after it had started, the noise stopped, but it had felt like an eternity of acoustic vulnerability. "Large ocean concept. God help us if that fails us. If any Iranian naval asset was nearby, these waters are going to get small really fast."

"I think that was bedrock, sir. Our luck with mud and sediment ran out for a while. On the bright side, it reminds us how lucky we are that the bottom is mostly soft."

Slowly, Causey nodded. "Agreed. But this is also a reminder that we need help. To your point about sending warships into Iranian water, the rules of engagement for the cavalry are someone else's decision, if the cavalry comes."

"I'm sure they'll do something, sir."

The *Indiana's* commander leaned forward and lowered his voice. "Get with the Cob, and have him check with the chiefs. Make a list of sailors, by name, who you'd send off the ship and in which order. There may be an opportunity for rescue and abandoning the ship."

"I'll do it, sir, but do you really think that's an option? I can't imagine the fleet letting us leave our ship in Iranian waters for them to take home and reverse engineer."

"I've got enough to think about without figuring it out for them, but shame on us if that's the order and we're not ready."

The executive officer furrowed his brow. "I suppose that could happen, and once we're all off, the fleet could blow up our ship to prevent the Iranians from having it."

"Maybe, but it's speculation. At this point, I'm committed to getting one hundred and forty-two sailors home with a salvageable ship. If it requires dragging us backwards all the way to Pakistan, that's what I'll do."

CHAPTER 7

His submarine rocking on the *Goliath's* cargo deck, Dmitry Volkov steadied himself against a railing. "Seasickness is one reason I prefer being underwater."

With the *Wraith* above the waves, its commanding officer needed little help in his control room, but he welcomed his friend's presence. The lithe form of his ship's dolphin trainer crouched, and pitying eyes looked at him. "You must feel terrible, Dmitry. You're turning green."

Volkov's nausea was persistent but mild. "I don't always get this way. It must look worse than it is."

"I'm sure that riding backwards doesn't help."

"It's the only way Terry can carry two submarines."

"Have you tried facing backwards, so that he's pulling you forwards?"

"I did for a bit, but it didn't help. I'll be fine once we submerge."

"That reminds me. My babies are probably unhappy with this incessant rocking. I need to check on them." The trainer stood and strode away.

The *Wraith's* commander stopped his friend. "Vasily?"

"Yes?"

"Are you ready to use your dolphins for this?"

Frowning, the lithe man placed his hands on his hips. "Why would you ask?"

"The water's shallow and noisy. It'll be hard for them to hear, and there may be a lot of targets to confuse them."

"Smart targets, like the Israelis?"

Volkov shrugged. "Perhaps. I don't want to underestimate the Iranians."

"Ever since Israel, I'm scared of losing my babies. But I believe I can talk them home from any distraction through the drones."

"You've gained confidence. That's good. You can't worry about every possible problem, or you'll go mad."

"But you look like you're worrying."

Volkov scoffed. "That's the burden of command."

"It's worse after what happened to the *Goliath*, isn't it?"

The *Wraith's* commander remembered the theft of the mercenary fleet's flagship. Doubt had pervaded his crew when an assailant had hijacked the transport vessel, but the dour mood of Volkov's sailors had been euphoric compared to the morbid victimhood overshadowing Cahill's men. "I believe our crew's fine. Terry's crew may be a different story. Three of his technicians quit after the hijacking, and he's barely had time to train replacements."

"All the crews have some attrition. Once a man has his wealth, he must decide if he's willing to stomach the ongoing danger. I can't fault them for leaving."

His nausea worsening with the increased rolling, Volkov grunted. "You are wise, Vasily. I trust that you and your dolphins have judged the continued risk acceptable."

"It's always scared me, but I admit I'm addicted to the adventure. May I check on my babies now?"

Volkov waved his hand. "Yes. Go. I'm sorry to have kept you from them."

Light on the balls of his feet, the trainer bounced away.

Turning to the monitors by his seat, the *Wraith's* commander saw his boss' face and attempted a greeting in English. "Hello, Pierre."

Renard impressed him by switching to Russian. "My friend, how are you?"

Volkov used simple phrases in his native language. "It's good to hear you speak Russian."

"You know I can manage when I must. Speak slowly, or I will fail to understand."

"I want to submerge." The *Wraith's* commander dipped his rigid hand below the surface of an imagery body of water.

"Why?"

"Sick." The Russian tapped his stomach.

"Soon." A shadow overfell the Frenchman's face. "I must say something important without your translator. I can buy new submarines. I cannot buy new people. Be safe."

Volkov interpreted the message as permission to live at the expense of the *Wraith*. "That's kind of you to say."

"It is true. It is false for the *Goliath*. Impossible to replace. It is true for the *Wraith* and *Specter*. I have friends and money. I can buy new *Scorpènes*."

"I'm coming back with your ship and your employees."

"I hope so. I told Jake the same."

"Good. Should I call my translator?"

"Yes. And your rider."

Volkov summoned his translator along with the guest from the American navy and then studied Renard's surroundings in the display. With bodies walking behind his boss, he placed the seated Frenchman in a busy conference room. "Where are you?"

"It's a special area for emergencies. They call it a 'crisis response' room."

Bleary-eyed from sleep, the translator arrived and sat next to his commanding officer. "Good evening. Or is it morning?"

"It's morning for us, evening for Pierre, I believe. He's in Bahrain with the American Fifth Fleet."

The translator looked at Renard, exchanged words in English, and updated his commanding officer. "It's almost midnight for him. He's hailing Jake and Terry now."

Moments later, a uniformed American naval officer who had surprised the *Wraith's* commander with the beauty of his pronunciation of Russian words, joined him in the control room. "Good morning, Mister Volkov."

"And to you, Commander Hatcher."

The faces of the other ship's commanders appeared on monitors, and the conversation became a drone of English.

The translator intervened. "Pierre wants us to be the rearguard. Jake will patrol ahead on the Pakistani side of the *Indiana*."

Volkov sipped soda water and burped. "That means I'm riding on Terry's back for another hour."

"I'm afraid so. He wants you to use the dolphins and drones to search behind you for Iranian submarines as you trail the *Indiana* eastward. Jake will search ahead. The American submarine *California* will hover over the *Indiana*."

"Hover and do what?"

"Jake's asking that question now."

The American requested, and the Frenchman answered.

"Pierre says the *Indiana's* making two knots eastward over ground by dragging itself backwards and will continue to do so until Terry loads it. The *California* will patrol circles around the *Indiana* listening for threats. Any threats will be shared by an acoustic datalink between all five ships, as distance permits. There will also be a constant broadcast of data via radio, available whenever you can raise a mast. The Americans have dedicated assets to continuously transmit a low-frequency broadcast so that we'll always have low-baud data, even while deep."

Volkov questioned the underwater datalink. "How proven is the submarine-to-submarine communications system?"

The *Wraith's* rider seemed confident, and as a submarine officer, he demonstrated his domain knowledge. "It's quite reliable, as long as the ships are in the same acoustic layer, which you will be in this shallow water. Any hydrophone on the equipped ships can listen, and it broadcasts from your bow and underwater phone systems. The coverage has proven effective in our usage."

While the translator summarized in English the American rider's assessment, Volkov recalled his testing of the digital acoustic communication system between the *Wraith* and the *Specter* before he'd boarded the *Goliath*. With cautious optimism, he considered it impressive but withheld final judgment pending its use in the real world. He returned his attention to the conversation among the commanders.

Renard spoke, and the translator relayed his words. "Expect the Iranians to have orders to sink mercenary ships but not American ships. They fear war with America but not with an upstart navy. Therefore, you and Jake are free to use slow-kill weapons liberally, not just in self-defense but also in defending the *Indiana*. And every submerged Iranian submarine is considered a threat to the *Indiana*. Use of heavyweights is restricted."

Volkov grunted his acknowledgement.

The translator continued reciting Renard's orders. "The *California* will be in charge of all ships. We'll take orders from its commanding officer, but if his order conflicts with Pierre's policies on weapons release or safety of ship, each mercenary fleet commander will give priority to Pierre's policies. The Americans have agreed to this."

The *Wraith's* commander studied Jake's face for signs of irritation in the *California's* primacy displacing him as the first among commanders, but the American showed no ire.

"When Terry has the *Indiana* in his cargo bed, he'll inform the *California*, and all five ships will escape to the south to international waters, and then the captain of the *California* will determine the best route to friendly waters, based upon threat assessments."

Trying to appease his uneasy stomach, Volkov shifted his weight in his seat. "Let's just get on with it."

"Do you want me to translate that?"

"No."

"Don't worry. Pierre just said we'll submerge after this conversation and then deploy Jake."

Taking solace in the pending relief from the rolling, Volkov called to the solitary watchman he'd stationed in the control room. "Pass the word to man the ship's propulsion and control watches."

An hour later, the *Goliath* dragged its two-submarine cargo below the waves while Volkov watched water slosh over the transport ship's cameras. The monitor portraying Renard's likeness turned black. Minutes ticked away slowly as the deck stabilized underneath the waves.

In English, Cahill mentioned something the translator relayed despite its obviousness. The Australian was releasing Jake's ship.

On the screens, Volkov watched underwater floodlights bathe his ship's twin, the *Specter*, in whiteness. Hydraulic rams rotated from the submarine, and then the freed vessel began its gentle ascent.

Managing the water weight underneath the departing vessel, Cahill shared his confidence in the *Goliath*. "Jake's free, and I'm maintaining depth control. No problem. I'm taking us down to sixty meters to clear under him."

Volkov's queasiness eased as the rocking subsided.

From a console with a black screen, Jake tested the underwater datalink. "Can you guys hear me?"

Letting the native English speakers talk, Volkov listened to their words and his translator's interpretation.

"Yeah, mate. You sound clear as a bell. How do you read me?"

"You sound great in digital clarity. Are you getting a data feed from me, too?"

"I've got it right here in front of me."

"How far's this thing supposed to work, again?"

"Your countrymen say it can push out to ten miles, but we've all set our power limits to three miles for this mission."

"So, I'll lose you before you deploy Dmitry."

"Right, mate. Happy hunting."

In silence, Volkov watched a screen of icons showing the *Goliath-Wraith* tandem move west while Jake took the *Specter* east. The data feed faded at three miles. "We're alone now."

The translator interpreted Cahill's response. "Not for much longer. We'll be within range of the *California* in the next ten minutes or so if we want to try communicating, depending where it is in its patrol circle."

Without Jake, Volkov assumed the Australian commander was in charge, but the patient expression on Cahill's face suggested he awaited an opinion, and the *Wraith's* commander provided one. "Let's not broadcast. We'd risk alerting the Iranians, and for what? To attempt to hail the *California's* crew when they should already know we're here?"

Commander Hatcher nodded. "They do."

"Alright, mate. I'll take you straight to your drop point."

While he rode the *Goliath* westward, Volkov tasked his sonar technicians with listening for submerged contacts, both friendly and hostile. He studied a display showing the *Indiana's* expected position five miles away, and the lack of sonic information concerned him. "Still nothing, Anatoly?"

Seated at a Subtics tactical console, the young sonar guru shook his head.

The American rider explained the silence. "The *California* measured sound levels from the *Indiana*, and it's undetectable outside two miles. With our background noise while tied to the *Goliath* at our transit speed, I'd be surprised if you'd hear it if we drove right over it."

The *Wraith's* commander recalled a briefing stating that the Americans had diverted two UUVs to mirror the *Indiana*. Nobody had mentioned the derogatory term for their roles, but the label "torpedo-sponges" cycled through his mind. "I had dared to hope to hear your robots, but I see that they're impressively quiet."

Commander Hatcher boasted of his navy's unmanned undersea vehicles. "They're impressive. They're much cheaper than building manned submarines, and there are too many Iranian submarines in these waters for our manned fleet to track. They've gathered invaluable data and were operating flawlessly until... well, we haven't confirmed if the malfunctioning unit failed or was sabotaged."

During the next thirty minutes, Volkov's tactical view showed the *Indiana*, circled by the *California* and mirrored by robots, moving to his northeast. As his attention shifted to dangers closer to his submarine, he stretched his legs and walked about the small compartment. With the *Goliath's* catamaran hulls worsening the background noise, the sonar displays were empty of hostile sounds.

From the monitor at the captain's console, Cahill's voice rang out.

The translator interpreted the command. "Terry said he's

slowing to deploy us."

Volkov walked to the gray-bearded veteran who controlled the flow of water, air, and communications throughout the *Wraith*. Tapping his shoulder, he leaned towards him. "Man the full watch sections, and have Vasily prepare his dolphins."

The gray-beard nodded and reached for a microphone.

"No. Do it quietly. Iranian submarines may be drifting out there, unheard." As the vibrations under his feet died with the decaying speed, Volkov walked to his commanding officer's console and sat in front of the Australian's image. "We're ready, Terry."

"I see that your weight distribution's good. When we're dead in the water, I'll let you go."

Volkov watched digits on his display tick towards zero. "Almost there."

"Let's kill off the rest of this speed with an upward glide." Cahill turned his face from the screen, and the deck took a subtle upward angle before settling. The *Goliath's* commander aimed his nose back towards the display. "We're drifting. Are you ready, Dmitry?"

"Da. Yes."

"Pump water off to make yourself light."

Volkov lifted his chin for his gray-bearded veteran's benefit. "Pump overboard from the middle drain tank." He then turned his jaw back to the screen with his Australian friend's image. "I'm pumping, Terry. I'm ready."

"Off you go. I'm deploying you now."

Through the *Goliath's* external cameras, the *Wraith's* commander watched hydraulic presses roll back and release his hull. As his ship rose and the laser communications lock with his host failed, the screens froze and then went black. But the borrowed American software allowed an acoustic link with Cahill's voice and low-bandwidth data.

"Can you hear me, Dmitry?"

"Very clearly, yes."

"Can you see data coming over the link?"

The *Wraith's* commander watched the *Goliath's* course, depth, and heading walk across the otherwise black monitor like tickertape. Other parameters rolled by, which he ignored. "Yes."

"Happy hunting, mate."

Volkov accelerated the *Wraith* northward into Iranian waters, losing the acoustic communications with the *Goliath* as distance weakened the link. When he reached the line he expected the *Indiana* had drawn in the mud, he slowed to follow the wounded American submarine with a zigzagging search. As his crew settled into the routine of looking for Persian threats, he walked to his torpedo room.

A man as lithe and graceful as the animals he trained hovered over a makeshift aquarium in the compartment's center passageway. The trainer kept his hand on a broached dorsal fin as he looked up. "Andrei's already in tube three."

Volkov saw the opened breach door and four sailors bending themselves around spare weapons to maneuver a tarp hanging from an overhead hook towards the centerline tank. He stepped back to let his men load the second bottlenose dolphin onto the sling. With practiced skill, the men lowered the canvas under the floating animal and worked him over it.

They hoisted Mikhail and swiveled him towards the waiting tube, exposing a blue harness wrapped forward of his dorsal fin that carried a camera, a sonic communications transceiver, and a small explosive device. The animal wiggled, exposing long rows of small teeth, and he fluttered his tongue while releasing a staccato screech.

Volkov snorted. "I can't tell them apart except for how animated Mikhail is."

Overseeing the sailors, the trainer nudged his way past his commanding officer. "Yes, yes. Mikhail the complainer and Andrei the stoic. It's so demeaning how you regard them like caricatures. It's not just you, but the whole crew. You may not think they notice, but you're wrong."

"I didn't mean to insult them."

Ignoring his commanding officer, the lithe man raised his

voice. "Slide him in behind Andrei."

Two sailors pushed the dolphin's fluke as two others slipped the tarp from under the animal. With the trainer's guidance, they closed the breach, equalized pressure, and flooded the tube.

Releasing the mammals, Volkov ordered the muzzle door opened, returned to the control room with the trainer, and then stood over his sonar leader's shoulder. "Hail them for a response. Minimum transmit power."

Anatoly called up the screen of recorded dolphin sounds and pressed the icon that invoked the chirps and whistles and demanded an immediate cetacean response. "They responded. Range, three hundred yards, based upon the roundtrip speed of sound."

"Send them to one o'clock relative to our position."

"I've sent them a command to swim at one o'clock relative to our position of twelve o'clock, and they've acknowledged."

Volkov gave the mammals time to swim and then grew impatient for their report. "Prepare to query them for submerged contacts."

The sonar ace tapped keys. "I'm ready to query them for new submerged contacts."

"Transmit the query."

Over loudspeakers, an exchange of chirps and whistles rang from the *Wraith's* bow-mounted hydrophones. After the animals responded, Anatoly shook his head. "They have nothing."

"This water's shallow and noisy. Finding contacts will be a challenge."

"Even for dolphins."

"Yes. And for humans, too. So, I want my best ears attuned to threats. Pass control of the dolphins to the trainer so you can listen."

Seated beside Anatoly, the lithe man looked up. "Yes, please. Let me control them."

"Have them follow us. This will be complex since we're trying to search behind us. It's a new geometry for them. Be vigilant."

"My babies will do their job, Dmitry."

As Volkov drew breath to order his drones launched to assist with his rearward search, his sonar guru curled forward and pressed his muffs against his head. A chill crept up the *Wraith* commander's spine. "Anatoly?"

"High-speed screws. Torpedo in the water!"

"Is it a threat to us?"

With fear in his eyes, Anatoly looked at his commanding officer. Blood fell from his face, and he resembled a ghost. "It's coming right at us. We need to run. Now!"

CHAPTER 8

New heights of fear terrifying him, Volkov shouted. "Torpedo evasion!"

Accelerating to flank speed, the *Wraith* shuddered and rolled through a sharp turn.

Ignoring his mortal danger, the trainer distracted his commanding officer. "My babies have a submerged contact, bearing–"

Volkov interrupted him. "I don't care where the contact is. Arm them, and have them deploy their warheads."

His face revealing betrayal, the lithe man looked up and pleaded with his eyes. "Dmitry? You're sending them away."

"I'm running from a torpedo. We've already lost them."

Tears welling, the trainer lowered his head and tapped a key, and the overhead loudspeaker issued an exchange of chirps and whistles. "They've acknowledged the order to arm themselves."

"Very well. As soon as they're armed, order them to deploy their warheads. Don't wait for my order."

In a room full of terrified men, the trainer alone revealed sadness. "I understand."

"We'll come back for them, if we survive." Volkov turned his attention to his sonar ace. "Is there a bearing drift yet?"

Anatoly shook his head. "It was still coming right at us when I lost it in our flow noise. No bearing rate. No bearing drift. No idea of range. It's a damned tail chase."

"Damn it." Volkov stepped behind the back of his seated graybearded veteran. "Prepare to launch one pair of gaseous countermeasures on my mark."

Through successive menus, the veteran tapped icons. "I'm ready."

"Launch countermeasures."

Anatoly pointed to a fuzzy trace forming on his screen. "The torpedo's behind our countermeasures."

"Then whoever shot it can't hear us, unless they've already

repositioned themselves wisely." Volkov returned to his sonar ace's side and crouched. "What's the status of my reactive weapon?"

Anatoly called up a screen. "Tube one's loaded with a slow-kill weapon. I've assigned it to run along the bearing of the incoming torpedo, range three miles."

To convey his seriousness, Volkov raised his voice. "I agree with the presets. Shoot tube one." The impulse launch popped the *Wraith* commander's ears as air displaced water within the tube. He verbalized his next order to his gray-bearded veteran. "Have the torpedo room cut the guidance wire to tube one and reload tubes one and three with slow-kill weapons."

Twisting his torso, the gray-beard faced him. "Do you want me to launch a noise-making countermeasure?"

With grave pessimism, Volkov pondered his escape, discerned hopelessness, and decided to hold his desperate course with the torpedo chasing him. "Launch the noise-maker."

The sonar guru announced the *Wraith's* second countermeasure. "I hear our noise-maker. It's transmitting our ship's recorded flank-speed frequencies."

"Very well, Anatoly." Volkov traversed the control room to his gray-bearded veteran's side and leaned into his ear. "Pass the word for all men who aren't staffing a combat or propulsion station to prepare to abandon ship."

Defeat loomed, but hope sprang from the last place the Russian expected as his American rider waved at him. "Mister Volkov! Come see this. It's the *California*."

Volkov marched to Commander Hatcher and studied English characters streaming over a black screen. He recognized the Latin alphabetical numbers, but the language's letters were unbreakable code. "I can't read all of that."

Seated beside the rider, the translator relayed the meaning. "It's a datalink from the *California* tracking the weapon that's chasing us and sending the *California's* new course and speed."

Digesting the interpretation, Volkov mentally ran the American submarine's new geometry relative to the *Wraith*, and then he looked to Commander Hatcher for context. "What sort of sailors behave like this, sprinting towards a hostile weapons exchange? What the devil are they doing?"

"It's not suicide, I assure you. I'm sure we'll know more soon. Just watch the datalink."

The *Wraith's* commander studied a tactical display showing a new icon of the friendly submarine and the updated American perspective of the incoming torpedo. The hostile weapon shifted backwards two miles to its true location, easing the constricting of Volkov's chest. "The *California's* six miles away. How can we hear its communications?"

With the imminent danger, Commander Hatcher offered his blunt explanation and shrugged. "The three-mile limit was imposed only on your fleet's ships."

"Can I respond?"

"Not beyond three miles, no."

Volkov turned his eyes to the English characters and noticed a new sequence. "What's it say?"

The rider handled the translation. "It's an order to come left to course one-one-five."

"I should bring the *Wraith* to course one-one-five?"

"Yes."

"That's too shallow of an evasion angle. How's that supposed to help?"

"Look here." The rider pointed at the tactical display. "If the *California* stays on course and speed... incredible."

Volkov noticed the American vessel outpacing him by ten knots. "What's incredible? The speed?"

"No. I know the *Virginia*-class' abilities. I commanded one. I mean its trajectory has it intercepting the torpedo in our stead."

"You said this wasn't suicide."

"Maybe I was wrong."

"Wrong or not, the *California* will take the weapon, and the orders are clear." Volkov raised his voice. "Come left to course one-one-five."

The deck angled and then settled.

"We're broadside to the torpedo, Anatoly. Can you hear anything?"

The sonar guru shook his head. "There's still too much flow noise. The torpedo's still too far away."

Tempted to slow and listen, Volkov instead watched the *California's* incoming gifted information stream across a screen. "What now?"

His face stone, Commander Hatcher remained stoic under the pressure. "Updates on the torpedo. The estimated solution is holding. Four minutes until it impacts us, unless the torpedo picks up the *California*."

Anatoly tapped his screen and raised his voice. "Active seeker, bearing three-one-nine. That's the incoming weapon. It just went active."

Volkov turned his head towards his sonar guru. "Listen for a Doppler shift as it acquires us and turns towards us."

The sonar ace nodded. "Doppler's already gone up, marking a fifteen-degree turn. The torpedo has acquired us and is compensating for our new course."

Volkov walked to the central table and looked down at the tactical scene. He grabbed a stylus and then extrapolated the undersea geometries to reveal the torpedo's potential timing to hit the American submarine. "If it acquires the *California*, impact is in six and a half minutes. Either way, the weapon hits a target."

The rider moved to the table. "We're missing something. This can't be a suicidal move. No offense, but your ships are the expendable ones."

"That's a bold statement for a man standing inside one."

"I'm an American naval officer on a nationless submarine owned by a French arms dealer that's staffed by Russians. I didn't expect this to be easy." The rider shifted his nose towards the streaming English characters. "Instructions from the *California*. A new course for you of one-five-five."

Volkov agreed with the evasion heading and adjusted the *Wraith's* direction. A minute later, he watched the icon representing the *California* breach the expected sonic acquisition cone of the torpedo's seeker. "We'll know soon enough if it's wire-guided. If it ignores the *California*, that will be telling."

Fed by the datalink, the chart showed the American vessel continuing into the hostile weapon's path, crossing to its cone's far edge, and then turning to evade.

Anatoly announced the failure. "No change in Doppler. The torpedo's staying on its course after us."

Raising his eyebrow, Volkov looked to his rider. "Your countrymen are heroic, but they're failing."

After waiting to allow the *California's* trajectory to shift the friendly submarine's icon back into the torpedo seeker's cone, Commander Hatcher responded. "Give them time. They're going broadside to the weapon now."

Volkov toggled a window to raw sound data and saw a cursor following the frequency of the hostile seeker. For a solid minute, the value remained unchanging, suggesting the futility of the American crew's effort to lure the weapon away. "Doppler's constant. Impact's in two minutes."

The rider gave a confirming nod.

"So be it." Volkov raised his voice towards the gray-beard. "Pass the word. Except for those manning propulsion and combat stations, all hands stand by to abandon ship."

Commander Hatcher raised an eyebrow. "You have a procedure for getting your crew off fast enough?"

The *Wraith's* commander impressed himself with his nonchalance. "In our fleet, we must be prepared for it. Lifejackets, inflatable rafts, small arms, satellite phones, radios… they'll all be assembled under our hatches within thirty seconds."

"Impressive."

"I've lost count of the hostile exchanges of weapons we've encountered. It's almost normal for us."

The rider scoffed. "If you say so." He read incoming characters. "The *California* recommends gaseous countermeasures."

Volkov agreed and elevated his voice. "Prepare to launch one pair of gaseous countermeasures on my mark."

The gray-bearded veteran tapped an icon. "I'm ready, Dmitry."

"Launch countermeasures."

On the chart behind the *Wraith*, a cloud formed representing the blinding bubbles. The *California* reached the gas field's edge and then disappeared behind it.

With ninety seconds to impact, the gray-bearded veteran shouted over his shoulder. "All hands are standing by to abandon ship."

"Very well."

"Do you want to come shallow?"

While assessing his options, Volkov ignored his veteran.

The gray-beard tried again. "Come shallow, Dmitry?"

"No. Stay on ordered depth."

Forty-five seconds later, the gray-bearded veteran revealed his fearful impatience. "We've got less than a minute."

"I know, damn it. Hold your tongue." Hungry for information, Volkov glared at the display.

As new characters trickled across the screen, Commander Hatcher announced the update. "The *California* has passed through our countermeasure field and is back in contact."

The American submarine's icon faded and reappeared in the *Wraith's* baffles. Its speed vector then veered to the southwest.

As the incoming torpedo's icon passed through the gasses, the sonar guru curled forward, pressing his earmuffs against his head in deep focus. "I hear the incoming weapon."

"Very well, Anatoly. Doppler?"

"Down-Doppler! I hear the seeker's frequency falling."

The rider's tone carried measured enthusiasm. "Confirmed! The *California* says the torpedo has turned away from us and has acquired its hull. The recommendation is for us to maintain course and speed until we're free of the acquisition cone."

Volkov reached for his whiskers and stroked their graying strands. "That's an easy decision for me, but I don't see a net gain. Like you said, our ship's expendable. The *California* is not."

Commander Hatcher's stoic tone returned. "There are several

tactical options remaining for my countrymen. I trust we'll be impressed soon with some decisive maneuvers." The rider's eyes followed the incoming data stream. "Gaseous countermeasures from the *California*. I don't expect further instructions for us. You can maneuver as you wish."

"The evasion's no longer our problem, thanks to your comrades." Volkov watched the torpedo's icon follow the American submarine out of his ship's baffles. He shouted. "All stop. Come to snorkel depth."

The deck rolled and then steadied as gravity and liquid friction slowed the *Wraith*. With the reduced speed, new sounds appeared on the sonar display, and Anatoly called out. "I hear the *California's* flow noise on broadband, barely, because I knew where to listen. I hear the torpedo's screws, too. The bearings align with the data from the *California*."

"Very well, Anatoly. Keep listening to the *California* and to the torpedo. Have the other sonar technicians listen for hostile submarines. We need to regroup."

"Understood, Dmitry." The sonar ace rattled off commands to the technicians seated with him at Subtics tactical consoles. Then he made another announcement. "Launch transients from the *California*."

"Countermeasures?"

"Possibly. I'll know soon... Yes. I hear bubbling. The torpedo's approaching the *California's* gaseous countermeasures."

Volkov grabbed a handle on the plotting table as the deck rolled under the waves.

"The torpedo's passing through the gaseous countermeasures. Also, I hear screws and propulsions sounds separating from the bearing of the *California*. It's probably a torpedo-launched decoy." A shadow overcame Anatoly's face. "No, wait. It's making turns for twelve knots."

Commander Hatcher gave an exuberant smile. "Excellent! It's a UUV. I knew there was a good explanation. The *California* sprinted towards a robot and took control of it. The sonar team will make it sprint towards themselves, they'll turn it broadside to the torpedo's seeker, and make it send out recordings of a *Virginia*-class propulsion plant. It's a brave move, but it's completely rational."

Volkov watched his sonar ace for a sign. "I pray it works."

Grinning, Anatoly looked at his commander. "Down-Doppler. The torpedo's turning towards the robot. And now the *California's* altering course away from the robot."

"Very well. It appears our heroes are saved."

A minute later, a loud detonation echoed through the *Wraith's* hull, and the sonar ace announced his findings. "The weapon exploded under the decoy. The *California's* slowing."

Slumping his shoulders in relief, Volkov let his head droop. Amid sighs and subtle cheers, he heard warranted praises for the bravery and cunning of the *California's* crew. When he looked up, the lithe form of his friend stood across the table.

The trainer's pained face was heavy ballast in an otherwise enlightened room. "My babies, Dmitry. They're gone!"

CHAPTER 9

The deck rolled in the swells as Jake took the *Specter* shallow. "Get our radio mast up, Henri. I need to hear from Pierre."

After a gentle click of a hydraulic actuator, the silver-haired mechanic bounced his voice off his panel. "The radio mast is up. We're connected."

Jake watched his boss' face appear on his monitor. Seeing a uniformed naval commander seated beside the Frenchman, the *Specter's* commander waited for Renard to speak first.

"Can you hear me, Jake?"

"Yeah, Pierre. Go ahead."

"I assume you know the outcome of the hostile torpedo?"

"I saw it on the low-frequency update. It sounds like a real close call with some ballsy moves."

"Indeed. Needless to say, the mood here was tense until the ships were safe. However, we must deal with the displacement of the *Wraith* and the *California* as well as the exposure of the *Indiana*."

"I should head back and hover over the *Indiana* until the *California* can replace me."

Renard looked towards the officer seated beside him. "That's the consensus here, and it will require some new software for you. With the recent changes to our tactical scenario, I've been moved to a private room, and Commander Johnson has been assigned as my personal liaison to the Fifth Fleet."

Jake noticed the lack of background noise and moving bodies as compared to his prior links. "Liaison? As in, he'll feed you whatever classified information you need without giving you full access to the tactical nerve center."

"More or less, yes."

"I guess they can't allow a Frenchman entrance into an American fleet's command center."

"Correct, but Commander Johnson has been quite helpful. In fact, he's shared an image with me I think you'll find interesting. A Predator drone is overflying your mission, and the Americans turned its camera over Dmitry when they learned of the torpedo. I'm sending it now."

An overhead view of the Iranian coast and the Gulf of Oman appeared and then zoomed in on two dark forms on the surface. Jake recognized them as dolphins wearing vests forward of their dorsal fins. "That's Mikhail and Andrei."

With a sardonic grin, the Frenchman's face supplanted the Predator's photograph. "No, my friend. I thought so as well at first, but if you look again, you'll see that there are no warheads, and their vests are black, not blue like those of our mammalian friends."

"No shit."

"It's true. Those are Iranian dolphins. The *California* will send recordings of its sonar system for analysis. We may be able to discern how the Persians control their dolphins and learn how to counter any future threats, like the Israelis did against us."

"Sure. Let me tell Antoine."

"Of course. We'll wait."

The *Specter's* commander aimed his voice at his sonar ace. "Antoine?"

"Yes, Jake?"

"The Americans figured out that the Iranians are using dolphins to find submarines, much like the way we use them."

The toad-head offered its profile. "No kidding?"

"That's how they found Dmitry. Can you review the last six hours of sonar for strange noises that could be dolphin commands and have the sonar team listen for them going forward?"

"Yes, of course."

Jake faced his boss and his American liaison. "When was the last time you saw the Iranian dolphins?"

A shadow crept over Renard's face. "They've disappeared again. You'll have to assume that they've been redeployed. You must consider them a threat."

"Shit, Pierre. I hardly know what to listen for until the Iranian dolphin code is broken, if we can even break it."

"I didn't say it would be easy, but while you're hovering over the *Indiana*, you'll have the luxury of defending water as opposed to moving at a searching speed."

"Hold on again. That reminds me. Let me turn towards the *Indiana*."

"Of course."

"Henri, left five-degrees rudder, steady course two-six-five. Set an alert in the system to inform me when I'm within a mile of the *Indiana*."

The French mechanic acknowledged, and the rolling deck took a subtle angle.

Jake looked back at his boss. "You mentioned new software."

"Ah, yes. I did. Commander Johnson?"

The naval officer's voice was higher-pitched than Jake had expected. "You'll need backdoor codes to control the UUVs. I'll have them sent to you. They'll be good for six hours from the moment the UUVs accept them."

"Not to be obvious, but the six-hour limit is because the *California* will be back to command them?"

"That's right. The *California* will be able to stealthily return to the *Indiana* well before that timeframe, and the *Goliath* will be on station by then as well."

"And not to be too obvious again, but these UUVs are out here primarily to be used as torpedo sponges, right?"

The American officer showed little emotion. "We call them 'sacrificial assets'."

"Understood. Can you send me the codes now while I'm shallow?"

"Yes. I'll have them sent immediately. They'll be an extension to the communications package you've already downloaded. They'll update automatically and give you a confirmation notification on your Subtics system. I need to send them from the command center. Excuse me." Commander Johnson stood and departed.

"So, we're alone. Or are we?"

Renard shook his head. "Assume we're always being watched. I see no reason why the Americans wouldn't record our links and assign someone to watch them in real time. I would if I were them."

"No secrets, then?"

"No enduring secrets. If you want a temporary secret, I don't believe anyone who's listening speaks French."

Taking the hint, Jake switched to his boss' native language. "Were Mikhail and Andrei deployed when Dmirty ran?"

"Yes, unfortunately."

"Maybe I can find them and convince them to come to the *Specter*. I don't have a tank, but I could keep them in a dry torpedo tube. I don't want to lose them. Are you okay if I send out their return-to-home message?"

Renard sighed in thought. "No. You can't risk having your broadcast overheard while you're near the *Indiana*. The Iranians obviously know a little something about dolphin management."

At the *Specter's* control station, the silver-haired French mechanic lifted his jaw. "The new package with the UUV codes has arrived."

"Have Claude make one of his geeks install it."

"What? You don't trust me to do it?"

"A man your age who can turn a wrench? No, Henri, I do not."

"Fair enough. I will find you a geek."

Speaking English, Jake returned his attention to Renard. "Then Mikhail and Andrei are at risk."

"Indeed. You should know, however, that Dmitry ordered them to plant their bombs on a submerged target. You may face an adversary who could be defeated with a simple detonation command."

"I'll keep that in mind, but I'm still concerned about retrieving Mikhail and Andrei."

"You can concern yourself with them later. They're in far less danger than you are, and you have more pressing matters."

Jake shrugged. "Should you let me go, then?"

"Yes. You've had your masts exposed long enough. Too long for my tastes, actually. I wouldn't have allowed it if not for the urgent need to communicate. Now, go protect the *Indiana* and await the *California's* return for additional instructions."

"What about Terry's timing?"

"He's still on schedule, last I heard, which was thirty minutes ago. I expect that he's deep now and maneuvering into position to carry the *Indiana*. It'll be slow and delicate work."

"I'm sure. I'll head back there to protect them. See you, Pierre."

"Prove to me once again that you are charmed."

"Lower all masts and antennas, Henri."

As the French mechanic obeyed, a black screen replaced Renard's image.

"Henri, make your depth thirty meters."

The Frenchman made the deck dip and level again. "Steady on a depth of thirty meters."

"Very well, Henri." Jake looked to Remy. "Antoine, get your team looking in three-hundred and sixty degrees. Standard search for Iranian assets, plus whatever you can dream up to listen for as dolphin commands."

Raising a finger to hush his commanding officer, the sonar guru curled forward and then pressed his muffs to his ears. Within his isolated world of watery sounds and auditory memories, Remy remained motionless.

Jake became anxious. "Antoine?"

The sonar guru's toad-shaped head turned. "High-speed screws. Torpedo in the water. No bearing drift."

"Shit."

"We need to run."

Adrenaline coursed through Jake's veins as he stepped to the central plotting table. "Torpedo evasion! All-ahead flank, cavitate!"

Rising from his seat at the ship's control station, the silver-haired mechanic grabbed a microphone and relayed the message over the submarine's public announcement system. "Torpedo evasion! All-ahead flank, cavitate!"

Jake called out to Henri. "Prepare to launch gaseous countermeasures."

The French mechanic tapped icons. "I'm ready."

"Launch countermeasures." While the deck shook with the acceleration to flank speed, the *Specter's* commander turned to the central plotting chart, grabbed a stylus, and hesitated in thought.

"Our course, Jake?"

The *Specter's* commander ignored Henri.

"I need a course. We're not on an evasion course."

Inhaling through his nostrils, Jake made his decision. "Is the UUV software installed?"

"I don't understand why you'd–"

"Answer the question!"

"I think so. Claude said it would take less than five minutes."

"Thinking's not good enough. Contact him, find out, and get it ready."

Henri's tone became accusatory. "I know what you're thinking, Jake, and I don't like it."

"You have a better idea?"

"*Merde.* I do not. I can only pray that you're still charmed, as Pierre says."

"You know what I want?"

"For both UUVs to make their maximum speeds towards us?"

"That's right." Anxious, Jake ran his hand through his hair. "And if you haven't figured it out yet, stay on the ordered course. I did the math in my head, and this might work."

"Might?"

"It'll be close." Jake looked at his sonar ace. "Antoine, I want two reactive weapons, one five degrees left, the other five degrees right of the bearing of the incoming weapon. How long do you need to program it?"

"Julien already has two weapons ready in the system and will update the offsets now. You only need to pick the torpedoes."

"Starboard side. Assign tubes one and three."

The technician seated beside Remy tapped keys to prepare the torpedoes. "Tubes one and three are ready."

"Shoot tubes one and three." The back-to-back impulse launches popped Jake's ears as the compartment gave its air to the torpedo tubes. "Who's handling communications with the UUVs?"

Remy swiveled his toad-shaped head towards his young associates. "Noah can handle it."

Two seats from the guru, the young technician tapped his screen. "I've got the American communications software system called up. I see a new menu for controlling a UUV."

"Connect with both robots and send them towards us at their fastest speeds."

Noah tapped his screen. "I'm trying now."

"Use maximum power."

"I'm transmitting."

Jake heard the *Specter's* bow-mounted sonar system whistling through the hull. "Watch for a response."

"Nothing yet, Jake."

"Shit. Keep trying every fifteen seconds." Jake called to the officer who rode his ship as a consultant. "Commander Martin, do you have anything to add?"

Standing behind Jake, the tall, slouching American rider stepped to the central table and spoke with a Texas drawl. "You're doing the right thing. They'll answer."

The young sonar technician tapped a key and forced the submarine's hydrophones to wail and echo throughout the control room. "No response yet."

"Keep trying, Noah. Antoine, do you have a solution on that incoming torpedo?"

The toad head shook. "I can make something up, if you'd like, but it's in our baffles and coming right for us. I have no idea of the range."

"Is it behind our countermeasures?"

"At the moment. When it passes through, I'll know the range."

Ignorant of the time to impact and lacking communications with his potential torpedo sponges, Jake tapped his fingers against the charting table. He wanted to ask for information but realized the futility. He needed to wait for it.

From Remy, the bad news came first. "The torpedo's through our countermeasures. Range four and a half miles. It's active, Jake. It has us."

A hostile weapon's icon appeared on the chart below Jake's nose. He grabbed a stylus, dragged it between the torpedo and the *Specter*, and read the outcome. Death was seven minutes away.

Henri broke an uncomfortable silence. "Do you want to launch a noise-maker?"

"No. I want the torpedo to focus on the robots. Where the hell are they, Noah?"

"Still nothing."

"Come on, Noah. We're only three miles from the *Indiana*. Get it–"

"I've got it! I have a response from robot twelve. It acknowledges our access codes."

Hope washed through Jake's bones. "Kick it up to its maximum speed and send it straight towards our track."

The young technician tapped buttons and the *Specter's* sonar system blared. "Robot twelve acknowledges the order. It's coming to our ordered course and making turns for eleven knots, its maximum speed."

"Can you hear it?"

"Yes. High-speed screws from robot twelve."

"Very well. Keep calling the other robot as backup."

"I've got robot eight, sir. It acknowledges."

"Send it towards our track at maximum speed, just like robot twelve."

The young technician hesitated before answering. "Robot eight can't reach us in time."

"Send it anyway."

Noah tapped icons, and the *Specter's* sonar shrieked. "Robot eight is coming towards us at eleven knots, too."

Jake tapped an icon to propel the icons on the chart into the future. The nearer UUV collided with the torpedo and the

Specter simultaneously, leaving him dead. He cursed under his breath. "Shit."

His rider leaned into his ear. "Those robots can actually make eleven and a half knots. See how they track."

The *Specter's* commander nodded. "That's good to know."

Henri appeared at the table and spoke softly in French. "Do you want to prepare to abandon ship?"

Jake scoffed. "You know that Commander Martin speaks French. That's why he's assigned to us."

"I know. It's just easier to speak my native language sometimes."

"No. I think we're going to make it." Tapping the screen, Jake updated the speed of the robots. "If robot twelve's really making eleven and a half knots, we'll make it by five hundred yards."

Five minutes later, the control room stank of fear, and the incoming torpedo's seeker pinged through the *Specter's* hull. The toad-head looked upward. "I heard robot twelve passing us."

Jake verified the collision course with the UUV and the hostile weapon. "Very well, Antoine. Noah, keep robot twelve on its course and speed."

"I'll keep robot twelve on course and speed, tracking at eleven and a half knots."

Thirty seconds later, the tactical chart showed the imminent merging of the robot and the torpedo. Jake rose to the balls of his feet, bent his knees, and grabbed handles on the central table. "Henri, pass the word to brace for impact!"

The French mechanic's voice rang from loudspeakers, and a tense ten seconds ticked away.

Then, the boom and the shockwave hammered the control room, and Jake held as the *Specter* reeled.

Breakers tripped, and the room went dark until emergency lighting invoked dim red glows.

In the silence, Jake glanced around the space. "Is everyone okay?"

Calm murmurs and affirmations confirmed his sailors' survival.

"Everyone check yourselves and the guy next to you to make sure you're in one piece. Henri, get a status from Claude on the engine room, and gather reports from all spaces."

"I'm on it, Jake."

"Slow us to three knots. It's time to regroup and find the *Indiana*."

CHAPTER 10

A harsh tug yanked Commander Causey from a dreamless sleep. When his awareness found reality, he gasped. The sloped deck plates serving as his harsh mattress vibrated with the pulsating energy of the *Indiana's* power plant. His neck ached from the poor head support of the rags he'd commandeered as a de facto pillow.

His second-in-command crouched by his side. "Sorry to wake you, captain. The divers have a visual on the *Goliath*."

"Good. How far are they from the *Goliath*?"

"About five minutes, sir."

"How long was I down?"

"An hour and a half, sir."

As he rolled to his side, Causey felt his tight muscles protesting. "I could sleep for a day and a half."

The executive officer surprised him with his initiative. "I could run things for another hour if you'd like. I don't expect we'll be connected to the *Goliath* until then."

The *Indiana's* commander teased himself with the proposal, but curiosity compelled him to his knees. "No, XO. I appreciate the offer, but I want to see this." He rubbed his eyes, stood, and then tiptoed over sleeping sailors who covered the deck in the engine room's middle level.

His second-in-command followed him. "If you want to freshen up, sir, the Cob set up makeshift heads outboard of the condensers in lower level."

"You mean like outhouses?"

"More or less, sir. There's some guys carrying buckets for disposal to work off punishments."

Causey cringed. "I hope the sailors had a choice in this?"

"Yes, sir. Two guys were on their way to you for non-judicial punishment, and I was going to recommend half-pay for three months for each. They jumped at the chance to do this instead."

"At least someone's making lemonade out of lemons."

"It's not pretty, but there's soap, towels, and toothpaste with flowing water."

After an unpleasant visit to the provisional toilets, Causey toured the engine room. Sailors slept, read, chatted and gave their commanding officer silent glances of cautious optimism. But the looming awareness of hidden enemy submarines and their near misses with their torpedoes curtailed the morale.

When he arrived at the upper level's aftermost reaches, his short sonar chief aimed his mustache at two technicians who listened through earmuffs and watched displays on laptops. "It's gone quiet, captain, except for the *Goliath* maneuvering behind us."

The update agreed with Causey's expectations. Tactical updates from the *Goliath* through the underwater communications system had allayed his fears of the two explosions his sonar team had heard through their towed array system. "Don't worry about the *Goliath* anymore. The divers have a visual on it. Just listen for threats."

"We're listening, sir, but the hydrophones don't perform so well getting dragged through the mud."

"There's supposedly a competent sonar team on the *Goliath*, but their towed array's hanging in the mud now, too. Stay alert and do your best. Any new messages?"

The sonar supervisor responded while checking a laptop equipped with the communications software. "No, sir. The *Goliath's* last communication was to maintain course and speed and to send our divers to the bridge. There's a magnetic induction communications system they've got staged for our divers which supposedly allows us to send data through the windows on our watertight doors."

"Got it. Thanks chief." Causey walked forward, greeting tired and concerned sailors with a confident smile until he reached the engine room's door to the tunnel.

Fatigue creeping into his bloodshot eyes, the burly diving officer faced him. "Good morning, sir." He stepped aside, revealing the portal. "Have a look."

Causey moved his nose to the circular window and saw

a waterproofed tablet tucked inside a dry case and hanging from wire wrap. The display showed the approaching brightness of the *Goliath's* bridge and floodlights. The transport ship's slight downward slope revealed its impressive construction and matched the *Indiana's* angle. "I've seen pictures at intel briefings, but that ship's quite a sight."

"It could be a tugboat for all I care, captain. As long as it gets us out of here."

"You're not seeing it for what it is. A ship of that size underwater, moving backwards, matching our course and speed. That's graceful power. I remember from a briefing about a year ago that it's got four outboards for stability control and supposedly has an amazing internal water management system. It's built to the task."

"Not that I'm complaining, but why in the world would anyone build a ship like that?"

"You're used to nuclear power plants because that's what we use. That gives us the speed and legs to get anywhere we want and when we want. But this mercenary fleet uses diesel submarines like most navies, because they're cheaper and simpler to build and operate, and they're good enough to protect local waters. So, when they need to get somewhere fast, which is how they make money, they need a transport ship. And there it is."

Standing next to the lieutenant, Senior Chief Spencer stepped forward. "Captain, we need to see what's going on."

Causey stepped back to let the divers see through the portal, but he held his ground behind their shoulders to retain his view of the action.

"Pardon us, sir. The lieutenant and I need to pay attention, but this should be straightforward. The guys inside the tunnel are in communication with the deployed team, and they'll let us know if something goes wrong, which it won't."

Causey grunted. "I'd agree with you, except for our recent run of bad luck."

Careless with his musculature, Lieutenant Hansen bumped his shoulder into the senior chief. "We need a status." He tapped on the window.

In the tunnel, hands slid a writing slate in front of the tablet. Causey recognized the scribbled numbers as a countdown towards the time the deployed divers needed to return, the estimated time left in their rebreathers, and their distance from the gash they'd exited in the *Indiana's* torpedo room.

Lieutenant Hansen tapped the window, and the slate disappeared.

The trio stood in silence as the tablet's video stream showed the *Goliath* getting larger in the lead diver's camera. As the swimmers reached the transparent hemisphere of the bridge, two men in white starched shirts became visible under the dome's lights. They pointed to a crossbeam arching over their heads.

The diver's lens focused on a clunky black equipment case mounted to the steel beam, and then his gloved fingers grabbed the device's handle. The screen turned dark as the swimmer turned his back to the transport vessel.

Lieutenant Hansen summarized the activity. "That's got to be the communications unit we need with the *Goliath*. He's bringing it back here now while his buddy spools the cable."

Causey verified his understanding. "It's got a magnetic induction pairing through the *Goliath's* bridge, right?"

The husky lieutenant looked over his thick shoulder. "That's right, captain, but it's even better than that. It's got multiple pairings. There's the one for the *Goliath's* bridge, but they've also given us one to use on our doors. We'll be connected to the real world through the *Goliath*."

Causey recalled having read the sonar-delivered message about the transport ship's gift of a hardline network connection. "We'll see if it really works. Any improvement in our communications would be welcomed."

"We'll know soon, captain."

Fifteen minutes later, the screen showed the solitary diver's flashlight beam casting its white cone on the forward compartment's door. Immersed gloves pressed a black box against the portal, blocking the light from the tunnel.

The display went dark, and then a hand removed the tablet from the engine room's window, and at the tunnel's far end the door opened. Gurgling water poured over the circular lip as the diver stepped into the makeshift decompression tank. With help from the duo within the reactor compartment, the arriving diver shut the watertight barrier.

After pressing another black box against the forward compartment's portal, the arriving diver streamed wire along the tunnel's floor to the engine room's door. Then suction cups blocked Causey's view of the window as another magnetic induction communications unit adhered to the transparent barrier.

The burly lieutenant faced Senior Chief Spencer. "Three minutes every thirty-three feet?"

The senior chief nodded. "I'll control the valve. Make sure the guys are ready."

Lieutenant Hansen rapped his knuckle against the portal and then indicated an ascent by jabbing his thumb upward.

With the communications box blocking the view, the diver inside the tunnel crouched to peek at his boss and then agreed with a nod.

The lieutenant glanced at his senior chief. "Bleed air from the reactor compartment for five seconds."

"Bleed air from the reactor compartment for five seconds, aye, sir." Stretching his lean frame into the cables and pipes paralleling the hull, Senior Chief Spencer reached into shadows for a valve. His voice echoed off the polished metal of an air reducer. "Bleeding air!"

High-pressure gas hissed, and Causey's ears popped.

Five seconds later, the sound died and the senior chief glanced over his shoulder. "How's that, sir?"

A writing slate appeared behind the suction cups.

Lieutenant Hansen shook his head. "I can't read it."

White-knuckled fingers grabbed the communications box and yanked it free, and then the writing slate appeared again with its values visible.

The officer addressed the senior chief. "That reduced pressure enough for this stage. You brought them up the equivalent of twenty-nine feet shallower."

A curious onlooker stood behind Causey. Too nubile to fear his captain's rank, the new arrival queried his commanding officer. "What's going on, captain?"

"We're equalizing reactor compartment pressure with the engine room. It's so the divers don't get the bends."

"Yeah. I felt my ears pop."

Causey grunted. "That reminds me. Get the engineer and tell him to come see me here."

"I'll find him, sir." The young sailor darted away.

A minute later, the engineering officer appeared. "You wanted to see me, sir?"

"Have you calculated how high the pressure will rise in the engine room after we equalize with the reactor compartment?"

"Yes, sir. It's going to get uncomfortable as people's inner ears adjust, but it's nothing dangerous."

"Alright. Thanks."

Twenty minutes later, the husky lieutenant cracked open the watertight door, and a gentle whoosh of air completed the equalization. A diver handed the final communications unit through the door. "Here you go, lieutenant."

"You're sure this one goes on this side of the door?"

"It's labeled, sir. Look."

The officer flipped the box and revealed bright stenciling calling out the engine room. "Good point."

"Looks like there's a laminated instructions card, too."

"Sure is." The lieutenant withdrew the card from a slip and read it. "Says there's a jump drive with software we can download and use with a USB cable. Says there's also a couple USB cables in here." He depressed a tab, opening a small chamber within the box.

"I think you're good, sir." The diver retreated into the tunnel and closed the door.

Fifteen minutes later, Causey examined the fruits of the labors of several technicians. Suction cups held induction units to the window, a USB cable connected a unit to a laptop balanced on an inverted garbage can, and custom software enabled the communications. "So, what do I do?"

The burly lieutenant's thick arm brushed his shoulder. "Let me try this." He unmuted the laptop.

An Australian accent rose from the computer. "Hello, *Indiana*? Hello, *Indiana*?"

Causey snapped at the laptop. "*Indiana*, here."

The Australian accent continued. "Hello, *Indiana*?"

"They can't hear me."

Lieutenant Hansen frowned. "Shit. We need a microphone." Again, he bumped the *Indiana's* commanding officer while reaching for the computer to mute the Australian voice.

Looking over his shoulder, Causey found a petty officer and tasked him with finding a microphone. The young sailor ran off.

After a five-minute search, the sailor returned with the headset belonging to an engineering lab technician.

Causey made a mental note to acquire a laptop with an internal microphone as he donned the gear and unmuted the connection. "This is the *Indiana*. Can you hear me?"

After a pause, an enthusiastic Australian accent filled his ears. "Good to hear from you, mate. Terry Cahill, here. Commanding officer of the RMF *Goliath*, at your service."

"RMF?"

"Renard's Mercenary Fleet. It's an unofficial title we use when we try to sound official, named for the man you'll hopefully be lifting a pint with later this week."

"It's encouraging to know that the RMF *Goliath* is nearby, Mister Cahill."

"Indeed, I am mate. Ready and waiting to help you out. Let's get your arses home."

CHAPTER 11

Hearing the foreigner's voice lifted Causey's spirits. "I'm Commander Andrew Causey, commanding officer of the USS *Indiana*. I'm pleased to meet you, Mister Cahill."

"Same to you, commander."

"I trust you have the details of an egress plan?"

"I do, but that'll have to wait. I have some news. The Iranians are using dolphins to find our ships. Your colleagues at your fleet headquarters saw them surfaced through a Predator drone, and they think that's how those mongrels targeted the *Wraith*. Your fleet wants you to send divers outside your hull to watch for them."

"Watch for them?"

The Australian paused before answering. "Kill them."

Causey tucked away his inherent pity for animals being used as tools of warfare. "Sure. If we can find them."

"Right. You've got men who can handle it?"

Studying the muscular lieutenant, Causey thought the young officer could strangle a dolphin with one hand, but he sought a definitive answer. "I need to ask my divers."

A young sailor appeared with a new laptop. "I installed the communications software. It's got a microphone. So you won't need the headset anymore."

The *Indiana's* commander reached for the first laptop's mute button. "Hold on, Mister Cahill. I'm switching laptops."

"Right. I'll wait."

The young sailor mounted the new laptop next to the first, swapped out the USB connection to the circuit, and then yelled into it. "Hello?"

The Australian accent rose from the new laptop. "Hello."

Causey removed his headset, angled his jaw downward, and raised his voice. "Can you hear me, Mister Cahill?"

"It's fine, commander."

"Standing next to me are my divers, Lieutenant Hansen and Senior Chief Spencer."

"Terry Cahill at your service, gents."

The burly officer bent towards the laptop. "We've got underwater rifles. They shoot barbs and will get the job done. The challenge against dolphins will be seeing them. They'll see us long before we see them."

"Right, mate. But we think they need to take pictures before their owners shoot weapons, which means they'll need to circle around to get an image that allows them to identify us. I imagine they've trained the dolphins to get some sort of broadside view from a known range. That might level the playing field, and they're also probably not trained in anti-swimmer attacks."

"Probably not. But they might be. This could become a battle." Lieutenant Hansen turned to his senior chief. "You'll have to run things in here. I'm going out there."

Senior Chief Spencer snorted. "Don't be a hero, sir. This isn't about power and size. It's going to be about reaction time. Our guys can handle it."

The young officer glared at the enlisted diver.

Unfazed, the senior chief held the glare.

Causey broke the stalemate. "Part of being an officer is knowing when to get out in front but knowing when to step back and keep the big picture."

Lieutenant Hansen relented. "Maybe you're right, sir, but who wants to stay behind when their guys are going into combat?"

"Let it go, lieutenant. Your guys are already suited up, and time is of the essence."

Senior Chief Spencer gave a sly grin. "I don't like it either, sir. I want to be out there, too, but the skipper's right. It's probably going to amount to nothing anyway. It's a big chunk of water for the dolphins to cover."

The officer flicked his fingers backwards. "Alright, senior chief. Send them out in port and starboard pairs."

Causey preempted the enlisted man's response. "Don't commit to that yet. I need to take in seawater from at least one side of the engine room."

The lieutenant faced the *Indiana's* commander. "Right, captain. I've already given the guys a depth floor. I don't want them going deeper than the decks of our upper level compartments."

Convinced the divers would remain safely above the water intakes, Causey spoke into the laptop. "Mister Cahill, did you catch all that?"

"It sounds like you're sending out four divers."

"That's correct. We've got one on his way back from your ship, and we'll have three men join him for a total of two pairs patrolling port and starboard."

"Send them as soon as you can. Dolphins are dangerous, and these Iranians know how to use them."

"I'm on it."

"While you do that, I'll move into position behind you."

The *Indiana's* commander frowned. "Aren't you already in position?"

"No, commander. I mean right behind you. I'll have me forward crossbeam three meters behind your propulsor."

Causey's internal insanity alarms blared, but he reminded himself the *Goliath* could handle operations he considered extreme. "That's asking for a collision."

The Australian's tone remained confident, indicating a businesslike approach to a situation Causey considered dire. "We are going to collide. That's what I'm here for. The only two concerns are making sure we're in the correct relative positions and making sure it's gentle and quiet when it happens."

The *Indiana's* commander sighed through his nostrils. "I have no choice but to trust you."

"Don't worry, commander. I know it's strange to you, but I load submarines into me cargo bed for a living. Maybe it'll help if you can watch what's going on. I have cameras covering the outside of me hulls. Can you see anything on video yet?"

Causey reached for the laptop and toggled through programs. A small window moved from the background to the foreground showing a grayscale rendition of the Australian's face under short dark hair. "I can see you now, Mister Cahill."

"Great. If you'll enable your laptop's camera, I'll be able to see you, too."

The *Indiana's* commander worked through a settings menu and clicked the checkbox enabling the lens. "Any luck?"

"Yeah. I see you. Now then, if your divers have standard five-pin RMK-to-RG-59 coax video cables, they can plug into the cable that's connecting our ships. Then we'll both be able to see what they see when they're out there. I'm told the bandwidth on our cable allows up to three video inputs."

The divers both nodded.

Causey stooped towards the computer. "We've got the cables."

Twenty minutes later, a new laptop had appeared beside the others on makeshift stands, giving three screens. One showed the Australian on the *Goliath's* bridge, and the others showed views from the cameras of the deployed dive teams. While the swimmers scanned the water for cetacean threats, the views were uninteresting shots of flashlights probing the darkness.

As one pair of divers completed a lap around the *Indiana*, Causey saw a huge school of tiny fish jetting in random but unified directions between long strands of kelp on his ship's starboard side. Beyond the brief view of undersea life, he saw only darkness, and he made a command decision. "Let's have them swim around the *Goliath*, too."

"Right, mate. Good idea. I'll shut down me MESMA plants while they swim, but we'll need to coordinate port and starboard. Me battery is tiny for a ship of this size."

"No need. They'll stay above your intakes." Causey glanced at the burly lieutenant.

The young officer nodded. "That's right, sir."

"Right, then, commander. Send them over."

Thirty minutes passed as the divers circled the transport vessel and searched the silent darkness. Convinced of his tenuous but intact stealth, Causey was ready to put his submarine into the Australian's care. "My divers are coming back to circle the *Indiana*. I recommend proceeding with loading."

"Agreed, mate. Let's get it done."

"What's the process?"

Cahill moved sideways, allowing his second-in-command to step into the screen. "Mister Walker will handle the systems for me while I oversee your loading. We'll do all the adjusting here on the *Goliath*. Your job will be to maintain a constant angle, course, and speed."

"I assume you need me to lift my stern."

"Right. I'll need at least ten degrees to give this a go. If you can give me twenty, that would be best. Any more, and me screws will break the surface. Any less, and I can't get underneath you enough."

Causey considered the torques and moments of shifting water throughout his submarine. "I'll see what I can do."

With the opportune sense developed over decades of submarining, the large-headed chief of the boat appeared when his commanding officer needed him. "I heard you're getting ready to have us loaded, sir?"

Causey scoffed. "I've been doing that for an hour. It's a slow process, but your timing's perfect. I want one phone-talker up here connected to the sonar team, and I want the executive officer stationed with the sonar team. I also want one phone-talker here connected to maneuvering. You know what... take out a pad and write this all down."

The Cob chuckled as he withdrew a pen and pad from his cotton jumpsuit. "You want one phone-talker with the sonar team, one with maneuvering, and the executive officer stationed with the sonar team."

"I also want local manual control of the trim pump and every trim and drain valve that's within reach. I want communications with all those stations through a phone-talker here. And I want all three phone-talkers on different circuits."

"Local manual control of the trim pump and every accessible trim and drain valve with a phone-talker. Three different circuits. Got it. I'll get help from the auxiliary division chief."

As the Cob stepped away, Causey leaned towards the nearest

laptop. "Mister Cahill, I'm stationing my men to create the angle on my ship. I'll need at least fifteen minutes to get this evolution going."

Tension crept into the Australian's voice as time ticked away their chances of remaining hidden. "As long as we don't hear any Iranian ships or see any of their dolphins, we're good."

The *Indiana's* commander recognized a risk of fratricide. "What about your team's dolphins? What if they show up here and we attack them by mistake? Is that deemed an acceptable loss?"

"That's already decided, mate. Your guys are to kill any dolphins that show up. They wouldn't have time to tell the mongrels' dolphins apart from ours, unfortunately."

"Understood."

"Right, then. We're ready when you are."

Fifteen minutes later, an entourage surrounded Causey.

A second-class petty officer he recognized from the auxiliary division wore a headset and lowered the sound-powered phone's speaker. "Sir, the trim and drain system's lined up to pump the after tanks overboard."

"Very well. To the trim pump operator, start pumping the after tanks overboard."

The petty officer repeated and relayed the order.

Causey faced a first-class petty officer from the sonar division. "Find out if sonar team hears anything abnormal with our pumping operations."

After the petty officer relayed the request, he announced the answer. "Nothing abnormal, sir, but the chief reminds you that our hydrophones are being dragged through the mud."

"Understood." Causey looked to the display showing the Australian's face. "Mister Cahill, can your team hear our trim pump?"

"We hear it, but our towed array's in the mud, too, and I don't have a bow-mounted system. The conformal arrays aren't showing an alarming sound power level from you, but me ship's much louder than yours."

"I'll keep pumping." Unsure if he discerned a gentle shift in the deck's angle, Causey looked at a first-class petty officer from his engineering staff. "Ask maneuvering what our angle is."

The sailor obeyed and reported. "Five degrees down, sir."

"We started at two-degrees down. This is taking too long." Causey thought of a way to accelerate the movement, waved his hand in the air, and raised his voice. "All phone-talkers, have the chief of the boat report to me."

Thirty seconds later, the large-headed master chief petty officer arrived. "Sir?"

"Round up every spare body and have them muster as close to the reactor compartment bulkhead as you can squeeze them."

The chief of the boat blinked.

"To help with the ship's angle."

"Oh. I see. I'll round them up, sir." The man turned to walk away.

"Cob?"

Stopping, the chief of boat swiveled his large head. "Yes, sir?"

"Quietly. Soft footsteps and minimal talking."

Five minutes later, one hundred men crowded the engine room's forward-most spaces. Murmurs flowed up and down through the three levels.

Along with those of his crew who faced sternwards, Causey leaned forward onto the balls of his feet. "How's my angle now?"

The engineering staff's petty officer queried maneuvering. "Nine degrees, sir. The engineer thinks mustering the crew forward helped."

"Good." The *Indiana's* commander spoke into the laptop. "Did you hear that, Mister Cahill? We're nine degrees down."

"That's good. Next, I'm going to try to slide under you. Can you slow to half a knot?"

"I can only measure my speed relative to the flowing water. I can't adjust for the current."

"Right. Forgot about your true speed. Let's instead talk in terms of how many turns you're making."

"I'm making turns for nine knots now."

"Try turns for four."

After giving the order to slow his ship's reverse crawl through the mud, Causey updated the Australian. "I'm making turns for four knots, and my angle's at down eleven now."

"Keep working your angle, mate, but the speed's good."

The auxiliary division phone-talker reported the bad news. "Captain, the trim and drain tanks are dry. The trim pump is shut down."

Causey nodded and then looked at Cahill's image in the laptop "I've reached my limit on the angle. I don't have any water left back here."

"Shit. I'll have to load you like you are."

"What if it doesn't work?"

"Then you'd have to send high-pressure air in your after ballast tanks, but let's not risk that noise yet."

"Do you need me to do anything else? Speed, rudder, stern planes?"

"No. Just keep them all where they are. I'll adjust." Cahill narrowed his eyes. "Are you ready?"

"Do I have a choice?"

"Not unless you want to spend the next seven days skulking along the bottom of the sea."

"Load me into your cargo bed, Mister Cahill."

"Right. I'll send you a different feed so you can watch what's happening instead of having to see me repugnant mug."

Causey chortled. "Try not to make any loud noises."

The Australian smirked, and then the screen switched to a view of the *Indiana's* propulsor. Running below both sides of his submarine's tapered stern, the *Goliath's* catamaran halves seemed inches from his hull. "Tugboats don't even get this close."

Cahill's voice issued from the laptop. "You're one meter from me cargo bed, and we're only going to get closer."

In the screen, the transport vessel quivered. "What was that?"

"Me bows just hit the bottom. Hold on." The Australian exchanged rapid words with his executive officer. "Alright. We've adjusted."

"Just like that? How?"

"The outboards and screws. Well, the two outboards I've deployed. I obviously can't use the forward two. It's all controlled by sonar range finders trying to keep the cargo bed a constant distance to your hull."

"That's impressive."

"And now I'm slowing... you'll drift into me. For what it's worth, brace for impact, commander."

The bump made Causey rock forward on his heels.

"You're in our bed. I'm closing down the presses. Keep your propulsion as it is."

In the laptop screen, hydraulic arms rotated from the transport ship's hulls towards the *Indiana*.

"We've got you, but don't celebrate just yet. I've only got you in sixteen of twenty-four presses."

"What's that mean?"

"It means that if you can't give me a higher angle, I can't get you any deeper into the bed. Now you have to pump water back into your after tanks to help balance you out."

Causey gave the order to flood the tanks and sent his sailors to the compartment's tail end, and then he turned his jaw back to the computer. "I'm flooding now."

"I'll wait until you're done."

When his tanks were full, Causey shared the news with the Australian. "I'm as heavy aft as I'm going to get."

"Alright. Come to all stop."

The *Indiana's* commander gave the order, and with the mud tugging his bow, the speed died instantly.

"You're stopped, commander. We're holding you. Everything's steady. We've got you."

"Then why do you sound doubtful?"

"Because the hard part starts now. We're going to try to rotate you back to a level deck."

"Slowly, I trust?"

"Yeah." The Australian's voice trailed off.

Below Causey's feet, the deck's angle receded, but then he heard alarms from the *Goliath*.

The Australian's voice boomed. "That's enough! Reverse our pitch, Liam!"

Causey felt the angle rise again. "What's wrong?"

"Too much stress on our presses. You're heavy forward. We can't lift you. We can't hold you tight enough to rock you back to level."

The *Indiana's* commander sighed. "Is that as bad as it sounds?"

"It bloody hell sure is, mate. This isn't going to work."

CHAPTER 12

Volkov lifted his head towards his American rider. "You're sure you've translated that correctly?"

Commander Hatcher exposed his palms. "My Russian's fine, and I'm sure I've translated it correctly. The fleet doesn't want the *California* to return to the *Indiana*. They say it's too dangerous now, and I agree."

"I hate to admit it, but I agree, too. Why risk a second American submarine when you can send mercenaries?"

"You're not going back."

"I know that, but two of my fellow mercenaries are there."

"Regardless, our opinions don't matter. You and the *California* are now tasked to clear a southern egress channel for the *Indiana*. These are the orders from the fleet."

Standing at the *Wraith's* central plotting table, Volkov straightened his back. The rocking deck vibrated with the rumbling diesel engines which fed his hungry battery cells. Leading a Frenchman's submarine against Iranian adversaries while following American orders challenged the Russian's paradigms. But he stayed true to the mission. "No plan survives engagement with the enemy. It's an understandable adjustment."

"But you sound like you hate it."

"It's embarrassing when two Iranian dolphins can defeat us."

"We're not defeated. Like you said. It's an adjustment."

Volkov leaned over the table and studied the consensus modeled on the tactical chart. The Americans suspected that at least three submarines were forming a barrier between the *Wraith* and his return route into Iranian waters. The barrier also trapped the *California* south of the *Indiana*. "If the Iranians are truly committing submarines to stop me and the *California* from returning to their waters, that reduces their search ability for the *Indiana*."

"Reduces, yes. But they have plenty of submarines left for searching. I think you'd better get down to the business of removing some of them."

Although coming from a foreign command structure, Volkov's orders aligned with his wishes–they allowed him to hunt. Hesitant to harass sailors of the fleet he'd once trained, he accepted the tasking for its tactical challenge. "Does the fleet have an opinion on a search strategy?"

"They left that up to you and the captain of the *California*."

"Which means, they left it up to the captain of the *California*."

The rider exhaled through his nostrils. "It could've been that simple, but the message from the *California's* captain is a recommendation for you to trail him northward. If his crew finds an Iranian target, you'll launch a slow-kill weapon against it. I trust you'll find that equitable and reasonable?"

"His being in front places him at more risk than me."

"But you get the shot."

"Of course, I get the shot. I'm the only one with slow-kills."

Commander Hatcher cleared his throat and gave a cold stare.

Volkov canted his head. "Maybe I've presumed too much. Perhaps I'm not the only one with slow-kills. I may not be privy to all knowledge of this mission."

"Let's not argue such details. The *California* already has a target for you."

Anticipation rose within him, but then the *Wraith's* commander sighed in resignation. His effort to learn English had been focused on the spoken word, and now the written characters from the *California* left him at a disadvantage. "Is that what it says?"

"Yes. It's the primary reason we believe they're setting up a barrier. The *California* solved for course and speed, and the target was probably in transit towards a position within the barrier."

"That's a reasonable response by the Iranians." Volkov turned his head and glanced at his trusted translator scribbling notes by the captain's chair. "Bring me what you have."

The translator ripped a sheet of notebook paper, darted to his commanding officer's side, and extended the scribbles.

"Your handwriting's atrocious."

"Fortunately for you, I specialize in real-time verbal translations so that your colleagues don't talk English circles around you. But I never won an award for my penmanship."

Volkov glanced at the scratches and conceded they passed as Cyrillic characters. "It's hard on the eyes, but I can read it."

"There's more coming. May I?"

With a wave, the *Wraith's* commander dismissed his translator and then digested his penned translations. They aligned with the rider's comments. "So, am I to attack this target the *California's* found for me?"

"If you can." The rider grabbed a stylus and tapped in the Iranian submarine's position. "The shot has some distance, but the target's motion is predictable. It's been holding course and speed for ten minutes."

"So be it. I'm ready to shoot."

"Then you agree with the overall plan? Follow the *California* and shoot targets as you receive the feeds?"

"If I'm also free to shoot what I find on my own."

Commander Hatcher frowned and gave a dismissive wave. "Yeah, yeah, of course."

"Agreed, then."

"May I send a response through your sonar team?"

"Hold on. How'd the *California* hear the target from its position? That's too far away, even for a *Virginia's* sonar system."

"You haven't read far enough into the data stream yet, but the *California's* deployed a drone."

Volkov addressed his sonar guru. "Anatoly? Who's listening to the *California*?"

The technician lifted his arm and pointed two seats to his left. "He is. But he didn't hear the drone being deployed, if that's what you're going to ask. It was too quiet."

The guru's clairvoyance surprised Volkov more than the quietness of the American submarine. "Yes. That's exactly what I was going to ask. Get both my drones ready to launch on forty-five-degree offsets."

"I'm getting both drones ready on forty-five-degree offsets.

Grigory will handle both drones."

Volkov aimed his chin at the technician beside his sonar guru. "Is he ready to handle two of them?"

"Yes. He handled one in Israel with one hand and half his brain."

"Hold off on the drones. I want to get a weapon out first."

"Tube one is ready, assigned to the Iranian submarine. Do you want to restrict the yield?"

Volkov realized the damage of twenty-four submunitions would be catastrophic to a vessel as small as a *Ghadir*. He opted for the humane solution, a subset of eight bomblets, half of which he expected to attach. "One-third."

"I've set the yield on torpedo one to one-third."

"Do you hear the Iranian submarine?"

"No. I'm just using the *California's* data."

"So be it. Keep this one quiet. I want it to swim out."

Anatoly tapped keys. "I've updated tube one to swim out."

"Shoot tube one."

"Weapon one is swimming out of tube one."

As the torpedo's icon formed on his tactical plot, Volkov turned his attention towards reconnaissance. "Are my drones ready?"

Muffs over his ears, Anatoly bounced his voice off his Subtics monitor. "Yes, Dmitry. Tubes five and six."

"Shoot tube five."

Anatoly angled his voice off the console again. "Drone one is swimming out of tube five. Drone one is clear of our hull and deployed on a forty-five-degree offset to the right. We have wire connectivity and confirmation of propulsion."

"Set the drone's speed to its maximum of ten knots."

"Drone one is at its maximum speed, ten knots."

"Shoot tube six."

"Drone two is swimming out of tube six. Drone one is clear of our hull and deployed on a forty-five-degree offset to the left. We have wire connectivity and confirmation of propulsion."

"Set the drone's speed to its maximum of ten knots."

"Drone two is at its maximum speed, ten knots."

The rider straightened his back. "Now, may I inform the *California* of your compliance with the plan?"

"Use drone two to avoid exposing our position."

"I'll have your technician aim the communication at the *California's* second drone."

"I don't see its second drone."

The translator ripped off a second sheet of notes, sped to his commander's side, and handed him his scribbles. "The second drone's listed here, Dmitry."

"Much as I appreciate this encrypted connection with the *California*, I hate being the last on my ship to know."

Nine minutes later, the torpedo's icon blinked, and the sonar ace announced the acquisition of its target. "Our torpedo has acquired the Iranian submarine."

"Very well. Any sign of evasion?"

"Just a course change. It was already making maximum speed. It's not going to matter, though. It's a good shot."

"Time to impact?"

"Fifty-seconds." A minute later, Anatoly announced the weapon's success. "The warhead has detonated. I can't hear bomblets... it's too far away."

"I'll trust the weapon."

"An explosion! Now another. Two more. And another. Five total."

Volkov felt anxious empathy for his distressed submarine brethren. "What about hull popping? Is it making it to the surface?"

"I don't know."

Calling out from the back of the room, the translator allayed his commanding officer's fears. "The *California* hears hull popping from its rightmost drone. The target's surfacing."

Commander Hatcher snorted. "You seem awfully concerned about your enemy's survival."

Volkov recalled a two-year tour of duty training the Iranians to use their *Kilo*-class submarines. "They're not my enemy.

They're yours. For me, they're just an opponent in a dangerous game."

"At least you recognize the danger."

For a moment, Volkov wondered if he could get away with shooting the rider out a torpedo tube. "I'm fully aware of it, commander, and don't doubt for a moment that I am. I've traded more weapons in hostile engagements than all your present submarine commanders combined. I also haven't forgotten that I just sprinted from a heavyweight torpedo and needed divine help from the *California* to keep my pressure hull intact."

"Good. Because you've removed only one submarine and are facing more than half a dozen more that are unaccounted for."

"But only three more can be standing between us and the *Indiana*. That's all I'm responsible for. And it can't be any more than three. The others are in port or were last seen too far away to cover the distance, per your fleet's intelligence reports."

"Don't get cocky, Mister Volkov. Three is plenty. Except for the one you just shot, they're all drifting. You and the *California* are searching, which means we need to move and make noise while they sit and listen. They have the positional advantage."

"But they don't use drones. Their small subs don't have the space to carry them, and their larger submarines are far away. I'm used to this sort of challenge, and I don't mean just in training scenarios. I'll follow in the *California's* wake and shoot weapons until this swath of water is sanitized."

Something within Volkov's message or the tone of its delivery appeared to bother the American, and he retreated to the back of the room.

Standing at the plotting table, the *Wraith's* commander stayed in the room's center. For thirty minutes, he followed a prescribed course and speed behind the American submarine, but Iranian targets eluded the teamed submarines.

The rider returned to Volkov's side and pointed at a stream of characters. "The *California's* going to slow down the search to four knots, and that goes for you and all drones."

The *Wraith's* commander grunted. "Four knots, and on a shallow approach angle. This will take forever."

"Would you rather commit suicide?"

Volkov conceded the need for caution. "No. Damn it. You have a point. I've lost my dolphins, and your robots are committed elsewhere. We have only our drones as advantages, and they have limits in their hydrophone loadout." He ordered his ship and drones slowed per the *California's* demand, and then he looked to the rider. "We all agree on moving slowly."

"I appreciate you being reasonable about this."

Volkov realized he'd been fighting his role as the American submarine's understudy and wanted insight into his ally. "Do you know the captain of the *California* personally?"

"I know him by reputation. He's by the book. He does as he's been trained, nothing outlandish, which I respect."

"Do you think he's tried using active sonar, in a micro-pulse secured mode, either from his ship or his drones?"

"I won't reveal anything about American tactics that I don't have to, but I'm sure you understand the value of secure active against drifting diesels. Why are you asking?"

"I want to make this go faster. Time is–"

A shadow overcame the rider's face. "Damn."

"What is it?"

"No need to hurry anymore."

"Why not?"

"It's the *Goliath*. Your colleagues sent a communications buoy. They tried loading the *Indiana*, but it didn't work."

"As in, a first attempt failed and they're delayed?"

"No. As in, it didn't work, and nobody has the first clue how to get the *Indiana* the hell out of here."

CHAPTER 13

Lieutenant Commander Jazani pleaded his case. "Sir, I want divers and dolphins."

The task force commander's tone was stern. "The divers are sapped. They just worked themselves into exhaustion scouring the bottom for the American submarine."

"Don't we have ships with side-scan sonar that can do that?"

"We do, but I'm searching with every asset I have. We use humans and technology to search."

Jazani leaned forward into his console and adjusted the boom microphone running along his jaw. "But it's all for nothing. Our lightweight torpedo hit something, but we can't find the American submarine."

"The conclusion is that we hit something else. That's the only logical explanation, and we've seen the Americans using decoys and robots to absorb our heavyweights."

"I know that, sir. I've read the reports. But when decoys and robots deceive our heavyweights, we hear them. Their whole point of their existence is to make noise and become targets, but I didn't hear a false target when the lightweight exploded. Nobody did."

"So, you think the first American submarine was hit?"

"I know it's hard to conclude that without evidence on the seafloor, but it must be considered."

"Then where is it? Do you propose that it turned into a ghost?"

The *Ghadir's* commander hesitated to share his theory and stalled. "I don't have a solid answer, but I have to speculate given the Americans' harsh response."

The task force's leader scoffed. "You call this harsh? One *Virginia*-class submarine, which, may I remind you, is likely the one we missed with the lightweight torpedo, is harassing us along with a mercenary mini-fleet. If you call that harsh, you'd be disappointed if we really infuriate the Americans."

"But then why the mercenaries? And especially why bring

their ugly railgun ship?"

As if being patient with a child, the task force commander sighed. "It's a measured response. The mercenaries have their less-than-lethal weapons, and you can't blame the Americans for making someone else handle their dirty work. As for that railgun ship, it's there to attack our shore-based military targets in case we overplay our response."

Jazani muted his microphone while groaning. He thought his nation's politicians had demanded the impossible by ordering the American submarine hobbled with a lightweight weapon. Now, they were reacting to the undesired outcome, and his task force leader's explaining couldn't hide the stench of desperation seeping into his new instructions. He unmuted his headset. "So, my orders are now to sink any mercenary vessel I find, but not at the risk of hitting said vessel in international waters, losing my ship, or hitting an American."

"Correct."

"Has anyone considered that the Americans want us to do exactly that? They may be using the mercenaries to bait our submarines into shooting and exposing ourselves to counterfire."

The task force commander's voice became deeper. "Your orders are your orders."

Jazani tried a new angle. "I want to keep searching for a bottomed American submarine."

"Absolutely not. Were you listening when I told you it's not there?"

"Of course, I was listening, sir. I mean to search farther east."

"I'm not following you."

"I mean, what if the submarine was damaged but somehow maintained propulsion?"

"Then it's already in Oman. I don't see your point."

"No, sir. What if it was limited in speed?"

The task force's leader sounded exasperated. "Then it's only half way to Oman but still out of reach."

Almost ashamed to share his theory, Jazani lowered his voice and pushed his boom microphone to his lips. "What if it had trouble with depth control? What if its commanding officer refused to risk the transit across deeper water because he's fighting a battle with uncertain shoring and with his drain pumps barely keeping pace with flooding? He'd want a nice, shallow, soft, flat bottom below him, wouldn't he?"

"Go on."

"He'd head east to Pakistani waters."

"If, if, if. Yes, I concede that if all that were true, your argument's logical. What do you want?"

"I want new orders to search waters to the east to look for the American submarine, and I want divers and dolphins to help me."

The task force commander hummed. "Huh."

"I hope that's a good 'huh'."

"It is. I can rearrange the patrol areas to give you the water. You can have the dive ship with two pairs of divers and side-scan sonar immediately, but the divers won't be available for ten hours, after they rest. I'm also keeping the dolphins and their mothership assigned where they are. We need them in the barrier that's keeping the Americans from re-invading our waters, and they're not trained to call out bottomed objects."

Jazani considered protesting the omission of the cetaceans for his agenda, but he conceded they were better used searching for the stealthy undamaged submarines. "Thank you, sir."

The task force's leader grunted. "Don't thank me. Do your job. Your primary tasking against the mercenary ships remains unchanged. This speculative hunt of yours is secondary."

"I'll carry out my orders."

"You're right, you will. I'll send you written details."

As the line went dead, Jazani tossed his headset to the console. While awaiting his updated patrol area, he reread the latest intelligence update explaining the unwelcomed interference from two *Scorpène*-class submarines and a catamaran railgun ship. As he reread the Russian man's name, he let out a lengthy sigh.

His executive officer's small frame twisted in the seat of his computer console. "What's that you got there, sir?"

"Just some background data on the mercenary fleet."

"You sounded like there was something more, sir."

Jazani hesitated to share but considered his executive officer and the two technicians who might overhear him trusted colleagues. "The captain of one of these mercenary ships is an old acquaintance who taught me tactics as part of a cadre of Russian officers. I was too young and naïve to realize it back then, but even when he was a junior officer, the senior Russians admired his skills."

The short officer swiveled in his chair and raised his eyebrows at his commanding officer. "Seriously?"

"Apparently, his career in the Russian submarine fleet has ended, and he's moved on to more lucrative endeavors."

"Which submarine is his, not that it matters?"

"Why doesn't it matter?"

"Because I trust you to not let it affect your judgment."

The *Ghadir's* commander grunted. "I appreciate the vote of confidence, but I fear you're overestimating me. I wouldn't call him a friend, but I remember him as a good man."

"And you refuse to kill good men?"

"Of course not."

"Then I still trust you to kill whom you must and lament it after the fact, perhaps in your second career as a poet-warrior."

After a deep breath during which he measured the weight of mortal responsibility, Jazani exhaled. "I don't know which submarine is his and which is the American's."

"Again, I trust you to kill whom you must."

"And there's the problem. My orders are liberal about killing–to the point of ambiguity."

"Orders to kill are always challenging, sir."

Reminding himself to honor the loneliness of leadership, Jazani measured his words to avoid complaining. "I've said too much already. It's just the normal burden of command. All the other submarine commanders have received the same order, and I doubt any of them are whining."

The executive officer baited his commander. "That doesn't make them any easier to follow, and I can tell that something's weighing on you."

Despite his desire to suffer in solitude, Jazani took the bait. "You're right. I'm sure you can see it on my face."

The short officer leaned into his boss and spoke softly. "And in your voice, and in your nervously tapping toes, and in your posture. You're practically curled over your console."

Made aware of his twitching foot, Jazani steadied it. "At some point, I may have to make a life or death decision, and you and everyone on this ship will have to obey me. If it happens, we'll all live with consequences, but I alone will have to live with the guilt if I get it wrong."

"Then let's make sure you get it right."

"How do you propose to predict the future?"

"Just talk it through."

"You've read the orders."

"True, sir. But we sort of ignored them while you challenged them and sought better guidance. But better guidance isn't coming. We're stuck with what we've got."

The *Ghadir's* commander shrugged. "Fine, then. I can sink a mercenary ship as long as it's within the twelve-nautical-mile coastal limit and if the attack has zero risk of sinking an American ship. But I should not take the shot if I believe I'm endangering our ship by inviting counterfire."

"What if you shoot but the target could evade to international waters before your weapon hits?"

"Unclear. You see my dilemma."

"I should've given our orders more thought already, sir."

"No. I should've instructed you to consider them more deeply already to train you for command."

The executive officer scoffed. "It's easy for someone sitting in a comfortable office to give those orders, but if you think about implementing them, any fool could see that they're politically-driven lunacy."

For hours, the delicacy of his orders had been running in circles throughout Jazani's head. "Much as they're challenging, I understand where they've come from. It's not all lunacy. I've been able to make some sense of it."

"If so, you're a better man than I am, sir."

"I can't do anything to an American ship because we've already sent our message with the lightweight torpedo, whether we hit our target or not. There's nothing else that needs saying to the Americans, and to take any hostile action against them would portray us as irrational maniacs."

The executive officer shrugged. "What's so bad about that? It would scare them and make them unable to predict our next moves."

Jazani realized his wisdom advantage over his younger second-in-command. "After the lightweight attack, they fear us more than they ever have. Any additional fear would turn them into frightened children with their fingers on the triggers of huge guns."

The short officer pursed his lips and remained silent.

"Okay. Maybe my argument about military escalation has failed to impress you, but what about the lifting of trade sanctions?"

The executive officer sneered. "Now, you're making sense, sir."

"We can't benefit from peace talks in Syria if we're starting a war. Do you want to reap the benefits of improved trade or not?"

"Someone should've thought of that before we launched that lightweight weapon at the Americans."

"That was a warranted reaction to them putting robots into our waters. At least it seemed like it at the time. I'm not entirely sure anymore."

The executive officer's pitch rose. "Then why can't we attack any other Americans? People get outraged when their sons and husbands die, and then an entire nation joins them–for about a week. Then they all go back to their private lives, especially Americans."

Jazani called the bluff. "You're sure of this? When's the last time a naval force attacked an American ship?"

The executive officer paused in thought. "The *Cole,* in Yemen."

"That wasn't a naval force. It was an al Qaeda suicide team."

"Okay, then. The *Stark.*"

The *Ghadir's* commander remembered history lessons on his nation's war with its neighbor. "That was an air force attack, and if memory serves, the American politicians claimed it was a lone Iraqi pilot's mistake. It's a poor data point for gauging American outrage on an intentional attack."

"What about the *Liberty,* then? That was intentional."

Jazani delved deeper into his maritime history. "That was more than fifty years ago, and American politicians would do anything to protect their little bitch sister Israel. So, they covered it up."

"Fine, sir. I can't think of another example."

"Then don't underestimate their anger. We might be able to explain away one attack with a lightweight torpedo. We can say we mistook it for a robot. We can say they got too close to a live-fire exercise and drew the weapon by accident. We can say anything with plausible denial. But if we sink a second, we can't claim anything but the intent to start hostilities."

The short officer's face flushed. "Even in our home waters?"

"Even in our home waters. We've already sent the message."

The short officer scoffed. "Bah! The message. And now they've used these mercenaries to sink two of our submarines."

Jazani considered the toll. After the *Virginia*-class submarine had helped a *Scorpène* evade a heavyweight, four of his navy's submarines had set an undersea blockade preventing the invaders' return. But the mercenary ship had hit *Ghadir-949,* slowly sinking it after it surfaced for its crew to escape. To the east, another mercenary submarine had crippled *Ghadir-961* after it had launched a heavyweight torpedo at the *Scorpène.* "They sank only one of them, and everyone survived."

"You know what I meant, sir. This is combat. Men are allowed to die. The Americans know that, especially when they're in our waters."

"Like it or not, you're deprived of the privilege of philosophy. You have only the duty to follow orders, which brings us back to ours. And they clearly state that we're not sinking Americans."

"Understood, sir."

"You're still red with anger."

The executive officer groaned.

"You're forgetting one thing."

"What's that, sir?"

"Within the bounds of this engagement, we're winning."

Frowning, the short man glared at his commander's nose. "How?"

"Assuming we find a damaged *Virginia*-class submarine, I guarantee you we've done more damage to the Americans than they have to us. Two damaged *Ghadirs* add up to nothing. They're small and easy to repair or rebuild, but a crippled *Virginia* is worth a fortune."

"Okay, sir. You're making a good point. I'll also concede that we accomplished something when we made the Americans bleed, if we did. They won't consider themselves invulnerable in our waters anymore."

"I'm not sure they ever did. Don't underestimate them. They're still the biggest and the best."

Looking away, the executive officer snorted and grinned.

"What's that for?"

"Bah. I'm overthinking this, sir. And you were right. You made a good point about the trade sanctions. It's strange that we're playing deadly cat-and-mouse games with their navy while we're hoping to expand our trade with them. It's like we live in different worlds on land and at sea."

Enjoying the shift to lighthearted matters, Jazani encouraged his subordinate. "Such is economics and warfare. So, if all of the American sanctions were lifted, what's the first thing you'd buy?"

"That's easy, sir. I want an iPhone."

"You can already get them."

"Yeah, but they're smuggled in and marked up in price, and I'm always a generation behind. I want the latest and greatest."

"No kidding?"

"No kidding. We have a great cell network, and I want to make full use of it. What about you, sir?"

Jazani envisioned a flat stretch of straight road outside the naval base of Bandar Abbas. "I want a new Dodge Charger SRT Hellcat."

"You could find one already if you tried hard enough."

"In my position as a submarine commander, I don't think I should be caught owning something from a gray market. I also don't want to throw my money away paying a gray-market premium."

"Well, at least you're dreaming large."

Jazani reflected over the latest model's specifications. "Over seven hundred horsepower. It can reach sixty miles per hour in under three and a half seconds."

"What's that? Ninety-six kilometers per hour?"

"Roughly."

"That's fast. And pointless. Why would you ever need such acceleration in an automobile?"

"For fun. And if you have to ask, you'll never understand."

A sonar technician called out. "I hear propulsion sounds of a *Virginia*-class submarine."

With a rapid spike of adrenaline, Jazani's attention returned to his submarine. "Any bearing rate?"

"Slight right."

"What's the range if you set the target's speed to zero?"

"Just under four miles, sir. We've been picking up their sonobuoy decoys at three and a half miles."

Jazani tapped an icon on his console. "I'm slowing us to all stop." The digital display showed his creeping submarine drifting to motionlessness. "Now what's the bearing rate?"

"Zero, sir."

"It's just another sonobuoy acting as a decoy. XO, radio this in and have a helicopter pluck it from the water. When you're done with that, get us back up to search speed and take us east into our new patrol waters."

Thirty minutes later, Jazani took *Ghadir-957* eastward, using his submarine's hydrophones to search for invaders while trusting the side-scan sonar of the nearby dive team's ship to search the water around him for a damaged American submarine's skulking hull. He steeled his endurance and patience for a long hunt.

His second-in-command stood and stretched his short frame towards the low overhead. "I assume you want me to run things during the midnight watch section, sir?"

Jazani nodded.

"Then you don't mind if I run off to get an early dinner and some sleep?"

"Not at all. Come back and relieve me before midnight."

The executive officer strolled past his commanding officer and out the back of the control room.

Alone with two young sonar technicians, Jazani led his submarine on a slow, disciplined, zigzagging search for hostile ships. Boring time passed without results, and then two new sailors replaced those seated before him.

Hours later, rubbing sleep from his reddened face, the executive officer returned. "What's going on, sir?"

"Nothing. No signs of anything except commercial shipping."

"I can't say that I'm surprised. I'll wake you if something unexpected happens."

Jazani stood and stretched. "The watch is yours."

After a quick dinner, the *Ghadir's* commander retired to his stateroom. His sleep was deep, and he awoke refreshed the next morning. When he checked the time, he realized he'd have divers available. He toweled himself down with moist wipes and then hurried to the control room and to his executive officer's side. "How was the night?"

The short officer was slouched in his seat. "Boring, except for the last hour when they deployed the divers."

"That's earlier than expected."

"Yes, sir. I think they're excited about the prospect of finding a wounded submarine. They're on the bottom now. You can call up their video if you want to come shallow."

Jazani sat. "Yes. I want to come shallow. I want as many eyes on the divers' feed as possible so that we don't miss any hard-to-find evidence." The *Ghadir's* commander took his ship upward, and the waves rocked the tiny vessel as he raised its radio mast.

His second-in-command toggled through screens. "The divers are looking at sediment."

"That's all they'll be looking at until they find something."

"But look here, sir. The dive ship has something on side-scan sonar."

Jazani looked at the brownish image of the seafloor and the sunken fishing trawler lying on its side. "That's no submarine, but it shows the impressive detail the side-scan sonar can render."

"Real impressive, sir. We could go a little faster if we rely exclusively upon the side-scan."

The *Ghadir's* commander shook his head. "No. Let's keep the divers in the water."

"Of course, sir. I'm going to get some breakfast, if you don't need me for a while."

"No. Go ahead."

The executive officer departed.

Alone, Jazani wondered if limiting his search team's progress to the speed of his divers created an unnecessary delay. After the first hour of searching yielded to the second, the second decayed into the third. His enthusiasm for finding the lost treasure of a wounded American submarine yielded to hope, and then hope decayed into doubt.

A report from a diver distracted the *Ghadir's* commander from despair. "I see a kelp forest to the south. We're going to check it out. Give us an extra thirty meters of line."

From the surfaced ship, the dive team's leader objected. "That's a negative. We need to continue on the search pattern."

Jazani shot his arm forward and tapped an icon to speak.

"Wait! Let them search. Your side-scan sonar can't see in there."

"No, but that kelp bed's too small for an American submarine to hide in. I've been over it enough times in my career. It's barely two miles wide now, and it's been shrinking over the years while the oxygen levels drop. This gulf is horrible for sea life and only getting worse."

The marine biology lesson annoyed the *Ghadir's* commander. "I want them to look regardless."

"As you wish. It's your search, sir."

Jazani watched the video as the diver approached the undersea foliage. His adrenaline spiked when he saw a matted section pressed against the seafloor.

A diver's voice carried enthusiasm. "Is that what you were looking for, commander?"

Leaning into his monitor with his unblinking eyes feasting upon a discovery, Jazani smirked. "Absolutely. Walk that depressed area from beginning to end and mark its heading. Tell me what direction that depression runs in. Once you've done that, you'll have solved for the direction of a damaged American submarine."

"We'll get it done, sir."

The *Ghadir's* commander switched circuits and hailed his leadership. "Task force commander, this is Shark One. Over."

A high-pitched voice issued from an overhead speaker. "Shark One, this is task force commander. Go ahead. Over."

Jazani recognized an underling on his task force leader's staff. "Where's the captain?"

"He's at the morning briefing."

"It's urgent. I'll wait while you get him."

Through the circuit, the man scoffed. "You seem to have forgotten the rank structure. If you want to schedule time with him, I'll put your request in the queue, lieutenant commander."

Jazani inhaled through his nose and exhaled slowly. "Alright, sir. I forgot that you outrank me. I apologize for any disrespect. I request that you have the captain contact me when it's convenient for him to see the evidence I've found of the damaged

American submarine."

"Why didn't you say that? Learn how to give a report." The staffer's speech ended abruptly, but background murmurs from the command center suggested an open line.

A minute later, the captain's deep voice came through the circuit. "Task force commander. Go ahead."

"Sir, I know that we wounded the American submarine with our original lightweight torpedo. I know where it's been, and I know where it's going. I found the evidence on the seafloor."

"Can you show me?"

"Yes, sir. If you can get a feed from the dive ship, you'll see what the divers found. Something dragged a submarine through a kelp bed."

The task force's leader aimed his words into the distance. "Get me the feed from the dive ship. Yes, at my console. Right here. Good." His voice returned to its normal strength. "I'm looking at it now, commander. Sensational... Excellent work. I agree it's on the bottom and dragging itself or being dragged through shallow waters towards Pakistan."

Prideful satisfaction billowed throughout Jazani's chest. "Thank you, sir."

"I'll send a helicopter team and a frigate ahead of the target to stop it from reaching Pakistan. I'll also send the submarines of our southern barrier northeast to give chase. Watch for the orders."

"What about me, sir?"

"Nothing changes for you. Keep going. You'll continue searching for the damaged target from behind. We've got it boxed in on all sides. But remember to search for its rescue team, both American and mercenary. They're sure to be coming."

CHAPTER 14

The prodding annoyed Jake. "Not yet, and stop asking me."

At the *Specter's* control station, the silver-haired Frenchman looked away. "Sorry, Jake. I'll be quiet."

A minute later, Jake looked at his colleague and thought the French mechanic might explode from the volcanic strength of his withheld opinion. "Is something on your mind?"

Henri winced as he pleaded. "If you don't shoot now, I..."

Seeing a chance to turn annoyance into frivolousness at the mechanic's expense, the *Specter's* commander smirked. "Yes?"

The Frenchman sighed and faced his panel. "I've never seen you move in so close for a shot... unnecessarily."

Seated at his captain's console, Jake glanced at the image in his display. Launched from a littoral combat ship and rendering a slant angle from its flightpath over Omani waters, an MQ-8 Fire Scout helicopter drone had captured a shot of the Iranian dolphins' mothership. The picture showed cranes swiveling one of the cetaceans towards its mate's exposed fluke in a holding tank on the fantail. "I'm not ready to sink it just yet."

The delay seemed to send the Frenchman into a subtle seizure. "I guess this is why you're in command."

Jake continued teasing his colleague. "No question about that."

Henri crossed his arms, stared at numbers on his panel Jake knew he'd committed to memory, and lowered his jaw towards his chest.

To avoid laughing, Jake bit his lip. But a chuckle escaped.

The Frenchman sent him a sideways stare. "What's so funny?"

"You want to call me names. You want to chastise me for crimes of omission and commission. You want to verbally skewer me. But you're trying to prove to me, to yourself, and to everyone that you have too much class to do it."

"I do have too much class."

"Bullshit. Let it out. Steamroll me with your angst, you old codger."

Henri turned and waggled his finger. "I'm letting you goad me only because you deserve it." The silver-haired mechanic caught the toad-headed sonar ace turning red and smirking. "Oh, mind your own affairs, Antoine. If you ever had the nerve to stand up to him, then maybe you'd become incensed once in a while."

"I just hear everything and report what I hear. No need for arguments from me."

"That's because I do all the dirty work, keeping him sane for all of us."

Jake interrupted the Frenchmen. "And as my unofficial therapist, you should know the value of expressing yourself. Let it out."

Henri's features softened as he pleaded. "For God's sake, man, if you're not going to shoot this ship, tell us what you intend to do instead. And if you're going to shoot it, would you please do so before you end up ramming it?"

"Oh, I'm going to shoot it, alright. Just not quite yet. And I'm not going to ram it, but don't put good ideas into my head like that."

"I fear for your state of mind."

Jake flicked his fingers and looked away. "You always worry about that."

"Yes. Yes, I do."

"Well, here's the plan." The *Specter's* commander stepped to the central plotting table and waited. "Are you going to join me or not?"

Henri sighed as he strode across the deck to accompany his commanding officer.

Jake aimed a stylus at an icon. "From Pierre's feed, we know this is the mothership. From Antoine's superhuman ears, we're locked in on it with sonar. It's a loud ship, and I'd bet my life that nobody onboard thinks we know of its existence, much less know its role in this conflict."

"From the sounds of it, you're betting everyone's lives on it."

Ignoring the jab, Jake moved the stylus. "Dmitry's here, ten miles away, trying to break this suspected underwater Iranian Maginot Line. The *California's* using its speed to go the long way around the barrier." He brushed his fingers toward the American submarine's icon, which had begun its transit northward towards its wounded sister ship after the *Goliath's* failure to load it.

Evidenced in his tone, Henri's frustration remained. "I understand all of this. You're still supposed to take out the mothership to disrupt the use of their dolphins. I don't see how anything you're pointing to in the geometry changes that."

"I'll sink it long before it can catch the *Indiana*. But I'm going to do more than that."

"Do tell."

"Based upon the time the Predator drone saw them deployed, I think the dolphins are south of the Iranian barrier now, looking for a target. I also think I can predict the timing of their return to the mothership, within a couple hours, based upon what the Americans have observed in their movements and from what we know about Mikhail and Andrei's cycles."

"So?"

Jake knew he was twisting his latest orders liberally, and he hoped his clever ploy would bear fruit to avoid embarrassment or worse. But he needed to work towards something besides another deadly weapons exchange. "I'm going to break their dolphin code."

"I don't like the sound of this."

"Your job will be holding speed, course, and depth right underneath the mothership. Antoine's job will be listening for dolphin calls. My guess is that if we're underneath that ship, we'll intercept some sort of communications between the dolphins and whoever's giving them commands."

Returning to his control station, Henri groaned. "I like the idea of ramming it better."

An hour later, Jake navigated the *Specter* underneath the dolphins' mothership. Creeping below the vessel at four knots, he allowed himself an upward view through his periscope. With the sun backlighting the keel, he saw protrusions he suspected housed hydrophones for undersea communications.

A swell swept the submarine upward, and Jake lowered the optics. "Careful, Henri."

"Sorry! That wave surprised me. They can't all be predicted, you know."

"I know. Do your best."

"This is exhausting. Do we have to be exactly underneath it?"

Jake canted his head and considered how the *Specter's* accidental noises, if created and overheard, would be mistaken as coming from the mothership. "I guess not. Thirty yards off the beam is okay." He had the French mechanic adjust the submarine's course and then waited for time and biological sounds to prove his theory of Persian cetacean communications.

Henri's impatience was obvious. "Are you sure you've calculated the dolphins' feeding and resting cycle correctly?"

Jake shrugged. "As correctly as possible. You know there's a lot of wiggle room in it."

"There's a lot more wiggle room in it than I interpreted in the orders from Pierre."

The Frenchman's verbal gamesmanship began to weary Jake. "Like you said, I'm in command. I've interpreted my orders."

"Are you sure you don't want to chance a discussion with Pierre for clarification?"

Jake recalled the consensus explaining the Iranian heavyweight torpedo that had required an American robot's sacrifice to protect him. "They're hiding electronic support measures suites on their merchant ships. That's how they found us and got off a good shot. I'm not giving them another free target by begging Pierre for permission to do what I'm already doing."

"They'll think it's coming from the mothership."

"Not if the mothership's the one catching us with the ESM."

Henri grunted and faced his panel. "Fair point."

"If Pierre really hated this delay in sinking the mothership, he'd question it, but he's just sending us tactical data on the low-baud feed as normal."

"Perhaps a communications buoy then, as a courtesy."

Jake inhaled through his nostrils and sighed. "I can live with that. Tell him we've taken station under the mothership to intercept and record dolphin transmissions. We'll sink the ship with at least two slow-kill weapons on our way out. Set a one-hour delay on the buoy and launch it when ready. I'll slow us for a few minutes so that we drift into the mothership's wake before the buoy surfaces. No need to let an attentive crewman on the bridge see it."

"Thank you, Jake."

The *Specter's* commander slowed his ship, drifted behind the targeted vessel, and allowed Henri to send the communications buoy. He then moved his submarine back into position next to the mothership and grew impatient. "Anything yet, Antoine?"

The toad-head turned. "I hear a lot of biological sounds. If you mean from the mothership specifically, nothing yet."

"How about chirps, whistles, or complaints from tired and hungry dolphins, possibly with a Persian accent?"

"Nothing yet."

"Damn. We'll keep waiting."

Apparently aware of his commanding officer's waning tolerance for open debate, Henri waited for a quiet moment to skulk to his side and lower his voice. "May we talk at my panel?"

Realizing the Frenchman's need to keep his eyes on his instruments to maintain depth in the shallow water, Jake followed Henri to control station. The status of trim and drain tanks spanning the *Specter* ran across a placard with lights and gauges showing their filled percentages, the status of their pumps, and the positions of the valves between them. "What's on your mind?"

Henri tapped an icon, opening a valve, flooding a central tank, and weighing the submarine deeper under the waves. "You need to decide now how long you're willing to wait. We may be temporarily safe hidden in plain sight under this mothership, but there are too many submarines, divers, and dare I say, dolphins that can detect us. These waters are dangerous."

Jake swallowed. "You're right. Forty-five more minutes."

"So that we can escape before our communications buoy sends its broadcast?"

"Yeah. Exactly."

"I'll set a timer to remind us."

Jake returned to his console and sat, but nervousness compelled him to his feet ten minutes later. He walked to the seated trio of sonar technicians and paced behind them.

A nasty glance from the toad-head told the *Specter's* commander that his presence bothered his team.

Jake stepped away and placed the central table between himself and his listening team. Fifteen minutes later, he noticed his fingers rapping against the chart as a burst of chirps and whistles echoed through the room. "Antoine?"

The toad-head turned. "Yes! That's it. From the mothership."

"Any response from dolphins?"

"Yes, at least I think so, but I'll need to analyze it later. It was a rapid exchange. I don't expect them to repeat it."

"Neither do I." Jake looked over his shoulder. "Henri, take us down gently to one hundred and fifty feet. Set us on course zero-eight-zero. Take us out of here."

"Gladly."

Half an hour later, Jake sensed renewed impatience as he glanced at his French mechanic. He moved to his colleague's side. "I assume that you want to shoot now?"

"The thought did cross my mind."

"First things first. Let's get another communications buoy to Pierre. This time, send him the recording of the dolphin exchange. Use a thirty-minute delay. Once it's launched, I'll shoot weapons."

"What if the mothership accelerates?"

"It won't. And we're still well within torpedo range if it does."

"I'll get the buoy launched. Should I also get tubes five and six ready, too?"

"Tubes three and five. It's a starboard nest shot. And keep it super quiet. Have them swim out."

The Frenchman tapped keys. "Tubes three and five are ready."

"Shoot tubes three and five."

Ten minutes later, the toad-head turned. "I hear our first weapon's warheads attaching to the mothership. At least half of them are hitting. I now hear the second weapon's warheads attaching as the first warheads detonate."

"Very well. Try to count them all."

"Too many to count. I'll need to listen to a recording if you want the accurate number."

The *Specter's* commander shook his head. "Just let me know what the mothership's doing."

"It's slowing and flooding from a lot of holes."

"But it's not sinking?"

The toad-head shook. "No. It's too big of a ship."

"Henri, ready tubes four and six."

The Frenchman tapped keys. "Tubes four and six are ready."

"Shoot tubes four and six."

As the second salvo sought its damaged prey, Jake saw the low-frequency feed confirm Renard's receipt of the recorded Iranian dolphin calls. "Pierre's received our message. If our ships play this call from a drone, we won't be dealing with Iranian dolphin problems anymore whether the dolphins can operate without their mothership or not."

Henri nodded. "I should've known better than to have doubted you."

Jake smirked. "Is that an apology?"

"I wasn't aware you were looking for one."

"I'm not. And I don't hold it against you. You'll doubt me again, I'm sure, and you'll be vocal about it. As usual." The fleeting joviality gave way to anxiety as Jake saw his sonar ace curl forward and press his muffs into his head. "Antoine?"

The toad-head rotated. "I just picked up a *Ghadir* from the south. It's moving."

"Bearing drift, bearing rate, blade rate?"

"Blade rate correlates to six knots. Bearing rate is zero."

Jake walked to the central table and watched an icon appear

with Remy's information. "Antoine, do you have it on the bow or conformal arrays?"

The toad-head shook. "Just the towed array."

"Alright. I'm slowing. Henri, all stop."

The silver-haired mechanic tapped his console, and the deck's gentle vibrations ceased.

Jake kept his eyes on the tactical chart. "Antoine, let me know when you've got a new bearing rate."

"Not yet."

"I don't like being at all stop while I'm running from a ship I just attacked."

"I said 'not yet'."

Holding back from tapping the hard surface, Jake wiggled nervous fingers over the table.

The toad-head turned. "Okay. I've got it. One-point-three degrees per minute to the left."

"Thanks, Antoine. Henri, make turns for seven knots."

"I've ordered turns for seven knots. The engine room acknowledges, and we're making turns for seven knots."

As Jake felt a gentle thrumming through his feet, he used a stylus to draw the discovered Iranian submarine's track. "Henri, get a note into a communications buoy for Pierre. Send him this new contact's course, speed, and location. It's too far away for me to shoot, and I don't like the way it's going."

"I'm preparing the message." In his unofficial role of psychologist, Henri added his leading questions. "What's not to like? Do you want to add a recommendation for him?"

Jake scoffed. "Yeah, I do, but I didn't want to tell him how to run his fleet, especially while he's working for a bigger fleet."

"Speak your mind and let him filter what he wants."

"Tell him that I think this submarine's got an idea of where the *Indiana* and *Goliath* are, but I have no idea how. We just found the dolphins, and they were nowhere near any of our other ships."

"That's to be verified."

The toad-head rotated upward. "I verified it. The dolphins

were returning to the mothership from the south."

Henri sneered. "Our superhuman sonar expert has verified the dolphins, but you said the Iranian submarine has an idea of our colleagues' location. It's not exact?"

The *Specter's* commander shook his head. "No. It's moving too far ahead to intercept them, but it's on the right trajectory for someone who knows our friends' course but has overestimated their speed. It seems like somebody figured out their direction towards Pakistan."

"I'm sure Pierre will see that, but I'll include your thoughts in the message anyway."

Jake considered his final teammate. "Yeah. And also ask him to send me whatever Dmitry's seeing. I wouldn't be surprised if there's more than one Iranian submarine on the move, trying to get ahead of Terry and ruin our mission."

CHAPTER 15

His adrenaline spiking, Volkov hushed his team. "Silence! Pass the word for everyone to stay still. Don't move. Touch nothing."

As an anxious tranquility enveloped the room, the gray-bearded veteran spoke repetitive commands into a sound-powered phone, compartment by compartment. "Everyone's aware to stay still, sir. Nobody's moving."

Disobeying his own orders, the *Wraith's* commander walked to his sonar team, stooped behind his expert, and lowered his voice to a near-whisper. The bright line of sound from the nearby Iranian submarine's reduction gears cut a hockey stick across the display. Overlapping the gears' signature, sounds from the propeller blades carved thinner strands across the screen. "How close?"

Anatoly kept his face aimed at his console. "Depends on speed. I'm factoring that in now."

"Don't you have blade rate?"

"I have everything. I'm still calculating. It came out of no-where."

Doing the blunt math in his head, Volkov tried to lead his witness to an answer. "A quarter a mile. Half a mile at most."

The sonar ace nodded his slow affirmation. "Yeah. Real close, but it's opening range now. We're no longer at risk of a collision."

"That's not what I was worried about."

Looking over his shoulder, Anatoly glared at his commanding officer. "You should've been."

Volkov silently conceded the point but concentrated on the present danger. "Keep tracking it. Listen for weapons launches."

Anatoly's voice rose above a whisper. "I'm listening. We all are." He aimed his nose at the technicians seated beside him. "There's no indication that we've been heard."

"Not yet, but no captain in his right mind would react at this range and signal that he did hear us. Any aggression would invite a one-for-one exchange. If he hears us and intends to shoot, my bet is that he'd wait until he's opened to at least three miles."

"I know you're not ready to shoot yet, but do you want a tube assigned to the new contact?"

"Yes. Tube one at one-third charge. Set it to swim out. I want a silent launch."

Anatoly nodded. "We'll make tube one ready." He tapped his colleague's shoulder and uttered the instruction for the junior technician to handle the weapon.

As his torpedo became available, Volkov evaluated his maneuvering options. Wanting to avoid the hydraulic and metallic adjustment sounds and the shifting flow noise of his rudder, he had one option. He crept to his gray-bearded veteran's side and attempted a telepathic link by mouthing the words while lifting his index and ring finger in a V-shape. "Two knots."

The veteran nodded. "Slowing to two knots, sir."

Volkov retraced his steps to his sonar ace. "That should make us harder to hear and let the Iranian drive away faster."

Ignoring the comment, Anatoly spoke to the man seated two consoles away. "Track the close-aboard contact. I hear something new." He aimed his jaw over his shoulder at his commander. "When you slowed down, I heard something else. There's another *Ghadir*-class submarine on the move. I'm assigning a cursor to it now."

After recovering from the shock of another phantom submarine's appearance, Volkov sneered. "That could be a good sign. Hopefully, the Iranians have received orders to withdraw from the area. Perhaps our close-aboard contact's driving away to a new patrol area, and not maneuvering to shoot us."

A silent, tense thirty seconds elapsed. "My initial solution has the distant *Ghadir* heading northeast as well. It's not the exact same course as the close-aboard contact, but they're both heading in a similar direction."

The *Wraith's* commander watched the lines of incoming sound from the nearby submarines steady on a constant bearing as the vessels slipped away. Watching the geometry and waiting for hostile action taxed his patience.

"Tube one is ready, sir."

"Very well, Anatoly. However, I'm not ready. We're still too close for torpedoes. The noise of the launch... the accuracy of a reactionary weapon. Not yet."

"Should I get a weapon ready for the second contact?"

Volkov lacked clarity on his ability to determine the distant *Ghadir's* fate, but he gave himself the option. "Yes. Tube three. Set it at one-third charge."

After furious tapping, Anatoly bounced his announcement off his display. "Tube three is ready."

"Easy now. These are slow submarines. No need to hurry."

"The close-aboard one's passing two and a half miles."

"Patience. I'll move us across the line of sight now so that our torpedo doesn't work as a tracer bullet in reverse."

"Agreed. I think we're far enough away from the target to maneuver without being heard."

Volkov risked raising his voice towards his gray-bearded veteran. "Make turns for six knots. Come right to course one-one-zero."

After the deck tilted and settled into the turn, the sonar ace's tone was impatient. "Three miles to the closer *Ghadir* and opening."

"That's good enough. Shoot tube one."

"Weapon one is swimming out of tube one."

"Very well. Now make sure our drones are still paralleling our course and speed."

"They are. They're still taking orders from the system."

While skulking through the Gulf of Oman with frequent turns, Volkov had set his two deployed drones to behave like robots mimicking his ship's course in their self-drive modes.

"Do you want to shoot the next *Ghadir*, Dmitry?"

"Show me the fuel prediction."

"It's insufficient. The weapon would stop half a mile short of the target, but you can close that distance before shooting."

Volkov sniffed a possible trap. "Of course, I could. And that may be exactly what they want me to do. Shoot a few gentle slow-kill weapons at their transiting submarines while their drifting colleagues stay hidden and use my torpedoes as tracer bullets to fix my position. There's a reason they built a lot of cheap, small submarines. Power in numbers."

"But if you let the second one get away, it'll become a risk to the *Indiana*."

Volkov frowned as he realized he'd been prioritizing his safety over the mission's success. "Damn it. You're right."

"Sorry, Dmitry. It's a difficult decision."

"Don't apologize. Reminding me was your duty. Deciding how much I'm willing to risk our Russian hides to save an American submarine is my duty." The *Wraith's* commander straightened his back and looked across the room at his rider.

Commander Hatcher raised his voice. "And what's the captain's decision?"

"I couldn't live with myself if I showed any cowardice. We're going after that second *Ghadir*. But we're doing it calmly and carefully. It's making six knots. I'll make eight to reduce the distance by a mile over the next thirty minutes and give myself a half mile of margin with my weapon. Then I'll shoot." Volkov gave his maneuvering orders to his gray-bearded veteran, and then the deck titled with the left turn to the northeast.

The American qualified his agreement. "That should neutralize the second *Ghadir* before it can tangle with the *Indiana*, assuming that nothing changes in its course and speed after you hit the first *Ghadir*."

Volkov glanced at a tactical display showing his first weapon racing towards its victim. "We'll know what the second *Ghadir* does soon enough. We've got its colleague pegged."

The sonar ace echoed his commander's sentiments. "Half a mile to impact. There's not even a reactive weapon yet. We shot from so deep in the baffles, I don't think they have a good bearing to our weapon, if their sonar team can hear it at all."

"Maybe not, but it doesn't matter. Have one of our guys listen for submunitions and for the *Ghadir* fighting to the surface after we hit it. The rest of you listen for submarines in hiding."

Seated next to the captain's console, the translator called out. "There's a note from Pierre on the low-baud feed. He says Jake sank the dolphins' mothership and recorded an undersea exchange he believes is the return-to-mothership command."

Volkov grunted. "Impressive. That could create some confused Iranian dolphins." He glanced around the control room and was thankful for the absence of his ship's cetacean trainer, who'd retreated to his bunk to hibernate after his babies' loss.

"Pierre says he's sending the dolphin command recording in a continuous loop on the high-frequency broadcast. It's there for you whenever you come shallow."

"I'm in a bit of a tactical bind here. It'll have to wait."

"Okay, I'm reading the data as it comes. He also says he'll send it in pieces over the low-frequency feed in between other updates. He says it should take about two hours that way."

"That's fine. Good thinking on his part, as usual. Once you've got it, loop it every five minutes from our drones. Half-power broadcasts."

"I'll set it up, Dmitry."

Volkov's translator seemed unhappy with the low-baud solution to the problem that had sent an accurate heavyweight torpedo at the *Wraith* two days earlier. "Can't you go shallow and raise an antenna?"

Commander Hatcher intercepted the question. "You've heard the crew talk about hull popping?"

"Well, yeah. I admit that I'd forgotten about that."

"Even in these shallow waters we're hearing it. If we go shallow, the water pressure drops, our hull expands, and our popping could be heard. High-frequency downloads will have to wait."

Anatoly's voice echoed off his console. "Our weapon has detonated under the first *Ghadir*. One, two.... three and now a fourth submunition has attached. And... now they're exploding."

Volkov folded his arms across his chest. "Perfect."

"Hull popping. The *Ghadir's* coming shallow."

"Watch the second *Ghadir* for a reaction."

"Six knots is its best transit speed. I don't think anything's going to change unless it plans to snorkel or surface."

The comment was like a punch to Volkov's stomach. "I've been an idiot. Of course, it's going to surface and snorkel for speed after I hit the other one. It's not hiding or hunting, and its nation controls the air and surface over its own waters. Damn it. All ahead standard, make turns for thirteen knots!"

Anatoly snapped his jaw towards his commanding officer. "I'm not sure I can track it with our own flow noise at thirteen knots."

"Do your best. Listen for hull popping. Listen for diesel noises. You may even hear it surface."

Commander Hatcher appeared by Volkov's side. "Shouldn't you finish off the first *Ghadir*?"

"Excuse me?"

"It has two torpedo tubes and is a functional warship. Your humane holes have just prevented it from submerging."

"There's a good chance that my former students are on that ship. Good men. I see no reason to expend a torpedo in battering their ship further. I've removed them from the undersea battle, and I believe that's sufficient."

"I don't."

Volkov mustered a stern tone. "If you want that submarine sunk, call your friends at the fifth fleet and have them do it. I have more important things to do. Am I clear, commander?"

The American rider revealed his strength by holding the Russian's glare. "Give me a communications buoy, and I'll do just that."

Volkov accepted the compromise. "Yes, but a fifteen-minute delay. I don't want to give an easy clue of our location. The Iranians are sniffing all radio noise."

The gray-bearded veteran hailed his commanding officer. "Fifteen-minute delay. I've got a communications buoy ready. I'm entering the *Ghadir's* coordinates into the message. Commander Hatcher can dictate to me whatever he wants to add."

Volkov canted his head towards the veteran. "He'll take care of you and your buoy. Let it be on your conscience."

The rider stormed away.

Anatoly's voice ricocheted off his console. "Hull popping. The second *Ghadir* is coming shallow." Thirty seconds later, he appended his findings. "And now I hear diesel noises. The second *Ghadir's* accelerating. Blade rate's increasing to its maximum speed of eleven knots."

"Damn it. Increase speed to fifteen knots."

The gray-bearded veteran relayed the order and added a warning. "Fifty-two minutes remaining on the battery at this speed."

"I'm firing in fifteen."

Anatoly added another concern. "The drones can't keep up. They'll be trailing us after fifteen minutes, but we'll still have them both under wire control."

"Very well. We'll reposition them later. Set them to send out active pings every thirty seconds."

The sonar ace looked over his shoulder. "Maximum power?"

"Yes. The entire Iranian fleet knows of our general location now, and I don't care if some distant vessel hears us. What's important is rousting the drifting submarines."

"With that logic, you could go active on our bow sonar."

Volkov considered it. "Tempting, but no. That incurs as much risk as reward. Just the drones."

"We're setting the drones to maximum power pings, recurring every thirty seconds."

The next quarter of an hour tested Volkov's patience, as he expected a hidden, drifting submarine to spring from nowhere and destroy him. But his fears proved unfounded as he reduced the distance to his next target.

The sonar ace brought the anticipated news. "We're within firing range of the *Ghadir*, with a half-mile margin of error."

Volkov double-checked the assumptions. "Verify the weapon has enough fuel while the target sustains eleven knots."

"Done. I had accounted for its maximum speed in my initial

torpedo fuel calculations."

"Then we're ready."

"Yes. It's time, Dmitry."

"Shoot tube three."

"Weapon two is swimming out of tube three."

Volkov called out to his gray-bearded veteran. "That's enough high-speed running. Slow us to four knots. Come right to course one-one-zero. Use the turn to slow us."

As the ship's vibrations receded, Anatoly curled forward in intense listening. He seemed mesmerized in hearing the world around him, but after several minutes, he shook his head. "Nothing. There's nothing new out there."

"What about the damaged *Ghadir*?"

"On the surface, running pumps to stay afloat."

"I can't wait to learn what Commander Hatcher's request leads to. I don't think his American colleagues are as aggressive as he is."

"You could come shallow and find out."

"Not yet. I don't want to give the Iranians our location. Just a single exposed antenna could do it."

"There's nothing around us, Dmitry. Not even merchants."

"And what about high-altitude reconnaissance craft? The Iranians use unmanned aerial vehicles, too. The consensus is that a merchant ship picked up Jake's radio broadcasts to target him. But I'm not so sure it wasn't a UAV."

"Under that logic, we're rolling the dice every time we expose any mast above the surface. Don't you at least want to download the dolphin calls? That's a tactical necessity now."

Volkov sighed. "You're right again. However, it can wait. According to Jake's findings, the dolphins are too far away to matter."

"That's true if there's only one pair of them."

The American rider interrupted. "You may be able to reduce your risk in broadcasting. We've got a destroyer stationed outside Iranian waters to control the sky, and we've got a littoral combat ship and a few riverine boats supporting it. You can use low-power, directional high-frequency broadcasts to contact any of them. Pierre's sending their locations periodically in his feed."

Volkov nodded. "I'll try that when I need to emit. First, I want to just listen."

"An excellent decision. We need an update."

"And I need to snorkel. I'll have to chance it." Risking the hull popping and the antenna exposure, Volkov ordered his ship shallow, raised his radio mast, and leaned over his tactical table. The dolphin call download arrived, followed by an update of known tactical assets in the battle. On the chart, the *California* appeared near the *Indiana*, its exact location a mystery. Iranian surface craft were racing east towards Pakistan, suggesting knowledge of the *Indiana's* long crawl towards safe waters. "Damn."

Beside him, Hatcher agreed. "They figured it out. That's why they gave up on this barrier and sent everything northeast. Taking out two *Ghadirs* will help, but it won't solve the problem. The *Goliath* has to find a way to load the *Indiana* and bring it out to the south."

"That's step three on my list. Let me hit the second *Ghadir* first before I worry about that. Then let me snorkel and charge my batteries."

Anatoly called out. "Our weapon has acquired the second *Ghadir* and is accelerating. The *Ghadir* doesn't have the evasion speed. It should happen soon."

Volkov waited.

"Detonation... bomblets are attaching. And... explosions. Three of them. The *Ghadir's* surfacing."

The American rider was bold. "Let me send another buoy about finishing that *Ghadir*."

"As you wish commander. Again, it's on your conscience."

"A fifteen-minute delay again?"

"Yes." Volkov had an idea, which became an order to his gray-bearded veteran. "Reload tubes one and three with limpet weapons."

"Limpets, sir?"

"I'll tag those two *Ghadir's* with sonic limpets so that I always know where they are, no matter what the Americans decide about their fates."

"Don't you think they'll be sunk soon?"

"If that happens, I won't shoot the limpets. Load the tubes like I said."

The translator stood and marched to his commanding officer with scribbled notes. "You'll want to read this."

"What's it say?"

"It's from the fifth fleet. They've received Commander Hatcher's recommendation of finishing off the first *Ghadir*. They're going in the other diplomatic direction and offering assistance to the crew. The Americans have two riverine command boats which are the closest vessels that could help."

Volkov scoffed. "I can't wait to see Commander Hatcher's response to that. In fact, I can't wait to see the Iranian response. This conflict's getting more bizarre by the hour."

"I suppose you now have a decision about shooting limpets."

"That's easy. I'll shoot them when they're ready. Pierre won't mind the expense, and there's little tactical risk."

"You'd shoot even if the Iranians accept the American offer?"

"Don't try to make political sense out of this, or you'll go crazy. The limpets don't make much of a difference, other than letting me know from far away if a wounded *Ghadir's* trying to move."

The translator shrugged. "I can't argue that."

"There are plenty of hard decisions ahead without having to stress over this one. I just wish that Terry could load the *Indiana* and get the hell out of here before someone makes the wrong decision and starts a fire that nobody can put out."

CHAPTER 16

With a black marker, Causey wrote the brainstorming session's latest contribution on a whiteboard. He hated the idea. Blow the forward ballast tanks, use the improved leverage to rotate backwards into the *Goliath's* cargo bed, and then evade. "Well, it's an idea, and it would work, but we'd announce ourselves to the entire world. It's a good idea to remember if we're in a pinch, though."

A brash junior petty officer called out. "You mean a worse pinch than we're in now, captain?"

Nervous laughter rose from the crew.

"Yes, I mean a worse pinch than we're in now. I can't say that I've seen worse, but I can imagine it. Keep the ideas coming."

Mustered around him, covering the widest opening in the engine room's middle level and arranged in varied postures, dozens of sailors faced him in silence.

The *Indiana's* commander cast his voice into a forest of pipes and machines that included a freshwater evaporator and high-pressure air compressors. "Come on. Anyone else? Don't be shy."

Heads shook.

Causey eyed his senior enlisted leaders one-by-one. "Division chiefs, anything to add from your breakout meetings?"

Again, heads shook.

The *Indiana's* commander faced his second-in-command. "XO, do I have all the ideas from the fleet on the board?"

"Yes, sir."

"Then that's it. Twenty-six ideas." Causey added a silent qualifier—most fruits of the extensive brainstorming sessions were rotten. Few caught his attention as better possible options than continuing east for six days to Pakistani waters.

A phone-talker wearing a headset challenged his hopes of staying the course. "Sir, Lieutenant Hansen says the *Goliath* urgently recommends coming to all stop."

Causey stepped to a handset, yanked it from a cradle, and lifted it to his cheek. "This is the captain."

The diver sounded urgent. "Sir, the *Goliath's* found something in the seafloor they don't like. A fissure, Mister Cahill called it, though I doubt it's an accurate description. I'd call it an underwater ravine."

"Like a valley?"

"Not that deep, but deep enough to matter."

"Big enough to make us stop?"

"That's correct, sir."

"I'll be right there." The *Indiana's* commander flipped the circuit to the engine room's command center. "Maneuvering, this is the captain. Come to all stop."

The reply came from the engineer. "Coming to all stop, sir."

"XO, pick the top ten of these ideas and take notes about their pros and cons. We'll review them when I get back." The deck's gentle rumble waned under Causey's sneakers as he marched toward the engine room's watertight door.

At the jury-rigged laptops, the dive team's officer pointed at the rightmost screen. "Check this out, sir."

Causey examined the underwater gully beneath the *Goliath's* floodlights. "Shit."

"I'm sending my guys to check it out, but I agree it sucks. It's deep enough to screw us. If we fall into it, we're not getting out."

"Lucky the *Goliath's* scouting ahead of us. God help us if we'd fallen..." Causey rubbed his tired eyes. "Never mind. We didn't fall into it. We just need to avoid it."

"No shit, sir. We either go around it in the shallow direction, go around it in the deep direction, or try one of our desperate ideas to avoid it altogether. But I don't see how we could cross it."

Cahill's Australian accent issued from the central laptop. "It looks like it goes on forever in either direction. If you go shallow, you'll expose your rudder. If you go deep, you'll tumble down the steep decline into the Gulf of Oman."

Causey revealed his concerns. "I was thinking about going deeper, even if it means going deeper than you can follow. The problem is, you're probably right about us rolling before making our way across."

On the laptop's screen, the *Goliath's* commander shrugged. "It only looks to be about three meters or so deep. You could try to power down one side and back up the other."

"The thought had crossed my mind." Causey met the burly diver's stare. "But I've heard dissenting views already about the chances of that working. Lieutenant Hansen and I were just convincing ourselves it was impossible."

"If you gunned it, you might reach ten knots before you hit the other side. It'd be an interesting outcome."

Causey disagreed. "It could get interesting with a big celebration on the other side, or it could get interesting with screams of terror if we roll. But you forgot to mention the possible outcome of us getting stuck in the rut. That's almost as bad as tumbling into the deep. Maybe worse."

"Right, mate. It's your ship, and I won't argue it. What if we put you back in me cargo bed and try pulling you across? Since I've got two hulls, the extra stability would prevent rolling, you'd have the *Goliath's* power helping you, and it would spread out the power over a larger surface area."

The suggestion sparked an idea. "Let's take it one step further. Let's use the ravine to get you deeper underneath me. Your bows are rakish, and you could press them up against the ravine's near side and lower your bed deeper below me."

Cahill nodded. "I see your point. I could very well get you deeper into me cargo bed than last time, but I don't see it making enough of a difference. You'd still be too heavy up front to rotate you back, I'm afraid."

"One of our ideas was to pump air into the forward ballast tanks to make us lighter up front while you load us again. If we combine that with you digging in deep, it might work."

"Yeah, mate. It might." The Australian's voice trailed off. "Wait. You don't mean blowing them dry with high-pressure air?"

"No. I don't want to announce ourselves to the world. It would be with our divers running hoses carrying hundred-pound air under the bottom grates."

The *Goliath's* commander furrowed his eyebrows. "I'm not sure one hundred pounds per square inch is enough. I'm doing the math in me head, and I think you'd be a bit short."

"Correction–I should've specified. We're using our hundred-pound line but adjusting the reducer to bring the pressure up to one-twenty. My auxiliary division assures me it's no problem."

Cahill nodded. "That'll get the job done, but you can't get to the grates unless you take a steep angle, or unless you have room underneath your keel."

"We'll have a little of both at the ravine."

"It might work. Yeah... it just might. Good thinking, commander. Brilliant, actually."

"It's amazing how sharp the mind can be when your life's at stake."

"Right. Let's do this, but let me first see if I can work meself into position. I don't want you committing to this until I know I can dig in there. I can back out of this easily. You can't."

While he trusted the Australian to maneuver the *Goliath*, Causey returned to the brainstorming session and examined the green writing his second-in-command had added to the whiteboard. "Looks like you got the top ten identified, XO."

"Just as you ordered, sir, with pros and cons for the top ten."

"Good job, but cut to the chase. Which one do you recommend?"

The executive officer blushed. "I've been gathering input from the crew, sir, running it like a think tank. I was waiting for you to return to order the ideas by priority."

"Understood." Causey ushered his second-in-command to the privacy behind the whiteboard and the refrigeration unit that served as an ad hoc wall. He lowered his voice. "But you need to have your own opinion."

"Of course, sir."

"Well?"

"I... uh."

"This isn't a drill, XO. I need your answer."

"Well, sir. I kind of got my own idea. Actually, it's more like an improvement to one of our good ones."

"Tell me."

Stiffening his back, the hesitant officer found his courage. "We start with the idea we've already shared about taking our maximum down angle and running hoses into our ballast tanks from the hundred-pound air system."

"Then what? What else have you got?"

"We can do even better, sir, especially while on the down angle. We should also release hundred-pound air into the forward compartment. But we have to be smart about it. We have to calculate the volume so that when we level out again on the *Goliath*, the air pocket doesn't fall below the upper edge of the damage to the torpedo room. Otherwise, it'll send a bubble to the surface. I figure even a few feet of clearance above the hole adds tons of buoyancy."

Causey frowned.

Shadows forming on his face, his second-in-command mimicked the negative gesture. "What's wrong, sir? You don't like it?"

"Maybe. I'm thinking." In Causey's mind, the *Indiana* rotated to its level deck atop the cargo ship. "I can't be sure. I don't think anyone can be. We don't know where our center of mass is versus the fulcrum of the *Goliath's* bed. I can't say if a bubble at the aft bulkhead of the forward compartment helps us or hurts us."

"Uh, yeah. I see your point, sir. I was thinking about our normal center of mass. Not this situation."

The conversation generated a new vision for the *Indiana's* commander. He chuckled.

"Captain?"

"You were hesitant to share your idea. I can't tell you if we'll end up acting on it, but I'll tell you it was a good one. You're a smart man, and you could be a good commanding officer if you'd shed your doubts."

The executive officer's eyes grew wide. "Sir, I don't know if now's a good time for a fitness report."

"Is it or is it not a good time for a fitness report?"

"I... uh, don't understand."

"You said you don't know. Hell, nobody knows everything all the time, but you know your own opinion, don't you?"

"Yes, sir."

"So, is it or is it not a good time for a fitness report?"

"If you see something I'm doing wrong that needs correcting, then yes. If not, then no. I think you should save it for later, sir."

Causey nodded slowly. "Good answer. But I disagree, and I'm the captain. So, here it comes. You've been carrying yourself through this mess like a naval officer should."

The executive officer cocked his head.

"Of course, I watch for that sort of thing. I have to. The other officers. The chiefs. The entire crew. If you looked weak or uncertain, it would kill their spirits. But somehow, this mess has erased every shred of doubt you have about yourself except when you're with me."

The man frowned and looked downward in thought. "Huh."

"Maybe you fear authority. Maybe you fear judgment. But based on the way you've been walking tall around here, like you're absolutely certain that you're going to get the crew home, you sure as hell don't fear death or failure. The men look at you like a beacon of hope, and I've never seen them do that before. Sustain it. Run the rest of your executive officer tour like that, and I'll end up recommending you for command."

The man of mediocre stature suddenly seemed taller. "I can do that, sir. I will do it."

Letting the rebuilt man have the final word, Causey led him back towards the waiting audience. While he walked, he visualized a new concept. "Come on, XO. I'm stealing your idea, but I'll give you partial credit. Wait until you hear the twisted version of it that just popped into my head. It involves garbage bags."

Thirty minutes later, Causey stood over the laptops.

Cahill announced his success in positioning his ship. "I'm ready for you, commander. Give it a go."

Balanced against the deck's down angle, the *Indiana's* commander faced the Australian's image in the laptop. Having dedicated his divers to tasks of buoyancy, he was blind to his stern's positioning. "You'll tell me when to slow, won't you?"

"Yeah, mate. I've got the rover deployed a hundred meters ahead of me. I'll be following you the whole way in. Can't see shit yet except your work lights, but I'm streaming the rover's video."

The *Indiana's* commander tapped the rightmost laptop's keys to toggle through feeds and invoke a new view. The lights supporting the work area where a pair of divers had rigged air hoses into the accessible ballast tank grates cast a blurry orb. "I see it. I'll back towards you now."

"Right, mate. Steady now."

Causey eyed his nearest phone-talker. "To maneuvering, make turns for all-back nine knots."

"Maneuvering acknowledges turns for all back nine knots, sir."

"Very well." The thrumming deck confirmed the submarine's movement.

"Are you in motion?"

"I'm just getting started."

"There you go. I see some sediment being kicked up. Your work lights just got dimmer."

"I see it, too." Causey turned his gaze from the laptop to a jury-rigged speed gauge his electronics division had set up near the watertight door. "We're at two knots."

Cahill nodded.

As Causey watched the luminous circle under his submarine grow, the sluggish journey went awry. "It looks like I'm tracking to your left."

"You are. Don't maneuver, though. I'll adjust." The Australian extended his arm and raised his voice. "I'm using me outboards to move five meters down the ravine."

The *Indiana's* commander watched the leftmost monitor follow the ravine's lip, which seemed to move northward as a camera under the *Goliath* slid southward above it.

"Bloody hell." In the central laptop's display, Cahill staggered and then recovered.

In the leftmost laptop, a cloud of sediment billowed underneath the camera. "Are you alright?"

Cahill released a nervous smile. "Never better. The waves above us are getting ornery, shoving us around a bit down here. That was bound to happen, I imagine. At least mud's quiet when you hit it."

As the glowing sphere grew, it outlined the silhouette of the tilted submarine. Causey thought he was watching his ship steaming in a slow-motion video. "We're playing a patient man's game."

"No kidding. Keep it steady. No rush. I'm moving another two meters to the left."

After a seeming eternity, Causey discerned his propulsor, rudder, and stern planes. Then he watched his ship's growing size steady as the moving lens matched its speed towards the *Goliath*. When the rover settled over the cargo ship, the *Indiana's* size expanded again.

"Alright, commander. Slow it down. Make turns for four knots."

The *Indiana's* commander relayed the order to his engineering team. "Time for even more patience."

"Coming left another half meter."

Mesmerized, Causey stood in quiet, trusting awe of the gentle dance between the hefty undersea vessels.

"Make turns for two knots, now."

Causey relayed the order to his engineering staff, and then seconds later he rocked back on his heels for balance as the deck halted.

"I've got you! All stop!"

"To maneuvering, all stop!"

"Maneuvering answers all stop, sir."

"Very well." The rightmost monitor showed hydraulic rams rotating against the *Indiana's* hull while the leftmost laptop became the blackness of the ravine's lip fusing with the *Goliath's* burdened keel.

"And now I've got you pressed into me cargo bed. Yeah... it's much better than before. This could work."

"I'll shift my water and people like last time and keep pushing air into the ballast tanks."

"It takes a while to blow them dry with reduced air, doesn't it?"

Causey appreciated the Australian's attempts at small talk instead of dwelling upon the dangers around them. "Forever." He grabbed a phone-talker and told him to have the executive officer shift water and people about the engine room to reverse the leverage towards the cargo ship.

Cahill furrowed his brow and reminded Causey of an offhand comment he'd made during their slow transit. "Commander, you said you had an idea to speed things up?"

"If you'll let me send you the feed, I'll show you. I'm already working on it."

"Alright." Cahill reached his arm forward, and then the screen with his image went black while his Australian accent remained audible from the computer. "Go ahead and send the feed."

Causey pressed keys on the central laptop, and a view of the two divers in his forward compartment's upper level appeared. Within the white cones from their flashlights, inflated garbage bags rose into the hull's insulation. The *Indiana's* commander aimed his jaw at the diving officer standing beside him. "How far along are they?"

"They're filling their eighteenth bag, sir."

"Sixty gallons per bag displaces almost five hundred pounds. So, that's about four and a half tons of buoyancy."

"I admit I haven't done the math, sir. I can see that they're not able to fill them completely since they need a lot of slack in the necks to tie them down."

The exchange gave the *Indiana's* commander a thought. "Damn it. Hold on. How completely are they filling them?"

"I'm not watching those details, sir. I'm just watching to make sure my guys have air, don't get stuck in there, and don't get the bends. Senior chief's in communication with them."

"We'll check with him later. We first need to consider what happens when we change depth. The *Goliath* needs the freedom to do that with us aboard."

His brows raised in realization, the burly diver agreed. "When we go deeper, the bags will compress and make us heavier."

"Exactly. I'm not sure if Mister Cahill will be able to adjust for that."

"He'd better, or else we're not coming home."

"We'll remind him of that before he'd take us down."

The Australian accent issued from a laptop. "I stand reminded, gents. In fact, I'm putting an alert in me system right now to warn me before we got below seventy meters. We'll see the same effect of compressed air in your ballast tanks, which I normally don't consider because they're usually flooded. So, yeah, I'm not taking you deeper unless I have to."

Causey leaned forward. "Much appreciated, Mister Cahill."

"It's a great point, mate. I'm glad you brought it up. Now that we're talking optimistically about me being able to carry you, I'm also going to set an alert at fifty-five meters so that I don't give your divers the bends."

"We'll get them back into the tunnel if we go shallow, but I appreciate the precaution. Which takes us to the worst part about the garbage bags—the makeshift balloons." Causey recalled basic physics effects. "It's going shallow that's a concern. We'll get lighter, which will be great until the bags pop. Then we'll become instantly heavier, and they'll make a lot of noise."

Lieutenant Hansen shared the governing equation. "Pressure times volume before a change in depth equals pressure times volume after a change in depth. If pressure goes down, volume expands, and boom. Shit, sir. I apologize. I should've thought of this. The bags in the lower level are at about one hundred and five pounds per square inch. On the surface, they'll still be under about twenty feet of water, so at about twenty pounds."

"Do the math and check it twice." Causey looked to the laptop and watched one diver shut a valve in the hundred-pound air line while his buddy pulled a floating garbage bag from the header and then knotted it sealed like a balloon. "We'll have to remind the divers about this."

"Before I run the numbers, I'm more curious about the ballast tanks, sir. May I?" Lieutenant Hansen reached for the laptop and flipped the view to a hose running under the *Indiana*. "Shit, that doesn't look good. Senior chief, has the external team reported in since we were loaded?"

His thin frame crouched and leaning against a bulkhead, Senior Chief Spencer spoke into a headset connected to the rightmost laptop. "Sorry, sir? What was that?"

The burly lieutenant repeated himself. "Has the external team reported in since we were loaded?"

"Hold on, guys. I need to brief the lieutenant and the captain." Standing, the tall diver flipped his boom microphone to his ear. "They said the air line to the aftermost ballast tank of the forward group is pinched by the *Goliath's* cargo bed. The other one's fine, though, still filling the middle tank."

Causey interrupted the divers. "So, that's it for the aftermost tank of the forward group?"

The senior chief shrugged. "Yes, sir. We got all the air into it we could before getting aboard the *Goliath*."

"Understood. We were up against a time limit on that tank, but we can stuff all the garbage bags we want into the forward compartment to help make up for it."

"As long as you don't mind sitting here waiting to be found, sir. I could speed things up and send the external team inside to help the guys with the garbage bags, but then you'd have no idea when the middle tank fills up."

Causey liked the idea of gaining buoyancy faster, but he hated the possibility of bubbles shooting from the ballast tank if it became dry while unwatched. "You're right, senior chief. That would speed things up, but keep it the way it is. We need to be patient. Which reminds me, Lieutenant Hansen and I just realized that we didn't account for the expanding gas in the bags when we go shallow. They could pop."

With a twinkle in his eye, the senior chief gave a wry smile. "We did, me and the dive team. It's already accounted for. They're eyeballing them to about one-third full. That should be good enough if we go shallow. Some of them may pop if we surface, but heck, we'd be surfaced, and so what?"

Causey grunted. "Good thinking. At least it wasn't a collective brain fart."

"And they're still pressing up against the overhead, but anchored so they don't drift aft."

"Great work, senior chief."

The Australian's enthusiastic voice rose from the central laptop. "Gents, no need to discuss it further. I've got you right where I want you."

As silence stifled the discussion, the *Indiana's* commander stared at his savior. "How do you know?"

A smile spread across Cahill's face. "I felt optimistic and gave it a go. The presses are holding you, and I've rotated you backwards half a degree. Are you blokes ready to go for broke?"

The *Indiana's* commander knew his ship was as ready as time had allowed. "Let's do it. Get us to a level deck and get us out of here."

"Here we go."

From the rover's overhead perspective, Causey watched the cargo ship rotate his submarine backwards with graceful control. As the deck leveled below his feet, a warm optimism filled him.

Then the world shook.

Cahill scowled. "Bloody hell."

As Causey staggered, he heard metal groaning and wailing. He regained his footing and met the stare of the senior chief. Both men shared a moment of despair.

They'd somehow become unstable and had announced their location to the known universe.

Causey yelled into the laptop. "What's going on?"

While righting the ships, the Australian ignored him.

"Talk to me, Mister Cahill."

"Sorry, mate. I almost lost you there, but I've still got you. The presses held. Barely."

"Did the mud crumble or something?"

"Or something. Liam's checking on it now, but I think part of that ravine's edge caved under the weight." A chagrined look consumed the Australian's face. "Was that as loud as I fear?"

Causey's stomach sank. "Yeah. It was bad."

The Australian narrowed his eyes. "Cut the air hose to your ballast tank and get your divers back in there. I'm putting you on an up angle to hold you while we move, and I'm getting you out of here. Now."

CHAPTER 17

Jazani dreamt.

A rumor of an attempt by the Revolutionary Guards' Navy, the maritime guerilla force defending the Persian Gulf, to procure a mercenary vessel with long-range railguns stirred his subconscious mind.

Was it true?

His dreaming brain rendered faceless shapes holding a debate within a black void, questioning if his countrymen had recently attempted to steal the *Goliath*.

If so, was the intent to intimidate the Americans, to threaten their fleet across the narrow strait?

Or was it part of something incursive–a plan of attack against chosen targets in the Fifth Fleet's home in Bahrain?

A shadowy voice of reason answered. No, not even the gutsy maritime guerilla force would strike the United States without provocation. Hadn't they returned the captured American boat crews in 2016, quickly and unharmed? Wasn't their leadership astute in the game of diplomacy?

But they had the moxie to attempt a grand theft, and a faceless voice said they had paid thieves to procure the *Goliath* as a muscle to be flexed for American awe.

However, the thieves had failed.

Within his dream, Jazani wondered if he himself had enabled sufficient intimidation by supporting the trap that had placed a lightweight torpedo on an American submarine.

Had the torpedo succeeded, or was he hunting a ghost?

A ghost ship. A spectral submarine.

Was he hunting pure hope?

An image of a *Virginia*-class vessel appeared but mocked him with its blurry blackness. In a waterless sea, it dodged an incoming lightweight weapon and then grew a humanoid mouth, which broke into a sardonic grin.

The American submarine spoke to him in English, but he understood. "How many times do you expect David to defeat

Goliath? Once in human history is enough. You can't beat the United States of America."

The frightened dreamer responded. "We found your robot."

Maintaining its moving lips, the submarine mocked him. "You did not. Dolphins did. Lucky. You can't control your waters based upon luck."

"But I–"

"But nothing. You have delusions of grandeur while your reality is failure. Failure to damage me, failure of your fellow *Ghadir*-class commanders to escape mercenary torpedoes, failure of your guerilla forces to capture the *Goliath*."

The *Goliath*. The mercenary catamaran with a cargo bed and railguns. A machine of far-reaching power menacing the waters of his homeland and his mind.

In his sleeping visions, the American submarine melted, and the deadly mercenary catamaran sped towards him. Impossibly sucking air into its powerful turbine engines while immersed in invisible water, it rotated vertically and aimed the leading edge of its cargo bed towards him like a sword.

Floating above himself, Jazani rose over *Ghadir-957* as the *Goliath* bisected his vessel and left its severed halves tumbling to the seafloor.

Falling towards his doomed submarine, he sensed himself drowning as his awareness returned to his cramped quarters.

"Captain!"

Jazani blinked as the passageway's light flowed over his executive officer's back through the opened door.

"Sir?"

"What?"

"We found the *Goliath*."

Wondering if he lingered within a dream, the *Ghadir's* commander inhaled a deep breath and rubbed his eyes.

"Sir, I said that we found the *Goliath*."

"Really? How?"

"Five sonar systems within the task force heard metallic transient noises. We even heard it ourselves on multiple organic sensors. The triangulation was perfect, and we're in the best position to attack."

Half asleep, Jazani tore the covers from his torso, shot his feet outward, and stumbled from his rack.

His second-in-command reached out with steadying hands. "Easy, sir."

The *Ghadir's* commander found his balance. Having slept barefooted in his uniform, he sought his footwear.

"Go, sir. I'll grab your shoes and catch up with you. You must see this and authorize the weapon's launch quickly, before the *Goliath* runs. Tube one's ready."

"Alright." Smooth deck plates under his soles, Jazani darted to the control room, sat at his console, and studied his waters. As they merged with his visual intake, his executive officer's claims proved true. Six and a half miles away, lines of bearing from multiple sonar systems within his task force intersected. "Who on our ship heard it?"

Seated at the consoles forward of him, two sonar technicians turned, and the thin, talkative one answered. "We both did, sir. It was loud enough."

"How'd you classify it?"

The talkative one answered again. "Creaking metal, sir. Like something strong was losing a fight with something stronger."

"Like straining gears?"

"Not quite, sir. More like, failing hydraulic joints."

The executive officer appeared and placed footwear on the deck. "Here you go, sir."

Jazani wiggled into his socks. "Failed hydraulics could be any control surface. Rudder, stern planes, bow planes. All of those could make such noises during a collision."

The thin sailor clarified. "There were multiple failures at the same time. The only logical explanation is that something hit the *Goliath's* support arms."

Jazani looked at his second-in-command sitting across the aisle from him. "Is that the extent of the evidence?"

"Yes, sir. But it's got to be the *Goliath*. Everyone agrees. Check the message traffic if you want."

"Never mind that. I'll trust your evaluation of the messages. Let me hear the noise for myself."

Turning towards his console, the thin technician tapped his screen. "I've got it queued up. I'll start the audio file for you, sir. And... it's ready."

Jazani placed headphones over his ears and listened. The rippling cacophony of groaning metal agreed with his crew's claims. He pulled off his listening equipment. "Who's got control of tube one?"

Raising his hand, the talkative technician faced him. "Me, sir."

"Tell me the parameters."

"Tube one is loaded with a Type 53 torpedo, programmed to swim out, run at forty-eight knots, run depth of thirty meters, ceiling at ten meters, floor at sixty-five meters, enable its active seeker at five miles, wire connection is good, targeted at the *Goliath*. The outer door is open. The weapon is ready."

With his target's position known, the *Ghadir's* commander tightened the noose. "Enable the seeker at six miles."

"Enable the seeker at six miles, aye, sir." The technician tapped his screen. "The seeker is set to enable at six miles, sir."

Jazani's pulse raced as he prepared to sentence dozens of men to death and destroy a billion-dollar machine. He rationalized away his doubt by reminding himself the mercenary ship's railguns presented an immediate threat to military targets and to civilians living along the coast of his homeland. That placated any guilt. "Shoot tube one."

The thin technician relayed the update. "Tube one is launched. The weapon is swimming out of its tube... the weapon is running normally. I have wire guidance."

A solemn silence overtook the room.

Relieved with the decision's passing, Jazani sighed and slumped his shoulders. "XO, bring us shallow and link me with the task force commander."

"I'm pumping water to bring us up, sir." The deck rocked in the shallows. "I'm raising our radio mast... making the connection. You're online, sir."

Jazani tapped an icon, put on a headset, and raised his voice into his microphone. "Task force commander, this is Shark One. Over."

A deep, anxious voice issued from an earpiece. "Shark One, this is task force commander. Go ahead. Over."

"Task force commander, Shark One. I just launched a heavy-weight torpedo at the *Goliath*. Time to impact, seven minutes, if the target remains stationary."

"Nobody heard your launch. Wait."

Jazani heard indistinct words through his circuit.

"I've had word sent about your actions. Well done, commander. I commend you on your decisiveness. I was going to give you three more minutes to take the initiative before ordering you to shoot."

Lingering doubts dissolved with the affirmation. "Thankfully, we were of similar mind, sir. It's taken care of."

"Indeed, it is. Send the data on the link, and we'll watch your weapon with multiple assets. Do you have wire control?"

"I do, sir."

"Restrict your maneuvering to make sure you keep it. That's a fast ship if it gets to the surface."

"I'm giving only half a mile of warning with the active seeker."

"Good." The task force's leader scoffed. "I must admit, I envy you, Jazani. This could very easily become the most important torpedo in our navy's history, and you fired it."

"I don't know what to say about that, sir. I'm just going to make sure it finds its target."

"Very well. Stay shallow and keep this line open."

A shadow of a thought cast itself upon Jazani's mind, grew into an impulse, and blossomed into a question. "Sir, are we telling the Americans about this?"

The task force commander's envy waned, and his voice became stern. "That's not your concern."

"Forgive my curiosity, sir."

After an uncomfortable pause, the task force's leader relaxed his tone. "Bah, there's nothing to forgive. I'd want to know, too, if I were in your position. I had my staff inform the fleet, and I've heard no word back on anyone's intent. I'll let them do whatever admirals and politicians do. I can only imagine the conversations that will take place in the next few minutes."

Jazani examined the display. A sunken dolphin mothership placed one mercenary vessel to his south, and two damaged *Ghadirs* placed one vessel to the southwest. Given the attacks against his countrymen, either submarine within the Frenchman's fleet could be close enough to hear his torpedo. "The mercenaries might hear it, if the Americans aren't close enough to hear it for themselves."

"Your only concern about that would be a counterfire weapon aimed back at you."

To quell his anxiety, Jazani watched the icon of a helicopter dipping its sonar along his torpedo's track. In addition to verifying that his weapon found its target, the airborne hydrophones mitigated the threat of an unheard hostile weapon coming back towards him. "I'm prepared for that, sir. The longer my torpedo runs without us hearing a hostile counterfire, the smaller the chance it'll happen. I'm also slipping sideways across the line of sight to make such a counterattack inaccurate."

"I sense that it's our day, commander. You needn't despair."

Despite his boss' assurances, Jazani did. An underlying anxiety unsettled him, and he hoped only the enormity of his attack caused it. As he glanced at a status showing his torpedo's journey one-third complete, he muted his microphone. "Any sign that the *Goliath* detects the shot?"

The talkative technician shook his head. "Nothing, sir."

Across the small compartment, the short executive officer also shook his head. "The task force's second helicopter holds the *Goliath* stationary, right where it's been since we heard it. It's... wait. Here we go. You should read this for yourself, sir."

As Jazani read the characters on a screen, he unmuted his microphone. "The helicopter hears something, sir?"

The task force commander's tone was tense. "Right. I'm hearing it now. I'm going to pipe it through to you directly, both the recordings and the aircrew's reports."

Over the earpiece, a rhythmic thump of rotor blades and the whine of a turboshaft engine became the background for a helicopter crewman's voice. "We hear both screws in motion now. The *Goliath* is accelerating."

Muting his connection to the task force's leader, Jazani called out to his technicians. "Are either of you getting the acoustic feed?"

The quiet one nodded as the thin one answered. "It's coming now, captain. I'm listening. I... uh something's strange."

"Go on."

"The helicopter crew didn't call out the *Goliath's* speed."

"I suspect they don't care. When you can outrun your targets by a factor of four and always drop your weapon in front of them, you don't worry about intercept shots or torpedo tail chases."

"I see, sir."

Jazani raised his voice. "The speed?"

"Sorry, sir. I was recalculating the torpedo's trajectory. It's not changing much. The *Goliath's* only making turns for three knots."

"But you're sure it's the *Goliath*? You've got a count of blades on two propellers of a submerged ship?"

"That's correct, captain."

Jazani crossed one quiet concern of his mental list. He then talked through another incongruity. "Three knots isn't a torpedo evasion. The *Goliath's* moving for some other reason."

"That's a fair assessment, captain."

The *Ghadir's* commander unmuted his microphone. "Sir, we correlate the audio information from the helicopter with our own and believe the *Goliath's* making three knots. That's not an evasion. It's planned movement."

"Wait."

Stunned by the terse order, Jazani watched his submarine's

tactical system increase his torpedo's time to impact by scant seconds based upon the *Goliath's* acceleration to a crawl.

The task force commander's deep voice returned. "The analysis here agrees with yours. Three knots. Keep your torpedo at runout speed with its seeker silent. Nothing changes."

"Understood, sir." Despite the tactical status quo, Jazani's mind became a hive of questions. What if the *Goliath* heard his weapon, surfaced, and sprinted into Omani water before his torpedo hit? Should the helicopter launch a weapon to divert the cargo vessel back into Iranian waters, or would that accidentally alert an ignorant crew to hidden danger? Was the small armada of American surface ships and aircrafts on the other side of the international boundary prepared to retaliate? "Sir, I..."

"What's that commander?"

"Nothing, sir. I appreciate the backup on my team's calculations."

"Of course."

Moving beyond the nagging doubts, Jazani verbalized his next question. "But I was wondering, sir, about the possibility of capturing the *Goliath*."

A loud snort preceded the answer. "A dozen other men with stars on their epaulets were wondering as well. But after we tried an approach that could be described as an attempt to capture the American *Virginia*-class, the admiralty's appetite for a repeated attempt is gone. And if there's anything interesting to capture, it's the railguns, which can be salvaged from the bottom. Perhaps good fortune will allow one of them to survive."

"I see, sir."

"You're the point of the spear, commander. Killing is never an easy task, but it's your duty, and it's my duty to make sure that you do yours. We've done our diligence, and the time for questioning your orders is over."

"Understood, sir." As Jazani gathered his thoughts, a final uncertainty invaded his head and stunned him into the silence the task force commander wanted. He opened his mouth to speak it, but his throat blocked the words, and the question morphed into a blend of fear and exhilaration. As he realized his alertness had shifted from half-asleep to tactical myopia since finding the *Goliath*, he understood why he'd missed the logical disconnect.

But now, clear.

His orders precluded him targeting an American submarine, but he wondered what could have caused the creaking sound in the doomed ship's cargo bed.

CHAPTER 18

Jake hovered over his sonar ace. "Nothing?"

Turning, the toad-head exposed a tight jaw. "I'll tell you if we hear something."

"It's not a matter of 'if', but of 'where'. Which asset shot at them? They must've taken the shot."

"Terry's not completely helpless. He can listen for himself."

"Yeah, but he doesn't have the superhuman ears of Antoine, Julien, and Noah on his team."

Ignoring the praise for his apprentices and himself, Remy turned his head, refocusing his attention on the waters around the *Specter*.

Taking the hint, Jake retreated to the central table and viewed the tactical chart. Below his nose, the latest feed revealed possible explanations for the delay in the Iranian response to the *Goliath's* damning noise exposure.

The display showed the Persian task force shifting eastward in anticipation of the *Indiana's* crawl to Pakistan. Two *Ghadir* submarines had eluded Volkov's reach on their northeasterly trek ahead of the American submarine, a frigate with helicopter support established an anti-submarine blockade at Iran's eastern nautical edge, and a Fire Scout helicopter drone had seen an Iranian *Kilo*-class submarine snorkeling forward of the injured *Virginia*-class.

As he'd watched the Iranian movements, Jake had wondered how his adversary had figured out the damaged American submarine's plight. He concluded they'd been lucky, had shown great instincts, or had simply stacked the correct assumptions together to discern their wounded adversary's most logical escape route. But the Iranian's skilled sleuthing worked against them as their conservative estimates drew their vessels far to the east.

With expected freedom to maneuver, Jake protected the northern flanks behind the absconding *Goliath* and its passenger, Volkov sanitized the escape route to the south, and the

California exercised freedom to hunt threats around its sister ship. If not for the accidental creaking from the cargo bed, the *Specter's* commander would have expected an easy path to safe harbors.

But the creaking was damning to any competent hunter, and the Persians had proven their skill.

Henri joined his commander at the table. "It's been five minutes already, but you still refuse to believe that fate would allow the noise mistake to be forgiven?"

"I'm not sure it was a mistake."

"What else could it have been?"

"Random bad luck. Cruel fate. Shit. I don't know. All I know is that it sucks."

"Not until the Iranians respond."

Jake refused to believe the Persian task force would ignore the *Goliath's* metallic groans, despite the thin and eastward-biased spread of their assets. "They're preparing to act. They'd be fools not to, if they're really out for blood."

The French mechanic shook his head. "I can dissect you with razor-like precision. But the Iranians? I admit I'm at a loss. I don't know if they mean to destroy us or simply to harass us at this point."

"They've got a right to be angry. Waiting for their wrath, not knowing if it's coming or when, is worse than having to react to it."

"I'm not sure I–"

"High-speed screws!" The toad-head turned its jaw upward. "Torpedo in the water! Bearing two-eight-eight. High bearing rate to the left. No threat to our ship."

Jake darted around the table to Remy's side. "Then who's it a threat to?"

"Terry."

Moving behind Jake, the tall American rider spoke with a Texas drawl. "That's Terry and the *Indiana*."

"Right. One torpedo shot at two ships." Jake studied the incoming lines of sound representing the weapon's propeller blades. The bearing and movement agreed with his sonar guru's assessment. "Antoine, enter your solution into the system."

Jake returned to the charting table and eyeballed an evasion course for Cahill. "Henri, get the system solution for the Iranian torpedo into a communications buoy, zero delay. Include a recommendation for Terry to run on his choice of one-four-zero or two-zero-zero. Launch it when it's ready."

"Zero delay communications buoy. I'm on it." The French mechanic tapped keys at his console. "The communications buoy is ready... the communications buoy is launched."

His teammates warned, Jake considered what else he could do for them, and distracting the shooter of a wire-guided weapon came to mind. He walked to the central table, grabbed a stylus, and shifted the hostile torpedo backwards in time to the moment the *Indiana* had stressed the groaning presses of the *Goliath's* cargo bed. Allotting the Iranians a three-minute reaction time, he geo-located the shooter and tapped in an adversarial submarine. "Antoine, do you see what I just added to the system?"

"Yes."

"That's the shooter. Can I borrow Julien and Noah to assign weapons?"

"Hurry. I need them to listen elsewhere."

"I'll be fast. Julien, assign tube three to a phantom target five degrees to the left of the shooter. Noah, assign tube five to a phantom target five degrees to the right. Got it?"

The two young Frenchmen voiced simultaneous affirmations.

Jake raised his voice. "Henri, ready tubes three and five."

"Tubes three and five are being readied."

As his gaze caught the tall Texan, Jake wondered about the roaming American submarine. "What about the *California*?"

The rider grunted. "It's on them to avoid your weapons. But be smart about it, and use long enable runs."

"Long enable runs for a target with shitty targeting?"

"You think the shooter's going to close distance towards our colleagues after shooting?"

"Maybe. I don't know what they're doing, but the sooner they know I've got weapons headed their way, the sooner their anxiety levels go up, and the sooner they might maneuver and break their wire."

"But if you warn them too soon, they may be able to evade without drastic maneuvers."

Jake moved between the two young Frenchman. "What's the default runs for your weapons?"

Their responses overlapping, the sonar technicians declared a distance of four and a half miles during which the torpedoes would cruise with their seekers dormant. The weapons were ready.

"Good enough?" Jake glanced at the American submarine officer.

Silently, the rider nodded his concurrence.

"Shoot tubes three and five." The back-to-back impulse launches popped Jake's ears. He walked to the central table, pressed his palms into it, and slumped over it. Below him, icons of his torpedoes raced towards his guess of the Iranian shooter's position. In a side window, Renard's low-speed feed confirmed receipt of the warning. "Henri, Pierre's acknowledging our communications buoy."

"I was going to mention it, but I noticed you reading it."

The *Specter's* commander digested his boss' response. Limited by the water-penetrating, low-frequency radio waves, the characters trickled like dewfall. As usual, Renard crammed meaning into few words. After a two-character system-generated code confirming receipt of the buoy's message, the Frenchman wrote: 'Terry evading'. "Antoine, do you hear any sign of Terry surfacing?"

"No.

"Do you hear him at all?"

"He's too far away and moving too slow."

"That doesn't sound like an evasion."

"Hold on." Remy pressed his muffs into his ears. "I hear him now. Making turns on both screws for thirteen knots, his maximum submerged sustainable speed."

"He must've received the note from Pierre just before we got ours. He was deep when he received it." Jake watched the *Goliath's* icon, waiting for its surfacing and its acceleration. And he kept waiting. "What the hell, Antoine? Is he holding thirteen knots?"

"Yes. I mean no, not exactly. He's making turns for thirteen knots, if that's what you meant. But he's moving slower because of the drag from the *Indiana*. You'll have to give the solution time to play out, but he's probably moving closer to twelve knots. And he's still submerged."

"Damn it." Jake recalculated the *Goliath-Indiana* tandem's evasion using the submerged speed limitation. "They won't make it. Impact's in six and a half minutes, and that torpedo should have almost ten percent fuel remaining. Something's wrong. They should be blowing the *Indiana's* forward ballast tanks and surfacing."

Henri announced an incoming message. "I think Pierre's latest feed may explain it."

Glancing at the trickling characters, Jake read the words 'Gunships over Terry', and then he recalled the Iranian airborne arsenal. "Shit. Sea Cobras. Twenty-two-millimeter cannons and rockets. Lots of rockets. Enough to put holes in all of Terry's compartments."

The American rider added emphasis to the lamentation. "And holes into the *Indiana's* only inhabitable compartment. You also need to assume there's at least one anti-submarine warfare helo out there and jet fighters in control of the air space. Our jets can't enter their air space without turning this into an unacceptable escalation."

"You're sure about that?"

The American's drawl was somber. "I was briefed. Yes. We're not sending our aircraft into their air space."

"Why not? What are they afraid of?"

After a slow sigh, the commander explained it. "The closer

you get to endangering civilians, the tighter everyone's sphincters get. I hate to say it, but if you sink a submarine, that's about the last thing anyone cares about. It's such a strange machine in the eyes of civilians, especially politicians, that it's almost like telling them we lost a spacecraft. We go out, we hide, we do shit they don't understand. God willing, we come back. If we don't, it's news until it ain't anymore."

Recalling the last catastrophe that took away his forty-three brothers and one sister, the Argentine submarine *San Juan*, Jake had to concede. It was a blip in international news, and he doubted that anyone except family members of the deceased, Argentine military enthusiasts, and his fellow submariners could remember the lost diesel boat's name. He slumped his shoulders. "Yeah. You're right."

"People care more about surface combatants because they can relate to big ships. Most people have sailed on cruise ships or know someone who has, and they know their consumer goods arrive every day on big ships. But when you get to aircraft, everyone flies, and nobody wants to see a jet shot down. It's too close to home, literally and figuratively."

"I think you're oversimplifying this a bit."

"Maybe I am, but not my next point. When you start pitting aircraft against aircraft, people get scared. They can see the battle. It's not out there on the distant ocean anymore. It's over their heads, Someone will videotape it. And they're right to be afraid. An aircraft can be over their houses in a matter of minutes, dropping bombs, launching missiles, or strafing."

"We can launch missiles from ships and submarines, too." As Jake launched his counterpoint, the thought of the *Goliath's* destruction weighed upon him. A moment of introspection revealed a desire forming within him–an excuse to quit Renard's fleet. If the heavyweight warhead destroyed the cargo ship, his French boss would have to end it all–evidenced by his tenacity to retrieve the flagship when militants had stolen it three months earlier. He hated himself for the selfish thought while his brethren faced their possible deaths.

"I agree, Mister Slate, because you're a hundred percent right, but civilians don't think that way. While this remains an undersea battle, it's safe from their perspective. If we involve surface ships, shooting guns and missiles, we let merchant ships and a few beach dwellers see it. But aircraft? No way. We can't invade their air. It would be too scary and too real for the Iranian people and for our politicians. I'm afraid that our friends aren't getting any help from above."

Jake glanced again at the chart and noticed a *Burke*-class destroyer racing towards the *Goliath-Indiana* tandem. "What about the *Laboon*? Shouldn't control of the sky be academic at this point with a *Burke* out there? Doesn't that get us around the argument of killer jets in the sky scaring the masses?"

The rider shook his head. "Check your radar horizon."

Obliging, Jake studied the distance between the destroyer and his colleagues. "Shit. I see your point. It's close enough to matter but too far away to light up the helicopters."

"My assumption's that the *Laboon's* keeping the helicopters below fifty feet. The Sea Cobras don't care about that, but it makes it hard for the Sea Kings to raise and lower their sonars, which slows them down to winch operations. It explains why the Sea Kings aren't able to get good enough targeting for dropping weapons."

Jake recalled similar limitations having helped Cahill in prior missions. Each commander in his mercenary fleet appreciated air cover against anti-submarine helicopters. "So, it's just a matter of time. A destroyer at flank speed... eventually the helos won't be able to hide at any altitude."

The commander shrugged. "Hide from the *Laboon's* radar, agreed. They'll be painted bright like a Christmas tree. But that doesn't mean they'll back down. I expect you'll see some increased military activity from the Iranians' army and air forces when the *Laboon* gets close enough to press the issue."

"Seriously? Who in their right mind would take on a *Burke*?"

"Don't kid yourself, Mister Slate. The Iranians have enough anti-ship missiles, attack aircraft, and shore-based launchers to give us fits. They know our strength, and they know how to counter it. If the *Laboon* gets aggressive, so will the Iranians, and even a *Burke* can be overwhelmed if its missile launchers are emptied. There's a lot to be said about homefield advantage."

Again, Jake checked the chart. "Shit. It doesn't matter anyway. The *Laboon's* not getting close enough before the torpedo hits."

"If Mister Cahill stays submerged, agreed. Unfortunately, like we just discussed, he can't surface."

"No. Not without changing the rules of engagement." Jake wondered if the Americans would really sacrifice a submarine and its crew to avoid unbounded military escalation.

"I know Mister Cahill's ship can fight an air battle on its own, but it'd take only two Sea Cobras to overwhelm him, and Renard said 'gunships', meaning at least two. Even without the *Laboon*, he'd be in trouble. I'm sure the Iranians did their homework, and if it came down to Mister Cahill on his own against them, they'd stay out of his Phalanx range and take their chances dodging his railguns. That'd give them plenty of chances to unload their magazines."

"I get it. He's screwed. They're all screwed."

"Can I talk to you in private?"

Jake followed the rider to his captain's console on the elevated conning platform. "What's going on?"

The Texas drawl turned ominous. "If Mister Cahill can't evade this torpedo, Mister Renard will order him to dump the *Indiana* back onto the seafloor and sacrifice the *Goliath* to the torpedo."

Wanting to be surprised, the *Specter's* commander found himself digesting the news as a foregone conclusion. He expected Cahill would obey the order and withdraw his crew to one hull while showing the torpedo his other hull. But against a heavyweight warhead, Jake worried. "And then what? We'd be back to square one with the *Indiana* stranded, except that the Iranians would know exactly where it is this time."

"At that point, we shift gears and negotiate."

Frustrated, Jake snorted. "Seems like you guys could've done that from the start without sacrificing Terry. You could've done that without making me and Dmitry risk our lives and our crews, too."

The drawl became placating. "Look, I'm just the messenger. These calls are made at levels so high it'd make your nose bleed."

"I'm sick of..." Jake's mind wandered towards the tactical geometry, and he glanced at the nearest display.

"I understand, Mister Slate. I don't like it either, but hindsight's twenty-twenty. We had to make the effort to pull out the *Indiana*."

"Yeah... we did." As Jake's mind drifted from the conversation to tactics, he tasted a new idea, chewed on it, and spat it out for its bitterness.

"Mister Slate?"

"I'm thinking." Regaining momentum, the idea returned into Jake's mind with tenacity, and after a brief resistance, he accepted it. He trotted to the central table and planned it. "Henri, all ahead flank, come left to course two-two-five."

"Jake?"

"You heard me."

"Indeed, I did. Coming to all ahead flank, course two-two-five."

The deck rumbled and rolled with the turn.

"Get a communications buoy to Pierre with our new course and speed and with instructions for Terry to come to course one-zero-zero. Zero delay."

Hesitating, Henri seemed to digest the meaning before responding in a solemn tone. "I'm entering our course and speed and a recommendation for Terry to come to course one-zero-zero. Zero delay." He raced his fingers across keys. "The buoy's ready."

"Launch it."

The French mechanic tapped a key. "The communications buoy is launched with zero delay."

Anxious, the rider masked his drawl with the rapid speech of worry. "What's the meaning of this?"

Jake beckoned him to the chart. "Come here."

The American obeyed but complained as he reached the table. "You can't have the *Goliath* change course that much. That's making it too easy for the torpedo to catch it."

"The torpedo's not catching the *Goliath*, and it's not catching the *Indiana*. It's catching us."

"You can't be serious?"

"We don't have an abandon ship plan on the *Specter* for nothing. Don't worry, commander. My guys will have you off the boat with at least a minute to spare before it blows up. Which reminds me." Jake raised his voice. "Henri, pass the word for everyone to prepare to abandon ship."

"I was wondering when you'd give the order. I'll pass the word."

His face pale, the rider shook his head.

Jake scowled. "What's wrong, other than turning ourselves into a torpedo sponge?"

"We're flirting with death."

"I don't like it, but it comes with the territory." Jake hated it. Exhausted by the torment of another self-inflicted bout of mortal terror, he wondered if death offered a peaceful alternative to his life's endless cycle of boredom and horror. He lied. "After you do it enough times, you get used to it."

"If this works, we'll be detainees or maybe prisoners of war."

"Again, it comes with the territory, and Iran's better behaved than you might think with this sort of thing."

"You're basing that on their treatment of Americans. Your crew is French, and you're French enough to fake it."

Overhearing the conversation, Henri chuckled. "As long as he doesn't talk."

Jake grimaced. "Bite me."

"Come on, my old friend. Your mastery of French is as impeccable as your courage in the face of danger. Your accent, however... not so much."

Dread rising under his cavalier veil, Jake continued to mask his fear to instill his team's confidence. "Bite me."

The rider remained somber while resisting the lighthearted mood. "French captives will be a new issue for Iran. I'm American, which could help matters, except that I'll ruin any chance of plausible deniability about this being a joint US-mercenary operation."

Jake saw value in an American naval officer's presence within his future group of detainees, but his mission was protecting the United States–not his team. "It's up to you, but you're welcome to put on our fleet's uniform and pretend you're one of us. I think Claude LaFontaine's got a build pretty close to yours."

Accentuating the rider's point, his Texas drawl came thickly. "You want me to pretend I'm French? If anyone's got a wretched American accent, it's me."

"We'll try not to talk." During a silence he found uncomfortable, Jake realized the gunships over Cahill might seek the *Specter* after its surfacing. Unsure how such a confrontation might unfold, he wanted his encapsulated anti-air weapons available. "Henri?"

"Yes?"

"Swap out tubes five and six with Sidewinders. Have the guys hurry and make all the noise they need. Get me at least one Sidewinder ready in five minutes."

"Five minutes will be tough."

"Push them."

"I will."

Beside the *Specter's* commander, the American officer grunted. "Encapsulated Sidewinders. A ship that can carry submarines underwater. Abandon ship procedures as business as usual. It's so bizarre, but it's logical. We don't consider any of this in our navy because everything's predicated on never being found. There's no need to exchange weapons. But you mercenaries have turned it into a business."

Jake smirked. "Guilty as charged."

Commander Martin sighed. "You know, Mister Slate, I didn't have much time to think about this assignment to your ship.

I'm the only post-command submarine officer who speaks French. So, I was ordered out here, and I have to admit, I didn't like the idea of working with mercenaries."

Jake grunted. "And now that you're getting the chance to be a torpedo sponge, you must be loving it."

"Not loving it but respecting it. You and your crew have got some balls–big brass ones."

"You're handling it well enough, yourself. Today, you're part of the team."

"It's an honor. And I'll take you up on that offer to go into spy mode. Where can I get some clothes from Mister LaFontaine?"

CHAPTER 19

Sanity eluded Causey like an itch beyond reach. Moving forward through the water, as opposed to dragging himself backward over mud, provided a scent of normalcy. But everything else was wrong.

The deck plates beneath his sneakers tilted upwards with his hull to provide gliding lift below his flooded compartment, he commanded his ship from his engine room's watertight door, and divers turned underinflated garbage bags into balloons in his flooded compartment.

Worst of all, he sprinted for his life.

But he wasn't sprinting. An Australian commander of a mercenary transport vessel sprinted for him, leaving him helpless on another man's back.

But it wasn't a sprint. The *Goliath's* underwater limits combined with the drag on the *Indiana* restricted the evasion to a light jog of twelve knots.

Standing beside his commander, the diving officer attempted optimism. "Maybe we'll get lucky, sir."

The *Indiana's* commander shook his head. "I never bank on luck. That loud creaking made the shot easy, and we're louder than a hurricane with all the jagged edges on the *Goliath*. Mister Cahill needs to get us out of here."

The Australian's voice rang from the central laptop. "I'm working on that, commander. And you won't believe the asinine idea me mate just proposed."

After Causey's recent run of bad luck, he thought he'd believe anything. "Try me."

"Mister Slate just offered to sacrifice himself to the torpedo."

The *Indiana's* commander thought he'd let a nuance of Australian English confuse him. "Did you say he'd sacrifice himself?"

Cahill was nonchalant. "We've done this a few times before, him more than anyone. I suppose I'll tell you about the highlights of our history, once things settle down."

The concept unnerved Causey. "You're talking about it like a standard operating procedure."

"I can't believe I'm saying it, but it more or less is. I've taken two hits in me port bow. Jake once gave up a submarine to save a *Burke*-class destroyer, though that was before I was on the team."

Waiting for others to solve his problems twisted Causey's stomach. "So, what can I do to help?"

"The most useful thing you could do is update your abandon ship procedure. We normally prepare life rafts, lifejackets, and small arms. But with our position in Iranian waters, I'm not sure if the presence of small arms would backfire."

Causey scowled. "You just said Mister Slate was sacrificing himself. Why would I need to abandon ship?"

The Australian's smile was sardonic. "You're in the care of Renard's Mercenary Fleet now. It's what we do when all else fails. Best to be ready."

The *Indiana's* commander glanced at a laptop showing a tactical rendition of his world. A trailing heavyweight torpedo loomed five minutes behind him, and a crew of French strangers raced to take the proverbial bullet for him. "Alright, what about the small arms? If we end up doing this, you'd say to go with our hands raised in hopes of diplomacy?"

"That's my guess. And it's only a guess, mind you. I'm not getting any guidance from above."

For a second, Causey thought the Australian referred to prayer, but he realized he meant Renard's data feed. "I'll bring the small arms. We can always throw them overboard if the Iranians want to show us hospitality."

A shadow overcame Cahill's face. "Bloody hell. We shouldn't have to be debating this. I'm tired of playing stupid games with these mongrels. Jake doesn't need to bother. We've still got time to surface and evade."

Another glance at the tactical feed from the *Goliath's* system showed Causey a small swarm of Iranian helicopters. Flow noise made the transport ship easy to hear, and gunships and anti-submarine aircraft hovered nearby. They promised a losing battle, and his ship would be the first target to breach the surface. "Two railguns and a Phalanx against four Sea Cobras and two Sea Kings? We'd be screwed."

The Australian's tone carried a hint of hope. "Hold on now. Pierre's update says the helos don't have us pegged. They're flying like they're still trying to find us."

"But they're close. You can hear them."

"Off and on, and not all of them at once. But yeah, they're close."

The *Indiana's* commander grunted. "The torpedo's following us passively, probably to avoid us tracking it and optimizing our evasion. Even though you turned and accelerated, you didn't go to the surface and hit an all-out evasion. They may be still be thinking they can sneak it in on us quietly."

"It's possible, but I wouldn't be surprised if it went active soon."

Causey allowed himself to entertain expectations of surviving. "With Mister Slate's sacrifice, we still shouldn't surface, and with the helos being some distance away, we don't have to worry about taking an air-dropped weapon. At least not yet."

"I'd still like to know why the helos haven't attacked us. I don't want Jake sacrificing his ship for our sakes only for us to get sunk by those Sea Kings. It could be that they're keeping their distance since they know our fleet carries anti-air missiles."

The *Indiana's* commander recalled his past briefings about the Frenchman's forces. "That's only the *Specter* and *Wraith*. You don't carry Sidewinders because you can't reload your tubes."

"But they may not know that."

"And I'm not sure I care why we're so fortunate. We can maintain course and speed, and time works in our favor as we approach the end of Iranian waters."

Apparently lost in the romance of speculation and analysis with his eyes aimed upward, Cahill continued. "It could be the proximity of the *Laboon*. I bet it's close enough to scare them."

The comment spurred Causey's memory. He recalled having

met the friendly destroyer's commanding officer while waiting in line to buy a bag of chips at the Naval Exchange. Reminded of the fellow officer who now protected his life, his submarine, and his crew, he suddenly remembered their last conversation.

A prior-enlisted sonar technician, the man had been given a choice as he approached his twenty-second year of service. He could command the USS *Laboon*, or he could retire from the U.S. Navy and begin another career.

During a slow walk to their cars in the exchange's parking lot, the prior-enlisted officer had admitted to the *Indiana's* commander the decision's difficulty. It had come down to a coin toss between joining his brother-in-law's software company as a sales representative or leading a ship through deployments across the world. Given the destroyer's timely air cover, Causey concluded the coin's landing had worked to his liking. "I bet it is the *Laboon*. Let's maintain course and speed and let the friendly air support get closer and stronger."

Cahill pursed his lips. "No, mate. That'll take too long, and I've dealt with this before."

Causey smelled a white lie. "You've dealt with a situation just like this? More helicopters than you can shoot down before they could vaporize big chunks of your hull and mine?"

"Well, no. But I need to test the waters, so to speak, by heading up there and taking the offensive. I won't let Jake wager his life because I was afraid to risk mine."

"You want to pop up there and start a gunfight with your slow guns against small, agile targets that outnumber you?"

"You forget, or you may not yet know, that I've got Stinger missiles. A lot of them, and I've got one launcher for each hatch. That's four teams, mate. Helicopters are the reason I've got them. I already have men staged, ready to climb through and shoot."

Impressed, Causey nodded. "That evens things up, I admit. It changes things and brings up a tough question."

"What's that?"

"How ready and willing are the Iranians to take you on?

They can talk about theories and plans amongst themselves, but you've taken out more aircraft in hostile engagements since the *Goliath* was commissioned than the rest of the world's ships combined. That's got to terrify any man who's flying low on one of those helos."

Cahill snorted. "There's only one way to find out."

Letting the Australian's confidence motivate him, Causey warmed to the prospect of challenging the Persians on the surface. "I should blow my forward ballast tanks first. You can't hold me above the water otherwise, and it would help our underwater dynamics."

The Australian raised his eyebrows. "You're right. As long as we're going up, the noise doesn't matter. I say you should do it now. The *Goliath* will adjust automatically."

Habit compelled Causey to respond with the traditional affirmation of 'very well', but he choked back the statement, realizing the Australian mercenary effectively commanded both of their ships. "Thank you, Mister Cahill. Give me a moment."

"Hurry, mate. I want to surface and get to top speed before Jake lets the *Specter* get snapped in half."

Causey looked at the diving officer. "Get your guys to blow the forward group."

"I'm on it, sir." Lieutenant Hansen relayed the order to Senior Chief Spencer, who verbalized it to the divers.

Remembering his other task, the *Indiana's* commander called out to a phone-talker. "Get the XO on the phone."

The young sailor relayed the order and responded a moment later. "The XO's on the line, sir."

Causey yanked a handset from a cradle. "Captain here."

"You wanted me, sir?"

"Yeah, XO. Get a modified abandon ship procedure together that gets us out of the engine room with small arms and communications equipment. Come up with something quick and dirty and rehearse it with the chiefs. You've got ten minutes."

"Ten minutes to develop it and rehearse it, sir?"

"With just the chiefs, yes. Iron out the details while you run through it with them. They'll have enough know-how to pull something together with you."

The executive officer's newfound confidence remained strong in his voice. "I'll take care of it, sir."

A distant hiss caught Causey's ear as he replaced the handset into its cradle. "Sounds like we're blowing."

Lieutenant Hansen confirmed it. "The guys reached the knocker valves, captain."

The Australian echoed the affirmation. "You're just starting to register lighter on the cargo bed's pressure sensors. I'll move water around to adjust. I'm going to reduce this annoying little up angle, too."

The deck leveled below Causey's feet. "That's fast water movement."

"It's what I'm built for, carrying submarines around."

The *Indiana's* commander reflected upon Cahill's words and his pending perilous trip to the surface. "Submarines, as in more than one at a time? I thought I remembered a briefing about you having carried the *Specter* and the *Wraith*."

"It's delicate, but yeah. Mercenaries, mate. It's cheaper to move all three ships together that way."

"Then... no, my logic's flawed."

"About what?"

"I was thinking that your hydraulic support rams could sustain loads in both directions, but that's not a logical conclusion. Your drag forces are always in the same direction despite whatever way your cargo's facing."

The Australian's eyes glanced at some display off screen, returned to the laptop, and narrowed. "I'm getting ready to surface and kick off a battle. If you've got a brilliant suggestion, now's the time. And yeah, the rams are mounted to handle drag in both directions. Pierre wanted this ship to handle reverse bells with cargo."

"Then why don't I power us out of here at high speed, still submerged? You keep making your best speed of thirteen, and the net stress on your rams shouldn't be any worse than it is now. It'll just be in the other direction while I pull you along faster than you can go on your own."

Cahill's eyes grew big. "God forgive me for being too stupid to think of that meself. Do it. Do it now. Accelerate slowly and let me watch the stresses. We'll go as fast as we can based upon whatever limit we hit first."

Causey yelled to his phone-talker. "To maneuvering... No. Never mind. They won't believe you." He pulled a handset from its cradle. "Maneuvering, this is the captain."

The engineer officer responded. "Captain, this is maneuvering."

"How long do you need to answer a forward bell?"

"I kept the propulsion train warm, just in case you needed it. That includes forward bells. I'm ready."

"Great work. Now, trust me. I'll explain later. Make turns, and I mean forward turns, for eighteen knots."

"Make turns for eighteen knots, aye, sir."

A vibrant hum rose behind Causey, and the world trembled. "How are you doing, Mister Cahill?"

"So far, so good. We're making fifteen and a half knots. The stresses are small. Give us a big push, will you?"

Causey clicked his handset. "Maneuvering, captain. Make turns for twenty-five knots."

"Make turns for twenty-five knots, aye, sir."

The hum's pitch rose, and the trembling increased.

Cahill seemed calm. "We're making twenty-one and a quarter knots. The worst ram's still only at seventy percent of its redline. Nothing else on the ship's breaking yet. Push it a bit harder."

"Maneuvering, captain. Increase your rated turns throttle setting one knot every five seconds to thirty knots or until I say 'stop'."

"I'm increasing my rated turns throttle setting one knot per five seconds to thirty knots or until you say 'stop'. Making turns for twenty-six knots... twenty-seven knots... twenty-eight knots."

Cahill interrupted the acceleration. "That's it!"

The *Indiana's* commander shouted. "Stop!"

"I've ceased my acceleration, sir. We're making turns for twenty-eight point four knots."

Causey saw the *Goliath's* commander glancing off screen. "How's it look, Mister Cahill?"

"Not bad. We're making twenty-three knots. Shit, it's been forever since I've gone this fast underwater, and never under a glass dome. If we hold this speed, we're going to get away from... shit."

"What's wrong?

"From Pierre, the Iranian shooter's steered the torpedo to an updated intercept course."

"How does he know? Mister Slate's sprinting too fast to hear it."

Cahill scoffed. "He didn't say, but it's got to be either the *California* or the *Wraith* listening for us."

"What's the verdict?"

The Australian aimed his eyes off screen. "Tight. Tighter than a gnat's ass, but the torpedo should run out of gas seven hundred yards behind us."

Causey's stomach churned acid. "That's tight."

The *Goliath's* commander faced the screen. "If it comes within half a mile, I'll take us to the surface and make sure we get away."

"And face the helo swarm?"

"Yeah. I'd rather do that than have Jake eat a torpedo."

"Shit! You need to let him know about our new speed. He has no idea. He still thinks he has to sacrifice himself."

"Bloody hell. Liam, get a communications buoy ready."

While the Australians hurried to broadcast the new plan, Causey reviewed the updated scenario. Factoring in thirty seconds to get the news to the *Specter*, he feared the sacrifice's fate.

The redirected torpedo would strike Jake Slate in two minutes.

CHAPTER 20

Crouched beside Henri, Jake lowered his voice. "I need to share an idea with you."

Apparently disliking his commander's tone, the Frenchman grunted. "Go ahead."

"We need to switch places. You, the captain. Me, the French mechanic who's going to keep his mouth shut after the Iranians take us into custody."

Henri raised his eyebrows. "You're certain we'll be taken? Even with the United States Navy only five miles away?"

"We're a warship in Iranian waters. So, don't count on the cavalry. Shit, we are the cavalry, and we're taking one for the team."

"I think you just mixed metaphors, but I understand."

Though Jake hoped the Persians would show restraint, a nagging inner voice told him he'd find incarceration with torturers and killers. "Commander Martin and I need to hide our links to the United States–me especially. If the Iranians have intelligence on me, they'd figure out…" Flashbacks played through his mind of sinking a Trident missile submarine and being declared a dead hero despite being an escaped traitor. "They might turn me into a political bargaining chip."

A shadow cut across the Frenchman's face. "They'll interview every man, captain or not. I'm sure they'll be thorough."

"But if I'm just a mechanic… shit, no offense."

A forgiving smile spread across Henri's face. "None taken."

"If I'm just a mechanic, I'll get a fraction of the grilling."

"Your pronunciation will still be poor."

Jake had predicted the protest. "Not if I stick to small phrases and act scared. Listen." He switched to French and rattled off rapid expressions. "I'm scared. Don't hurt me. I don't know. It's just a job. I work for the money. I want to go home."

Henri raised his eyebrows. "Not bad. A non-native speaker may be fooled. Your ploy may work, but I don't suppose anyone else could handle the job of pretending to be you. Perhaps Claude?"

Knowing the commanding officer bore the greatest burden of a captive crew, Jake pursed his lips to hide his shame. "Are you trying to help me decide, or are you trying to wiggle out of it?"

"Wiggle out of it."

"Can you picture Claude explaining our tactical decisions? Whoever's pretending to be our captain will have to tell them something about our mission, or else he'll just piss them off. Claude's blind and deaf about anything forward of the engine room, and he'd beg for mercy if they deprive him of cigarettes for twenty minutes."

Henri straightened his back. "I'll do it, but only because nobody else can. You'll stay by my side, though? I would welcome your advice."

"Yeah. Of course. And Commander Martin will be a sonar technician. I already talked to Antoine about it."

"If I survive this, remind me to berate Antoine for going along with your ploy to put a target on my back."

The torpedo alarm chimed, and Jake sprang to the nearest free console. The frequency of the active seeker matched his expectations of the Iranian inventory, and the bearing equaled that of the weapon he sought to intercept. He silenced the alarm. "That's the hostile torpedo, right where it should be. Antoine, watch for it to switch to range-gating."

"Of course. It'll happen soon."

Henri looked to him. "It's time to head shallow."

Agreeing, the *Specter's* commander qualified his response. "But not time to surface. We need to keep our speed. Make your depth thirty meters. Come left to course one-seven-five."

"Coming to thirty meters, course one-seven-five."

As the deck rose and rolled, Jake stepped towards the elevated conning platform and reached for a handset. He brought it to his lips and keyed it. "Everyone, this is Jake. If we end up in the hands of the Iranians, which is likely, we're going to hide that fact that Commander Martin and I are American citizens." He lowered the handset and let the news sink in.

From his control station, the silver-haired mechanic laughed nervously. "I thought the CIA revoked your citizenship?"

Seeking levity to hide from his fear, Jake scoffed. "No. Dying revoked my citizenship. I'm legally dead, which is one reason you're taking my place in the crew's most uncomfortable role."

"Do you need to remind me? Why do you think I have this sickened look on my face?"

Jake lifted the handset and continued updating his sailors. "Until I say otherwise, you'll all refer to Henri Lanier as our commanding officer, and you'll refer to me as the best French mechanic you've ever known. We're switching places. Furthermore, Commander Martin is no longer an American naval officer but one of our sonar technicians pilfered from *la Marine Nationale*. His name is Michel DuPont. Make sure you remember this. Remind each other."

Henri nodded slowly. "Well said."

Keying the microphone, the *Specter's* commander issued his final order to the bulk of his crew. "Everyone outside the control room, prepare to abandon ship. Muster the Stinger teams and have them go first. Be ready to defend against helicopters from topside. Bring at least two reloads each, duct tape life jackets around them, and assign strong swimmers to get them to the rafts. That's it. I'll see you all in the water. Move out!"

The toad-head exposed its jaw. "The incoming torpedo has changed its ping cycle. It's acquired us. Per system solution, the time to impact is three minutes, fifteen seconds."

"Understood, Antoine. We'll wait a bit longer."

"Three minutes to impact. I think we should surface."

"Not yet.

"Two minutes, forty-five seconds."

Jake yelled. "It's time! Henri, drive us to the surface."

"You don't want to blow the main ballast tanks?"

"No. Use our speed and a thirty-second high-pressure air blow to both tanks. Don't touch the emergency air."

The Frenchman called out while adjusting the stern planes on his console and then reaching for high-pressure air levers. "Understood. Thirty-seconds of high-pressure air to both tanks.

Do you want to use Sidewinders? Possibly with a delay to account for the transit time of helicopters?"

Jake wanted to avoid angering the Iranians by shooting a fire-and-forget weapon. "I don't. The Stinger teams will have to suffice."

"Understood. I'm driving us to the surface, pumping trim tanks."

As the deck rocked in the shallows, Jake dismissed the majority of his control room. "Everyone except Henri and Antoine get out of here. Join everyone else at the after hatch. Henri, call Claude and make sure men are heading topside."

As the room emptied, Henri yanked a phone from its cradle and lifted it towards his cheek. "I'll tell him. By the way, we're surfaced. Do you want to take a look around and get on the radio?"

Realizing he'd let his tactical brain lapse into a coma, Jake sneered. "Yeah. May as well hear Pierre whine about losing his submarine. Connect me. I'm raising the periscope." He strolled to his console and tapped a key to raise his photonics mast. A quick rotation brought him a sunlit panorama.

The low height of his optics shortened his horizon, but the upper halves of three helicopters appeared above the water in the *Goliath's* direction. One's rounded contours suggested an anti-submarine aircraft while the others' sharp edges portended armored gunships. A final item caught his eye–the thin, dark cross of a *Burke*-class destroyer's mast jutting from the waves.

Henri yelled across the control room. "I briefed Pierre. I'm sending him to you on the open microphone."

Renard's voice filled the room. "Jake?"

The *Specter's* commander yelled. "I'm here."

"I don't suppose you have one more evasion within you?"

Jake's mind raced for context but found none. "What the hell?"

"Terry's using the *Indiana's* propulsion to make twenty-three knots. He can escape without you sacrificing your ship."

The *Specter's* commander sneered as his heart sank. "Too late. The torpedo's locked in, and we're getting ready to ditch."

"I feared as much. I can see the first among your crew jumping overboard through a Fire Scout. I'm also tracking the weapon through Dmitry's data link."

Jake had forgotten about his Russian colleague's support and welcomed the reminder of the *Wraith* lurking below him. "Sorry, Pierre. I'm about to waste... what? Three hundred million of your dollars?"

"Roughly, but you made the right call. I can buy a new *Scorpène*, but I can't replace the *Goliath*, and I don't need the Americans hunting me down for failing to protect the *Indiana*. Save yourself and consider my property a tax write-off."

Jake scoffed. "But you don't pay taxes, you drowning rat."

"Speaking of drowning, get your charmed ass off my ship before you get dragged under with it."

Agreeing with his boss, Jake yelled. "Say goodbye to the *Specter*, boys. Let's go."

A gloomy déjà vu fell over Jake, and he noticed the insanity of his repeated jumping from doomed submarines. He recalled giving the ocean's depths a rented submarine to protect an American destroyer, and he recalled an unnecessary evacuation of the *Specter* a decade earlier off the coast of a Taiwanese islet.

Slapping Jake's back, Henri broke the nostalgic trance. "Since I'm pretending to be the captain now, I should be the last one off."

Taking the hint, Jake followed Remy out of the compartment, past the crew's dining area, and to the cone of natural light beaming through the opened hatch. He grabbed a lifejacket from a pile and slipped it over his chest. After putting on his Bluetooth earpiece, he withdrew his global satellite phone from his pocket and dialed Renard while climbing into the salty air. Heat rising from the submarine's black paint engulfed him as he squinted to protect his irises from the sun.

Bobbing in the *Specter's* whitewashed wake, floating sailors were a collage of white shirts, orange lifejackets, and splashes as they swam towards and climbed into inflated circular rafts.

Renard's voice filled Jake's ear. "Good to see you, my friend. You have a minute and a half. Get off."

"Can you hear me, Pierre?"

"Yes. I said, get off my ship. Why are you still standing there?"

Shouldering a Stinger launcher with lifejackets taped around its length, a lone, lanky straggler stood in front of Jake, Henri, and Remy. Claude LaFontaine called out to his shipmates. "How much time do we have?"

The *Specter's* commander glared at his engineer. "Ninety seconds. But we need to be off in thirty to avoid the shockwave."

"Then we have a problem." The launcher swinging beside his ear, LaFontaine twisted his wiry frame. "They can't get good footing to hold the other launcher steady."

Jake watched three men gyrating about each other, struggling for equilibrium. With waves rolling under their raft, they rested the wobbling launcher over a hunched man's back, but the weapon slid off its human mount as a trough took the survival craft. "Shit."

"It gets worse." LaFontaine swung his launcher towards the other horizon. "That Sea Cobra's coming for us."

Jake had missed the helicopter upon his arrival topside. "Damn it. Give me that." He stepped forward and yanked the Stinger off his engineer's shoulders before the lanky man could protest. His strong arms bore the weight through a lifejacket's clumsy bulk as he swiveled the weapon next to his ear and shouted. "All of you. Go!"

Henri protested. "I'm masquerading as the captain. I should be the last man off. I'll take the launcher."

"I'm still in charge, and I'm ordering you off my submarine."

The Frenchman's eyes softened. "Jake. You can't."

Unwilling to yield the gunship uncontested access to his sailors, Jake stifled his racing thoughts and the unidentified emotions colliding within him. "I can, and I will. Do you want to argue, or do you want to swim away from the big torpedo?"

Heeding the advice, the silver-haired mechanic slapped his

commanding officer's back. "Luckily, I learned how to swim. I agree with Pierre and somehow believe you're still charmed. See you later, my friend." Henri sprinted three steps and leapt into the water.

Remy tapped the back of Jake's arm. "Don't test your luck. I would be saddened if you mistime this." The toad-head lowered as the sonar ace sprinted and jumped.

The lanky engineer raised his voice. "I have no idea what's running through your mind. God willing, I'll see you in a life raft soon." LaFontaine cast himself overboard.

Standing alone, Jake faced the incoming Sea Cobra. Thankful someone else had turned on the Stinger launcher, he checked the status in its optics. His eyes focused on phrases in plain English stating the missile was armed with its heat seeker ready to track a target. He knew he could point at the helicopter and fire, but he forgot how to enable the laser guidance for overcoming the countermeasure of flares.

"Jake?"

"Not now, Pierre." Jake needed to think. He aimed the Stinger at the helicopter in hopes of tapping his memory of the weapon's function. But his mind went blank. "How the heck..." Caressing the handle, he worked his fingers around a guard and the trigger. The touch invoked his muscle memory, and he remembered how to use the laser guidance.

The voice in his ear nagged him. "Are you listening, Jake?"

"Not really."

"Get off my submarine."

"How long now?"

"Forty seconds. I told you to get off my submarine."

"Not yet."

"You're about to commit suicide. I won't allow it."

Jake wanted to be scared, but a swirling mix of emotions made him numb. He wondered if he'd become arrogant by expecting to survive every mortal danger or if he'd flirted with death so often that he'd grown receptive to its promise of peace and beyond. "The pilot needs to see my resolve."

"Damn it, man. He's going to see your shattered carcass if you wait any longer."

For fleeting moments, Jake considered death a viable option. The fury still simmering deep within him would disappear. The futility he felt during boring times aboard the *Specter* between terrifying battles would evaporate. The fear of a meaningless life beyond the mercenary fleet would end. The fatigue of constant brushes with death would become permanent rest. "I can't–"

Renard raised his voice. "You can't survive if you're blown up! Get off my submarine and figure out how to fire the Stinger while treading water if you must. I'm not losing you!"

The *Specter's* commander scoffed. "Well, shit, Pierre. After all these years, you really do care."

"Yes, damn it! What must I say to get you off that ship? Do I need to say 'I consider you my son' or 'I love you'?"

The comment reminded Jake that he believed in something more than himself, the *Specter*, and Renard's Mercenary Fleet. His boss did love him, and he wasn't the only one. "Nah. I already know all that." He hurled the launcher into the waves, leapt overboard, and swam for his life.

CHAPTER 21

A hive of conflicting thoughts buzzed in Jazani's head as he toggled his gaze between two screens. The lower display streamed video from a drone overflying the mercenary submarine while the lower showed the telemetry data and control icons of his torpedo. With fifteen seconds to impact, he emitted a thoughtful groan.

With a morbid silence over the room, his second-in-command glanced at him but then lowered his gaze.

Despite the three men accompanying him in the *Ghadir's* control room and the background voices in his earpiece, Jazani was alone.

His task force commander withheld clarification of how to proceed with his life's critical next quarter of a minute. Therefore, his orders stood.

And they were ambiguous. Freedom to engage a mercenary vessel, but no obligation to do so. Restrictions on endangering an American vessel, but no definition of endangerment.

The burden of the command decision was his. The glory of getting it right or the shame of getting it wrong would carry his career to lofty heights or haunt him forever, and he had no idea who would serve as his judge and jury–other than his own conscience.

During an instant, a replay of recent events flashed in his mind.

Helicopters had kept the *Goliath* submerged, but the cargo ship had attained a faster speed than his intelligence reports predicted possible. The mercenary catamaran breaking twenty knots without exposing its air intakes was unexpected–unfeasible, but it had happened.

He'd speculated how. Had the ship found a way to store high-pressure air for running its gas turbines in bursts? If so, why didn't he hear jets wailing underwater? Was something else accelerating his targeted vessel?

A clue had arrived when his sonar team had heard a straining

Virginia-class power plant on the same bearing.

But two minutes ago, he'd stopped caring.

He'd discarded the riddle when a *Scorpène*-class vessel had offered itself. Shocking Jazani, the mercenary submarine had sprinted onto the torpedo's track in an obvious act of sacrifice. The brazenness suggested a suicidal adversary or one who'd developed comfort toying with death.

The drone's video had proven the latter.

With urgent efficiency, the ship had surfaced, the aft hatch had flipped back, and a tall, lanky man had bounded onto the deck. By the time the drone's camera had been aimed at the *Scorpène*, a Stinger missile had appeared, wrapped in lifejackets, and had steadied on the first sailor's shoulder. Before the Persian fleet's air assets could respond, their prey had grown teeth. Life rafts had also appeared, landing in the water with sailors who inflated them into escape pods.

Tactical data showed the United States abstaining from influencing the mercenary's fate. The American fleet behaved as it should, honoring the international twelve-mile boundary, but a destroyer, its escorts, and several fixed and rotary winged aircraft stood by to overwhelm Jazani and his comrades if ordered.

Afraid of the unseen American submarine he suspected lurked nearby, he let fear bring his thoughts back to his present concerns aboard his *Ghadir*-class vessel.

He took a final view of his targeted crew's evacuation and realized they'd escaped mortal danger—except for the lone cowboy who'd considered himself unbreakable against a heavyweight torpedo. Unable to escape the pending shockwave, the man who'd just followed his Stinger missile into the water had delayed his evacuation to the brink of insanity.

Ten seconds.

His finger hovering over the shutdown button, Jazani considered his torpedo laughable overkill in snuffing a solitary man's life, that of the straggling cowboy, but he considered the would-be victim responsible for his own pending death. Freed of the mortal ramifications of his decision, the *Ghadir's* commander weighed the tactical value of shattering the *Scorpène's* keel.

A demonstration of power, aimed at the American nemesis, targeting their illegal mercenary lackeys, and captured on video for the entire world to view.

The easy answer. The traditional move. The expected decision.

But Jazani considered himself a thinking man capable of discerning possibilities beyond the expected.

So, he thought.

Eight seconds to detonation.

Nothing changed. He kept thinking.

Seven seconds.

Reckless destruction. Necessary?

Six seconds.

Who would mock and shun him if he spared his target?

Five seconds.

Would his military brethren consider him weak for showing mercy? Would it ruin him?

Four seconds.

Setting aside pride and self-preservation, he considered the outcome. If someone above him overruled his mercy, the helicopters could finish the submarine. A hedge, if he opted for mercy.

Three seconds.

A helpless submarine. An unmanned submarine. A vessel steaming with its throttles pinned open heading towards a wall of American assets poised to receive it outside Iranian waters. Five miles to international waters giving time for friendly assets to board it. Take it. Capture the *Scorpène*. Acquire a submarine to compensate for the American one that got away.

He tapped the button, and then a blinking line of text signaled the torpedo's shutting down.

Standing, the short executive officer protested. "What are you doing?"

"I shut down the weapon."

"Why?"

Giving the insubordination an appropriate unsympathetic response, Jazani turned his shoulder to his executive officer and unmuted his headset. "Task force commander, this is Shark One. I shut down my weapon."

The deep voice sounded startled. "Understood, Shark One. You had the leeway, but I'm... surprised. Why'd you do it?"

"We can still take that submarine as our own."

The task force commander grunted. "Good idea. We already have a commando team scrambling on that, but there's no guarantee that they'll arrive in time. That's why I let you continue as you wished."

"If a boarding attempt doesn't work out, we can damage or sink it with the helicopters."

"A contingency plan for that's in place as well."

Relieved to escape beratement from his immediate supervisor, Jazani probed further into his military's intent. "What about the *Goliath*, sir?"

"The American submarine's too close. We're letting it go. Our target's the *Scorpène*. I'll reserve my judgment on your decision while we're in the heat of battle, but I do commend your courage on making a tough call to spare the *Scorpène*."

"Thank you, sir." The affirmation that a senior officer could perceive his move as brave comforted Jazani. His anxiety's ebbing allowed him to conceive an idea. "You could drop a man from a Sea King, sir. I imagine you could even land a Sea King on its back."

Another grunt. "Considered, as well. But you must also consider that an armed team remained aboard to prevent just that."

"Suicidal men, sir? That's unlike the Americans or the Europeans or whoever's on that ship."

"We don't know who staffs that ship. Would you be willing to jump into confined quarters with a pistol and no armor against waiting riflemen?"

His curiosity piqued, Jazani gave the question deep thought. "I'm not sure. Maybe. I don't think it's as dangerous as you might expect since the man topside would hold the high ground over a narrow upward climb. And what would such men gain by killing a single airman?"

"They'd retain control of their ship."

"This is complex gamesmanship."

"Indeed, it is. Fortunately for you, your moves are complete. But I have to make a final call."

Jazani took the bait. "What's that, sir?"

"When I asked if you could do it, it wasn't hypothetical. I wanted an objective opinion. Five seconds after I hang up on you, I'm going to talk to my air commander. Within those seconds, I need to decide if I'll order an airman to risk his life and take that submarine. I appreciate your point about the high ground."

As the line went silent, Jazani looked up at his second-in-command. The short officer scowled. "What'd he say, sir?"

"They'll try to retake the *Scorpène* with a commando team, but he sounded doubtful if they could reach it in time. Or maybe they'll do it with an ad hoc man from a Sea King."

Apparently calmed that actions had been set in motion after his ship's torpedo had gone dormant, the executive officer sat and snorted. "Wow."

"You really wanted me to crack that submarine in half."

"Yes, sir. I don't see what harm it could've done. Mercenaries are scum without loyalty to anything but money."

"I won't argue their motivations or their character, but what if they weren't here?"

"The mercenaries? I don't know, sir."

"Think, man. How would the Americans have reacted without them? How would they have defended their flooded ship?"

The short officer's face darkened. "I can't say."

"You can't say because it's an ugly answer. They'd be defending their wounded asset the only way they can, by overpowering us. The submarines they paid mercenaries to damage with their humane weapons would've instead been shattered by American torpedoes–with their crew vaporized. I don't know how much I considered this in my final decision, but it must've been in the back of my mind."

"I guess so. I see your point."

Jazani's final thought about the spared submarine reached the forefront of his mind. "Oh, and since I'm sure the Americans were watching, I may have done us a favor in the trade negotiations."

The short officer snorted. "You mean so I can get my iPhone?"

"Yes. And I also want my Dodge Charger. My stupidly fast, gorgeous SRT."

"Maybe I'm wrong, sir. You might be lauded for this."

As Jazani's mood softened, a haunting, shrill echo poured ice water over his warming innards. Then two more pounded the control room. Active sonar pings. "What was that? Identify!"

His talkative technician squirmed. "Identifying. It's close. Oh, no, sir. I'm..."

"What?"

"I'll send it over the loudspeaker."

In perfect Persian, an English-accented voice issued orders. "...shutting down your torpedo a wise and gracious choice. We are speaking to you from a drone and have you targeted. Do not attempt any further launch of weapons. You must let the surfaced submarine escape to international waters. I repeat, we are watching you. We consider your act of shutting down your torpedo a wise..."

Shocked by his instant defeat in the invisible game of undersea cat-and-mouse, Jazani's heart sank into a melting mix of panic and embarrassment. He pointed at the overhead speaker. "Keep recording this."

"Yes, sir." The talkative technician turned his face towards his console, seemingly content to hide his shocked expression.

As he recognized the immediate need to react, Jazani swallowed his emotions and accepted the uncomfortable necessity of his next conversation. "XO, listen in case the message changes. I need to contact the task force commander. I believe a crucial decision's been made for him."

CHAPTER 22

Volkov swore. "*Suka blyad!*"

Seated beside him, his translator shook his head. "That sounds bad to anyone, whether they speak Russian or not."

As the high-frequency feed streamed through the *Wraith's* exposed radio mast, Renard frowned. "And that's the first curse I learned in Russian."

"Sorry. It's just–"

"No need for apologies." Renard switched to English, and then the translator's interpretation hummed along with the Frenchman's discourse. "I was impressed myself. The shooter was a *Ghadir*-class, as you might expect from the law of averages."

"Such a small submarine."

"It takes only one torpedo to alter the tides of war."

"And it was so close. Seconds, Pierre. I was afraid for Jake. Did the *California* threaten them to shut it down?"

"It's possible, but I can only speculate. The Americans aren't sharing all their private information anymore. There's no more need, since our mission's complete, except for sneaking the *Indiana* back to Bahrain and recovering the *Specter*."

"Sneaking?"

"Submerged and undetected. Let the world's speculation begin in Bahrain, but no sooner, when a damaged submarine returns home on its own power on the surface. Onlookers–and spies–will wonder. Did it hit an uncharted wreck? Did it collide with another ship? Nobody will know after a tarp's been laid over the damage."

"The forward compartment's flooded. I assume there's a plan to change that?"

Renard smirked. "Terry will lift the *Indiana* and get the damage above the waterline. Then pumps will drain the compartment, and our client's submarine will once again be seaworthy."

"You're sure the hole is high enough?"

"The lower portion will be shored as best as possible, and the tarp overlay should be watertight enough. The pumps will keep pace with any ingress. Now that the conflict's resolved, the crew needn't worry about the noise. Of course, Terry will be submerged nearby to catch the *Indiana* if it starts to lose seaworthiness."

Satisfied that his team had achieved its goal while he added mission kills to his personal fleet-leading tally, Volkov shifted his thoughts to the *Specter*. "What about Jake? Are the Iranians resisting?"

Renard shook his head. "No. This campaign has evolved into its nonviolent phase. The Iranians were quietly moving in on the rafts to retrieve the *Specter's* crew, likely to gain some sort of advantage by detaining them. But shortly after the *California* announced itself to the *Ghadir*, they became suddenly receptive to hailing and invited the American ships to participate."

Volkov raised his eyebrows. "An invitation into their waters?"

The Frenchman's grin bordered upon the sinister. "Yes. The Iranians will play it up as goodwill during the peace talks in Syria and in the ensuing trade negotiations, but they and the Americans will silently acknowledge each other's awareness of the *California's* role in the outcome."

"I never want to be a politician."

"I think you'd be a horrible one, given that you're a world-class man of action."

The comment warmed Volkov, but a lingering concern about the runaway submarine cooled him. "Who's getting the *Specter* back?"

"The Iranians have agreed to let it drive itself into international waters and let the Americans board it. The Americans are sending helicopters now to get the *Specter* while riverine command boats retrieve Jake's crew."

"That's great." As a swell rocked his shallow ship, Volkov checked a chart. Three miles separated him from international waters. "Can I surface when I'm outside Iranian waters?"

"Uh... no. Sorry, I admit to not having considered your immediate future yet, but I believe it's best that you remain hidden and stay far from the *Laboon* since it's the American task force's capital ship in this campaign."

The *Wraith's* commander scowled. "Could they really think I'll turn on them now, after saving their..." Catching himself, he trailed off his voice. He remembered that destroyer sailors found discomfort with any submarine below them. "Never mind. I'll come up with a track to get to Bahrain, and I'll avoid the *Laboon*."

The Frenchman frowned, and then a calmness fell over his face. "I'm tempted to believe it's over. In fact, I can't think of a reason to entertain further pessimism. We've succeeded."

Knowing the mission's high stakes, with its expected monumental monetary payout, America's forgiveness of Renard's lifetime of gray market dealings, and newfound favor with the United States in the global intelligence community, Volkov recognized decades of worry lifting from his boss' face. "That's wonderful, Pierre."

"Indeed. I'm still trying to grasp the magnitude, but I dare say that this is the mission I've spent my entire life pursuing. Three months ago, I was terrified that my future was steaming away into oblivion with my stolen flagship. Then while I was still licking my wounds, providence delivered me a distressed American submarine. Multiple lifetimes of planning couldn't have created this opportunity. It was... a divine gift."

"It's a complete win."

Color flushing his face, Renard nodded. "The Iranians will believe they'd already won when they damaged the *Indiana*. The Americans will believe they achieved a draw by mitigating the damage and salvaging the *Indiana*. Our involvement was, allowing for the normal adjustments of battle, flawless."

The *Wraith's* commander sighed, and a gentle sadness crept up his ribs. With Renard's tone making him wonder if he'd disband the fleet after reaching his pinnacle achievement, he drew breath to ask his boss about the possibility. But then he thought better of it and let the Frenchman enjoy his moment. "Yes. We did well."

"We played to everyone's strengths. Jake, my fearless champion. Terry, my clever chameleon. You, my assassin."

"I... thanks, I guess."

Renard continued his sentimental tone. "This would've been perfect if not for those still missing in action."

Confused, Volkov calculated the cost. Every man would come home alive after the Americans plucked the *Specter's* crew from the water. But then a wave of awareness washed over him. The men would come home, but not every teammate. His sadness wasn't just fear of the fleet's potential disbanding. It included the loss of the dolphins. "*Suka blyad*! I'd forgotten. May I stay in the area and search for Mikhail and Andrei?"

"I'm sorry, but no. It's time to leave this theater. You need to bring your rider home, and I want my entire fleet in Bahrain as a reminder of our success while I negotiate our final compensation."

"But they're so valuable, and they're part of my crew. And poor Vasily. He's been bedridden since we lost them. He's inconsolable."

"This situation must be diffused in agreed-upon, choreographed steps, and that won't allow you to linger. You must bring the *Wraith* back here directly."

Volkov withheld his commentary about the dolphins being the solitary blotch on the mission's otherwise perfect result. Instead of lamenting the loss, he chose to delay grieving his cetacean comrades in favor of starting the multi-day journey to his next port of call. He jammed his chagrin into his belly and turned his attentions to planning for a voyage to Bahrain.

Three days later, he stood beside his translator within the entryway of the Fifth Fleet's waterfront officer's club. Remembering the final years of the Cold War from his childhood, he grasped the irony of being a career Russian submarine commander enjoying American hospitality.

Wearing the beige pants and white collared shirt uniform of the Frenchman's fleet, Cahill seemed a refreshed ball of energy.

He extended a hand. "Where've you been, mate?"

Volkov shook his colleague's hand. "I couldn't match your speed in my mortal diesel boat. That must've been nice, getting that extra boost from the *Indiana's* power plant underwater."

Cahill watched the translator's lips and chuckled. "Thanks to nuclear power, I got here last night and slept over a floor of solid concrete. Got me shore legs back already."

"I don't think I'll be here long enough to get mine."

"Really? Plans already? Where are you heading?"

"I'm trying to plan a fishing expedition."

Cahill frowned. "What are you fishing for? I didn't know you were a fisher."

"I'll tell you more after I talk to Pierre. I still need his help arranging it."

"Sure, mate. You're the last to arrive. The rest are already in there. Let's go make the introductions." Cahill pushed through a double-door into an austere dining hall. With the building reserved for the submariners' private event, the Australian led him to the room's solitary populated circular table.

As he approached the other diners, Volkov recognized half of them. Jake sat between Henri and Renard, who sat next to Commander Martin. The *Wraith's* former rider had blown his hair dry and appeared like a new man in his starched white uniform. Four unfamiliar men in American uniforms, a captain and three commanders, sat together. After introductions, Volkov sat with his translator while Cahill took a seat facing the Russians.

The captain, an overweight man with a second chin, asserted control of the conversation. "As the task force commander, I'm honored to entertain our guests tonight. I was running the mission from the command center, and I must say it was impressive work by everyone. Introductions... I believe you know the post-command riders we assigned to your ships, but Commander Causey and Commander White of the *Indiana* and *California* respectively are new to most of you, although it seems that Mister Slate and Commander Causey were classmates at the academy."

As his translator completed his interpretation, Volkov raised his eyebrows. "It's a small world."

Jake specified. "We were even in the same company. We roamed the same floor together studying to the wee hours of the morning getting our engineering degrees."

The obese captain interjected his opinions. "Despite differences in nations and fleets, we're submariners first. But it's nice when we realize some of us have history. To those of us who fight below the waves." He raised a glass of wine.

Volkov lifted his beverage with the rest of the table, added his gratitude to the *California's* commander for his bravery, and clanked his vessel with the others'.

A shadow fell across the captain's face. "As a reminder, we don't talk about classified matters outside secure facilities. Mister Renard has said that his staff will risk such discussions, but as a matter of practice, we don't do that in the United States Navy. So, keep our conversations unclassified tonight."

The *Indiana's* commander spoke. "I have to thank you all. I'm not sure where my crew and I would be without you. Now, the *Indiana* will continue to serve the fleet for decades."

The hefty captain seemed impressed with his knowledge of history as he added context. "This won't be the first American nuclear submarine to be flooded and recovered. The *Guitarro* was accidentally sunk by the pier during tests prior to its commissioning. Don't ask me how the shipyard workers managed that, but someone decided the cost of raising and recovering the ship was worth it. So, we'll salvage the *Indiana*, especially since it was only half-flooded."

Volkov remembered his nation's similar case study, which he shared through his translator. "Of course, as a general rule, we Russians always outdo you Americans in mistakes driven by haste and carelessness. For example, you had Three Mile Island, which harmed nothing outside the containment barrier, but we had Chernobyl."

The preamble to his anecdote begot polite chuckles.

He continued. "You may have had the *Guitarro*, but we had the

K-429. Sunk and refloated not once, but twice. And, of course, we managed to snuff out more than a dozen lives in the process."

After a moment, the hefty captain nodded slowly and then shifted the conversation. "I think we've all had enough talk of sunken submarines. Why don't we talk about something more lighthearted while we order some food? Mister Renard, I'd like to know how you manage your sailors' logistics when they live where they want and you homeport your ships around the globe."

Volkov noticed his boss had been oddly silent, like a man with nothing left to prove. Reluctantly, Renard opened his mouth. "It was nothing really. Just overhead expenses, like a consultancy in which one must be liberal about spending money to keep the staff happy. Chartered flights, top-rate hotels, great food. Add that to excellent salaries, and the men worried about little other than succeeding and coming home alive."

Hoping he'd misheard, Volkov whispered to his translator. "Did he just speak in the past tense?"

"Yes. I'm sure of it. It surprised me as well."

Volkov remained quiet during the meal and sought signs in Renard's body language that the rescue mission had changed his boss from a man of action to a retiree. But other than unprecedented silence, the Frenchman withheld hints.

After dinner, the American captain ushered the group to a lounge for cocktails. A bartender took orders, and remaining on their feet, the submariners broke into cliques. Volkov saw a choice between joining members of his team or the Americans, and he selected the familiar faces.

Holding a highball glass, Renard stirred ice cubes with a toothpick running through an olive. The gesture seemed slow, as if intended to build a dramatic effect. He inhaled thoughtfully and then looked at each man. "I've been making a difficult decision, and I believe I've come to it. I don't want to destroy what I've built–what we've all built together–but I don't have the energy to continue, at least not at the moment."

Among groans, Cahill protested. "What's that mean, mate?

You're not quitting on us, are you?"

"Quitting? I hate such a term. I'm going to call it a sabbatical."

The Australian seemed calmer. "Well, at least a sabbatical is temporary. Is that what you mean?"

"I'm not entirely sure, but I think so. I intend to put our ships into dry dock for a year and give everyone a holiday. Believe me, this isn't anything I'd planned, but with this recent success, I..." Tears welled in the Frenchman's eyes. "Such good fortune. The opportunity. The outcome. It's all too perfect. I can't see what else there's left for me to achieve."

As the group's newest commander and rising star, Volkov identified himself with the fleet. He hated the discussion. "But you said there were other missions awaiting us."

Renard blinked to clear his vision. "Indeed, I did. But each of them can wait. They're strategic in nature, and my prospective clients can wait, despite their certain protestations to the contrary."

The Australian challenged the logic. "But if you've achieved perfection, you'll end up retiring for good and making them wait forever. Not that they're anyone I care about, but you see where I'm going with this. Your sabbatical's starting to sound like forever."

"I'm not sure. I honestly don't know. It's all too sudden."

Surprising Volkov, Cahill shifted into a pensive tone and allied with Renard. "That's fair, I imagine. You've been at this longer than any of us."

"Thank you, Terry."

"No problem, mate. Alright then. I wasn't sure when to tell you guys, but I may as well blurt it out. Ariella and I are engaged. We were waiting for a good time to get married, and I suppose now we can plan for it."

Happy for his colleague, Volkov shook his hand and then stepped aside while the others congratulated the Australian.

Breaking his self-imposed silence, Slate spoke with a tone that threatened Volkov's desire to retain command of the *Wraith*. "May I share what we talked about, Pierre?"

Renard nodded. "Go ahead."

"It's not just Pierre. I'm tired of this, too. I never really had a choice about joining this fleet, like you guys did. With me, it just sort of happened. It started with revenge, and then it's been a long, long road to redemption. After what we just did, there's nothing left for me to do, either. If anyone still thinks I owe them anything, they'll never be satisfied. And if I haven't forgiven myself by now, I never will. I need time to figure out if I can do that."

Volkov challenged Jake. "But what would you do? A man of action. You can't be satisfied with less."

His translator offered the look he'd developed when doubting the Russian commander's intent to repeat his sentiments in English.

"Go ahead. Tell him."

After the translation, Jake gave a sheepish grin. "I need to do something I've been putting off. I've been researching it, and I'm going back to school." He paused for effect. "I'm enrolling in a bible study program and getting my Masters in Divinity."

Renard answered some of the questions swirling in Volkov's mind, starting with the involvement of his high-ranking CIA contact. "Miss McDonald has assured me that Jake can enroll without fear of his background being discovered. She created a fake background for him that will enable his acceptance, and she'll also make sure he's accepted wherever he applies."

Volkov felt his future crumbling. "Can't that be done part time? I'm afraid that if we take a year off, we may never reunite, just like Terry said–especially with Pierre's frame of mind."

For the first time that evening, Renard spoke with authority. "My mind's made up." As the translator relayed the message, the Frenchman gave Volkov an apologetic look. "I must be honest with myself. I can't consider another mission without time to reflect upon my identity, my family, my legacy."

Volkov's chest tightened. "There's nothing I can say to stop this? What if this is the end? What if we never get back together?"

Renard smiled. "If we do get back together, we'll know that our enduring union was meant to be."

A week later, Volkov stood on the bridge of a Bahraini fishing boat. Renard had helped him find a ship with a bilingual captain, and the Frenchman had also funded the trip. The sting of possible forced retirement still hurt, and he appreciated the distraction of the open sea. "Where did you learn Russian?"

The middle-aged fishing captain kept his eyes on the horizon. "At home. My mother is Russian and immigrated two years before I was born."

"Lucky for me. I don't know how else I'd be getting along."

The captain scoffed. "No. Lucky for me. Your boss paid me for more than I could hope to catch, and I brought only half my crew. And they get to rest and play cards the entire trip. This is almost a paid vacation."

Volkov turned towards the cabin's rear. "Can I refill your coffee?"

"Sure." As a voice rose from the captain's hip, he lifted the radio and responded. "Hold the coffee. Your friend's calling for you."

"Oh, really? Excuse me." Curious, Volkov headed aft through a dank corridor until he stopped in front of a door. As he reached for its knob, it flung open.

Wide-eyed and giddy, the lithe trainer reached for Volkov's shoulders. "I heard their response! I checked three times!"

After days of the ship's fishing sonar belting out dolphin calls without results, Volkov had feared their expedition's failure. "You're sure it's them?"

"A mother knows!" The trainer darted out the aft door to the weather deck.

Volkov followed his friend outside into the pleasant, warm air. "What direction were they?"

The trainer pointed off the starboard beam.

Calm seas and sunlight made searching the surface easy, and Volkov scanned the waters with his naked eyes. "I don't see them."

"I know they're coming. They have to come."

Volkov encouraged his friend. "They might make the entire trip underwater." Despite his own words, he kept his optimism in check.

Five minutes later, dolphins surfaced, and the trainer howled in joy. "That's them! They've got their vests."

One dolphin raised his head above the water, exposed long rows of small teeth, and then fluttered his tongue while releasing a staccato screech.

"It's Mikhail!"

Happy their search had succeeded, Volkov guffawed. "Unbelievable. Of course, it's Mikhail. Andrei's too cool to talk."

"Get the crew! Get the nets! Get them to fill their holding tanks! We need to get my babies aboard!"

"Right." Volkov turned to the door.

"Wait! Look! Two more with vests."

Volkov saw two dolphins wearing black harnesses covered in Arabic characters. "*Suka blyad!*"

"They're Iranian. They look like the ones from the American reconnaissance images. My babies have made friends."

Thirty minutes later, the ship drifted, and the trainer treaded water in a wetsuit while ushering a dolphin into a net. "Come on, Mikhail. This is the only fishing net I ever want to see you in, but get into it for me."

After the mammal obeyed, a crane lifted him and swung him over the deck. Deckhands guided him into a tank with Andrei. Then the crew lowered the netting to retrieve the first of the Iranian animals.

Seeming to trust the process from having seen the Russian dolphins commit, a Persian cetacean wiggled over the netting. As the crew lifted it, the animal's underbelly became visible.

Without announcing his intention, the trainer ducked his head below the water and disappeared. Before the first Iranian dolphin joined Mikhail and Andrei in the tank, the lithe man reappeared and shouted his discovery. "I didn't think to check until I saw the underbelly, but the Iranian dolphins are females."

Volkov chuckled and then yelled to the water. "Your babies didn't make friends, Vasily. It looks like they've found themselves wives!"

"That's wonderful!"

Volkov took the union as a positive sign. "Now your babies can make babies, and you can train the newborns to be super-dolphins for our fleet." He lowered his voice and completed his sentiment to himself. "God willing, we'll have missions for them, if my friends can admit their addictions and realize they can't escape this life."

THE END

EPILOGUE

Three months later, Jake lifted his chiming cell phone to his ear. "Your Majesty?"

"*Yulla.* Hurry up."

Jake patronized his wife. "If Her Highness requests the honor of my presence, she should've sucked it up and climbed the mountain with me."

"I don't miss you. I'm hungry, and you said you'd get back in time for lunch."

"I'm sorry, Your Grace, but it seems that age has been cruel to my colleagues. Henri's doing okay, but Pierre and Claude are dragging their asses. Claude in particular looks like he was ridden hard and put away wet."

Linda chuckled. "That's funny."

"Well, I meant it to be funny, but it's not really. I think smoking has caught up with him. Lucky for Pierre that he cut back a lot. But it looks like you're going to have lunch without me."

"When will you be back?"

Sitting on the concrete base of the six-meter-tall Croix de Provence capping Montagne Sainte-Victoire, Jake scanned the verdant foliage covering the rocky slopes that fell upon the small village of Château de Vauvenargues. The breathtaking panorama was serene. "It's nice up here. Maybe I'll stay forever."

"Hah hah. You know you can't live without me."

"Yes, Your Eminence. You've called my bluff."

"Did you walk ahead of the bodyguards?"

Jake grunted. "Two came with me, Henri, Noel, and Julien. They're back in the cabin waiting for the slow pokes. The other two guards stayed back with Claude and Pierre."

"That doesn't help with my hunger, and since you lied to me about lunch–"

"I didn't lie! The old farts are taking forever. They aren't even here at the top yet."

She giggled. "Since you lied to me about lunch, I'm going to see if I can break your credit card while I shop in Aix-en-Provence today."

"Oh really? You're going to buy an entire building?"

"No, but I can do damage with shoes and purses on the Cours Mirabeau, and that's after I order the most expensive thing on the menu at the most expensive restaurant."

"Your husband forbids it."

"My husband's out of luck."

"Aren't you late for a Disobedient Wives Club meeting or something like that?"

"Hah! After that smartass remark, I'm going off-menu at lunch to really jack up the price."

"Have fun, Your Excellence."

"I will. And then you're taking me somewhere nice for dinner."

"Where?"

"You tell me. You're the man."

Jake snorted. "Hell, no. I'm not falling into that trap. You're the most finicky foodie on the planet. Even if I guessed what you wanted now, your mood would change by dinner."

"Hah. You're right. I'll pick a place, and it's going to cost you."

The line went silent, and Jake slid the phone into his jeans. As the June sun warmed his cheeks, movement below him caught his attention.

Renard strode up the rocky path, ascended the final slope, and sat next to Jake. Given their location, he started the conversation in French. "Sorry to keep you waiting."

Respecting his friend's homeland, Jake responded in the indigenous language. "I'm fine with it, but be aware that Linda may tease you when you see her. She just called me."

"Ah, and how's Linda. What did she say?"

"She said she's going to abuse my credit card for missing our lunch date."

The Frenchman shrugged. "Sorry. You can blame that on me."

"Already done. But don't worry. She's not really mad. Just playing with me. This is our first vacation since school started, and she wants time alone with me. But she understands that I needed my climb with my French buddies."

"Indeed. Our lives together didn't exactly start on this mountain, but this is where it pivoted from a solitary mission of vengeance to something magnificent. I struggle to define in words what we've accomplished."

Saddened by the group's disbanding, Jake sighed. "Yeah."

"Are you okay? How's that ancient anger of yours doing?"

"Better. It's still simmering down there, and I may never be completely cured. But our last mission helped ease a lot of pain, and my studies are taking all my extra energy. I mean, I love it, having professors to add context and fellow truth seekers to explore the material with, and the effort brings a sort of tiring peace. Like the end of a long run."

"That's wonderful. We all needed this time to reflect."

Jake gave his friend and mentor a hard stare. "Do you plan to ever bring us together again?"

Renard held his gaze but then aimed his face at the dirt. "I still don't know." He reengaged Jake's stare. "And that's the truth."

"Well, shit, Pierre. If all this time off is supposed to somehow reinvigorate you, why are you dragging your ass up this mountain so slowly and letting Queen Linda get upset?"

"Part of the reason was to accompany Claude so that he wouldn't feel singled out. He was struggling."

"Okay. What was the other part? And don't blame Claude for the rust in your joints, you old geezer."

Renard smiled and then surprised Jake by laying on his back below the cross. The Frenchman had never shown such a vulnerable posture. "I've been coming up this mountain all my life. I've taken this climb at least fifty times."

Analyzing the Frenchman's mannerisms, Jake wondered if his friend had undergone a life-altering transformation. "Yeah. And?"

"And this is the first time I've ever stopped to look straight up at the sky. It's blue, you know."

"So I've heard."

"Well, there's no need to blame Claude for anything. I took my damned time climbing this mountain to enjoy the scent of the lilac, the green of the slopes, and the cry of the terns."

"You're a poet now."

"Not a poet. Just exploring a life free of burdens. Free of that gnawing need to accomplish something. I'm discovering contentment." After answering, Renard sprang upward and then crouched forward to reach for Jake's feet.

"Um... what do you think you're doing?"

"Preparing you for the descent."

"Are my laces untied?"

"Don't worry about it. I'm taking care of it. As for this retirement, I'm finding it wonderful. Will I never bring our fleet back together? Like I said, I can't say. But never say never."

"And Olivia's keeping quiet?"

"Miss McDonald assures me that all debts are paid. You and I are clear, per her ledger. I verified this with Congressman Rickets. Her power is still growing, but it's not unchecked. Even if she were to change her mind, those in power within the American intelligence community have acknowledged our cleared ledger. In other words, neither Miss McDonald nor anyone within the CIA shall ever bother you or me again. At least, that's the message today. I won't be so naïve as to expect a permanent guarantee."

Jake felt hard tugs around his insteps. "I can live with that. I guess I'll have to."

"And if you question my vigor, I'll offer you this. If you can beat me down the mountain, I'll cover all the charges Linda places on your credit card today."

"Seriously?"

With youthful exuberance, Renard sprang forward and raced down the mountain. Ten steps away, he stopped and turned. "Are you going to question the opportunity, or are you going to capitalize upon it?"

"You asked for it, old man." As Jake stood and stepped forward, his foot stopped. Glancing down, he saw two double knots tying his boots together. He looked up.

The Frenchman gave a sardonic grin and shrugged before turning and disappearing down the path.

As he knelt and recovered his footwear, Jake knew he could catch the Frenchman. But after all Renard had done for him, he questioned if he could exploit his friend for another dime.

About the Author

After graduating from the Naval Academy in 1991, John Monteith served on a nuclear ballistic missile submarine and as a top-rated instructor of combat tactics at the U.S. Naval Submarine School. He now works as an engineer when not writing.

Join the Rogue Submarine fleet to get news, freebies, discounts, and your FREE Rogue Avenger bonus content!

Rogue Submarine Series:

ROGUE AVENGER (2005)
ROGUE BETRAYER (2007)
ROGUE CRUSADER (2010)
ROGUE DEFENDER (2013)
ROGUE ENFORCER (2014)
ROGUE FORTRESS (2015)
ROGUE GOLIATH (2015)
ROGUE HUNTER (2016)
ROGUE INVADER (2017)
ROGUE JUSTICE (2017)
ROGUE KINGDOM (2018)
ROGUE LIBERATOR (2018)

Wraith Hunter Chronicles:

PROPHECY OF ASHES (2018)
PROPHECY OF BLOOD (2018)
PROPHECY OF CHAOS (2018)
PROPHECY OF DUST (2018)

John Monteith recommends his talented colleagues:

Graham Brown, author of The Gods of War.

Jeff Edwards, author of Sword of Shiva.

Thomas Mays, author of A Sword into Darkness.

Kevin Miller, author of Raven One.

Ted Nulty, author of Gone Feral.

ROGUE LIBERATOR

Copyright © 2018 by John R. Monteith

Braveship Books

www.braveshipbooks.com

The tactics described in this book do not represent actual U.S. Navy or NATO tactics past or present. Also, many of the code words and some of the equipment have been altered to prevent unauthorized disclosure of classified material.

ISBN-13: 978-1-64062-061-2
Published in the United States of America